THE LIFE OF PINKY JENKINS, VOLUME I

H . BEDFORD-JONES

# THE LIFE OF PINKY JENKINS, VOLUME 1

## H. BEDFORD-JONES

ALTUS PRESS • 2016

© 2016 Steeger Properties, LLC, under license to Altus Press • First Edition—2016

EDITED AND DESIGNED BY
Matthew Moring

PUBLISHING HISTORY

"When Fate Wore Chaps" originally appeared in the December 18, 1920 issue of *Western Story Magazine* (Vol. 13, No. 5).

"A Stranger and Took In" originally appeared in the April 9, 1921 issue of *Western Story Magazine* (Vol. 16, No. 3).

"Where the Railroad Ended" originally appeared in the April 23, 1921 issue of *Western Story Magazine* (Vol. 16, No. 5).

"Fast Work in High Valley" originally appeared in the June 25, 1921 issue of *Western Story Magazine* (Vol. 18, No. 2).

"A New Deal in Double Ace" originally appeared in the First July, 1923 issue of *Ace-High Magazine* (Vol. 12, No. 1). Copyright © 2016 Steeger Properties, LLC. All Rights Reserved. Reprinted by arrangement with Steeger Properties, LLC.

THANKS TO
Cathy Clark, Everard P. Digges LaTouche, Judy Lloyd and Nick Martorelli

# TABLE OF CONTENTS

WHEN FATE WORE CHAPS

# CHAPTER I

## THE GIRL IN THE LIMOUSINE

IT ALL happened because Steve was a betting fool. I was fool enough to stick with him, being a friend and partner, and so forth, besides half owner of the H Bar L.

We went down to that rodeo at Salinas in style. That rodeo knew we were there! We furnished all the H Bar L boys with purple chaps, yellow handkerchiefs, and a general color scheme, which was a riot. To show that we weren't too stuck up to join, Steve and I shared the general ensemble. Steve was entered in the roping, and I went in for the riding.

That rodeo was a sad affair for us. Steve bet on me, and I bet on Steve, with unfriendly results. When we had got rid of our glad rags and came back to the big Elite tourster we had driven from the ranch, we found Bowen, one of the Miller & Lux managers, waiting for us with a grin of sympathy.

"Now, that's what comes of being ranch owners," says Bowen, shaking his fat head at us. "You boys have grown fat and slushy with prosperity! Same with your outfit. Bet you the H Bar L don't take down an event!"

"Name the amount! You're on," says Steve promptly.

Bowen chuckled. "It ain't an amount, Steve Moran. If you win, I'll shove a peanut all the way up the San Juan grade with a toothpick. If I win, you and Tom Jenkins ride clear home to the H Bar L in your rainbow punchin' outfit. Are you game?"

I allowed not. It was a double-barreled bet and unfair. Besides, our ranch lay halfway across the glorious State of California, and the touring car looked a sight more comfortable than horse leather. But Steve poked me in the ribs and agreed to the fool bet.

"When we win, Bowen," says he, "there'll be a crowd to watch you up the San Juan!"

"But when I win," retorted Bowen, "you gents will have a send-off to remember!"

To cut a sad recital short, one thing happened after another, and three mornings later we bade a sad good-by to the silver-mounted flask in the door pocket of the big Elite. We set forth along the highway, and I pass in silence over the send-off the boys gave us. It was complete and left nothing to the imagination.

Neither did we. Steve had a yellow handkerchief, I had a purple one; he had green-dyed chaps, I had white angoras that like to sweat me out of the saddle; our shirts were bright red, and we wore two guns, tied down like a movie hero. Not to mention other trimmings, such as banded Stetsons and so forth. The particulars still hurt.

Finally we were clear of the bunch and sloping along. Steve was cheerful, as usual; nothing could make that boy's mouth turn down.

"This is a lark, Pinky!" he said, addressing me by my usual handle.

"That's because you got a college education," I allowed gloomily. "My sense of the fitness of things ain't been interfered with. We look like plumb fools."

Steve grinned. "We are plumb fools. Half the joy of living consists in being a fool when you feel like it!"

"You feel like it too frequent, Steve Moran," I says. "If I was a lanky, red-headed rooster with a bad eye and a fool disposition, an Irish name, and a reputation for raisin' Cain, I'd get me into a roping contest with a bunch of kids."

"You entered in the riding, Pinky," he cut in. "So ride!" And with that he gave my bronc the quirt—and, believe me, I rode!

We sauntered along most of that day without anything more exciting than smiles. Every automobile in California was on that stretch of highway, and we put 'em all in good humor. Along in the afternoon we met a fine large roadster with two fat gents who had more tongue than sense. They hauled up alongside and kidded us the wrong way.

Pretty soon Steve got sore, and he started in to shoot. Naturally, I joined him. The guns were loaded with blanks, but they were wadded double for noise—and we shot straight. Those two sports thought they were getting real shot up, and they departed thence at sixty miles an hour or better.

"Now," I said, as we went on, "this is a heap more satisfactory, Steve! So long as I get one or two more chances to laugh my own self, I ain't going to mind this trip."

Steve looks at me down his nose.

"Those two gents are bad medicine, Pinky," he stated. "Bet you fifty they get the sheriff or constable after us! They could telephone back, you know."

"Taken," I said promptly. "Get ready to cut loose from fifty."

Well, about five miles farther on we came to a signpost that said this was the county line. I pointed it out sadly to Steve, remarking that if we had come in the Elite, we'd have passed this signal station about seven hours previously. Just then a dusty streak came up from behind us and turned into a gent mounted on a motor cycle. He slowed down and stopped between us, with his feet on the ground, and shoved back his goggles.

"Hello!" he said. "I'm lookin' for you two guys."

"Look real hard, partner," I returned, "and if you ain't blind, we'll show up right in the foreground. Seen us yet?"

"Just for that," says he, "I'll take you in here and now."

"Go slow!" spoke up Steve. "Go slow! What's the big idea?"

"You got gay a while back and shot up two men in a roadster," stated the gent. "I'm one of the county officers, and you can turn around and hike back with me."

Steve reached out. "Pinky, I'll trouble you for that fifty."

I extracted the money and handed it across the cop's head. Then I looked at the signpost, and Steve caught the look.

"See here!" I said to the cop, and he gave me his attention.

"Now see here!" says Steve, and the cop looked the other way into the muzzle of Steve's gun. "All right, Pinky—take his weapons away."

I leaned down and went through the poor boob, got a fine gat off his hip, and unloaded it before returning same. He was right peeved about the whole affair, seemed to think it was anything but legal, and began to threaten us up and down and roundabout. So, at that, Steve leaned over and blew daylight through his rear tire.

"Get us good and plenty—if you can!" said Steve. "Beat it, partner."

We were just over the county line, and the cop judged he would take our advice. He spurred up his motor cycle and went limping away.

"Now we've done it!" I told Steve. "The next town we hit will be waiting for us with a rope—unless some more speed cops run us down first."

Steve grinned and reloaded his gun. "We're having fun, aren't we?"

"We ain't going to have much fun when we tell the judge about it," I predicts.

"Bet you fifty we don't get pinched."

"Nope," I responded, after thinking it over. "I see your game. You figure on leaving the highway and cutting over the hills, eh? I ain't payin' any more fines for poor judgment, Steve. Go ahead, and let's reach a hotel somewheres."

"No hotel within twenty miles," he stated. "We'll get there some time to-night."

I groaned to myself and settled down into the saddle. The more I thought about that cop and his threats, the more I began to think that we were plumb fools for monkeying with the buzz saw. But there was no backing out now.

By this time, late in the afternoon, there were few tourists on the road and we had things pretty much to ourselves. We had about three more days of it ahead of us, and the prospect was not pleasing. Think of us, sober, respectable ranchers, backed by the H Bar L and seven thousand head of cattle, not to mention thirty thousand cool in the bank, riding across California in a regular circus get-up!

Unexpectedly, we came around a curve in the highway to find that an irrigation ditch had broken and spilled a lot of water across the asphalt ahead. We were not the first to discover that pleasing fact, for a limousine had come around that bend and had gone squeegee into the ditch—skidded. I recognized the car as one that had passed us, with a pretty girl driving; it was an Elite, so we had remarked it.

"There's our make of limousine," I says to Steve, as we drew rein and stared. "And she's ditched! Couldn't have happened very long ago. Where's the girl?"

Steve was already shoving forward, and I joined him. Not a car was in sight on the road, and evidently we were the first to come upon the scene of accident.

We dismounted and investigated. The limousine was right side up and seemed to have suffered no great damage outside of shell shock. It was another matter with the girl, for we found her lying under the wheel with a bad bruise across her forehead, knocked out.

"She was flung about, eh?" said Steve. "Hitch up the broncs, Pinky, and pull out the car while I attend to her."

"Hitch up—" I says. "I'd like to see you hitch these broncs to anything, much less this car. She ain't dead?"

"Not yet."

I noticed again that the girl was right pretty, and I guess Steve had been noticing it for some time. While he tried to work over her I looked at the license tag fixed up beside the driver's seat.

"Look here, Steve!" I said, pointing to it. "Here's the whole story: Elite limousine and so forth, owned by Elizabeth Abbot, of Pacific County! This here is Elizabeth Abbot, and likewise Pacific county, savvy? That's the Abbot ranch, about ten miles off the highway and ahead of us. Remember, we put through a deal last year with John Abbot for those thoroughbred Guernseys you were so stuck on?"

"By gosh!" said Steve. "I guess you're right!"

"Now you're talking sense," I told him. "Never mind holdin' her hands any longer—she don't know it and you're wasting time. The Abbots are high society folks, anyhow; the old man used to be a regular feller, but his son and daughter ain't in our class now—"

"Shut your fool mouth, Pinky," and Steve lifts the girl to the rear seat. "Let's try and drive this car back on the road. We can get her home by dark."

The girl showed no signs of life, beyond a high color and mighty pretty features. We gave our attention to the car.

Nobody else came along to help us, and we had a job of it. But nothing was broken, so presently we got the big glass box out on the asphalt again and ready to step off. I told Steve we had better take it slow and lead the broncs, but he was frightened about the girl.

"Forget the broncs! Let's go. They'll wander home some day."

"You go on, then," I said, and got out of the car. "I'll follow. I ain't goin' back on old Pinto Ben for all the girls that was ever born! And you're a nut of a cow-puncher to be talking thataway, Steve Moran! That just shows what a girl's face can do."

"Go to thunder!" says Steve, and throws in the gears.

He went away from there in a hurry, and I climbed back into the saddle. As I said, I have a notion of what's due a horse. Besides which, I'd heard a lot about John Abbot and the way he was raising Cain with the old man's money, and I didn't like it much. If there was any gratitude coming, Steve could have it all.

Cattle raising is business, not foolishness. Old man Abbot was business clear through. But when his kids went to carrying it on, they played a new game—built a fine big house off to itself, with Filipino servants and such things, and entertained city folks all the time, while a foreman managed the ranch. That ain't my style.

So there we were, with night coming on.

## CHAPTER II

### OBJECT — PARADISE

STEVE TOLD me later what happened when he got to Abbotsford, which was the name of the Abbot mansion.

The house was a huge affair, built of adobes plastered over, a regular palace with gardens and porches and stables. Dinner had been waiting half an hour for Elizabeth Abbot, and there was a house full of guests, so everybody piled out when Steve arrived.

I never figured which was the worse flustered, Steve or the crowd. Steve stammered something about finding the car on his way home from the Salinas rodeo, and then everybody was talking at once and carrying the girl upstairs. John Abbot took Steve by the arm and brought him inside, and then the crowd stared again!

You see, the Abbot vaqueros were mostly greasers, and there was no striving after style on that place. So the guests had been disappointed with Abbot's punchers, and when they saw Steve in all his glory, they cottoned to him. They were all city men, five or six of them, and as many girls. The chief guest of honor, however, was the Honorable Felton Courteney, an Englishman and a great pal of John Abbot.

Courteney surveyed Steve through a monocle, and after that Steve wanted to commit murder on him, I judge. Anyway, Courteney thought he had found something rich and rare. He starts in to questioning Steve, while John Abbot looked after his sister.

"Sure," says Steve, looking real simple. "I'm a pore cowboy out of a job, and—yes. I don't mind if I do, thanks."

One of the Filipinos showed up with a tray of cold refreshments, and Steve drank six.

Well, you can figure for yourself what happened, with that devil Steve enjoying life and Courteney out to amuse himself with a poor, ignorant American. When I got to the house, they dragged me in to join the party at dinner. Naturally, in my rigging, I showed up good alongside Steve, and those folks were having the time of their lives. Just then John Abbot showed up with word that his sister was not hurt to speak of, but would not appear until the morning. Then, having met me, he shook hands. He was not so bad as I had expected, but I judged he was a bit inclined to the booze. A young fellow, too.

"I owe you two gentlemen a big debt," he says, and he meant it. "Stick around with us, will you? There's no formality here, and my sister will want to thank you to-morrow."

I saw that he was really a decent sort, and I was going to tell him who we were, but Steve shoves me into my chair.

"Much obliged," he answered. "We'll stick, thanks. Ain't it terrible how everything is dryin' up this year, Abbot? It's playin'—"

His language had me roped and hog tied, but it seemed to tickle everybody else. It was the first time I'd ever heard Steve go the limit that he went. Why, the boy talked like the orneri- est sheep man you ever heard! It was his talk that gave me the idea he was putting over some kind of a game.

I had been pitchforked into the business, feeling so much like a blamed fool in the outfit I was wearing, that I played clam. There we were, chaps and all, while everybody else in the room was dolled up to the nines, and Steve spreading his elbows over the tablecloth and putting down fizzy wet goods like mad! At least, I shared the general impression that he was putting them down until he slid a glassful down my boot top by mistake.

Well, Steve certainly cut loose. I was not so popular, because I was hungry and gave my attention to the grub in sight. By this time I was hoping nobody would ever find out who I really was. Little by little, they drifted out to another big room, where somebody started a music box and there was dancing. Steve went with the crowd, acting like a regular wild hombre who had never seen a polished floor.

Presently only Courteney and a couple of other fellows re- mained with the wet goods and me. John Abbot stayed, and he was looking worried. Now, they overlooked a bet then and there. Maybe I ain't up to Steve's mark when it comes to education, but I was raised by old "Frenchy" Nicotin on the Silver Circle and Frenchy taught me to talk French like a frog. Besides which, I had brushed up considerable during the recent disturbance along the Belgian border, where I held down a job as interpreter. It didn't show to speak of, in my rodeo garments, but it was there.

So and thusly, when Courteney leaned over the table and spoke to Abbot in French, I got an earful of what went on.

"Listen!" he says, his bored-looking face taking on an expression of interest. "We want to keep these two men for a few days, John. They are the most delicious scoundrels I've ever seen."

Abbot looked at him sour enough. "They are my guests, Courteney," he answered. "And I owe them gratitude for a great service. I do not propose to have you fellows make a laughing-stock of their ignorance."

"Not at all," cut in Courteney smoothly. "We shall amuse ourselves, yes; but, of course, we do not mean to let them see that they are being made butts. Besides, they haven't the perception to see it! What harm will it do?"

The other two boys spoke up and backed Courteney's play. Now, John Abbot was a fair sort, but he had been hitting that private stock, and it looked to me as though Courteney sort of had him under his thumb. Like the rest of them, he seemed to look up to Courteney as a little tin god on wheels, simply because he was a lord's son or something.

I did have a notion to cut in with a line of French on my own account, but it looked too bad to crab the game that way. So I kept quiet.

"Well, have it your own way," says Abbot at last. "But remember this, gentlemen—I will stand for nothing that's raw! Have your fun, but remember that these men are my guests, and that if you impose too far upon their ignorance of social usages, there will be trouble."

Right there I agreed with Abbot all the way.

"You say you're out of a job, Jenkins?" said Abbot to me, as though he wanted to get rid of Courteney's high-falutin' ways.

"Worse'n that," I says. "I wouldn't be a bit surprised if the police came along to hunt us up and give us a job. Steve and me had a little argument with a motor cop to-day, and if you ask me, he was sore about it."

I told them of what had happened, and they went into a yell of laughter. That drew in some more of the crowd, and I had to tell it all over again. Also, I won't say but what a shot of hooch helped some with the story. Then, all of a sudden—

*Blam! Blam!*

That was Steve, in the front room, showing how his gun worked. They explained to him that such things weren't done in houses that had wallpaper and electric lights and fancy furniture, and he was real apologetic about it. When I came in, he was perched on top of the music box, telling stories about the rodeo and gouging the mahogany sides with his spurs, which he still wore.

We did pull it a little rough that night, I admit. All the time, I was growing madder and madder, knowing the crowd thought we were two fool simpletons and were playing us for ignorant bundle stiffs. At last, however, we agreed to hit the hay, so Abbot took us to a room he had fixed up for us. Our saddle rolls had already been taken there.

"Look here, boys," he said when he showed us to the room, "most of these people never saw a real puncher before. They don't know they exist in California. If they get kidding you, just you go the limit, savvy? I'm ranch raised myself, and I'd like to see you hand 'em something."

Now, that was sure white of him—whiter than we knew at the time, for then we did not know how Courteney held John Abbot under his paw. So we thanked him and said good night, and the door shut.

"I bet they'd like to be peekin' in," I says, "to see how the wild men take to sheets and such things." Then I said a few things more, but not for publication.

"Hello!" and Steve stared at me. "What's got your cussing streak started, Pinky?"

At this I told him about what Courteney had said in French. He was not a mite surprised, but just nodded his head, and his eyes crinkled up.

"I suspected as much from the first. And to be honest, Pinky, you can't blame 'em much! If two ordinary ranch hands walked in with the rescued damsel, they'd probably get the glad hand, a big feed, a shot of hooch, and some cigars—and outer darkness. But we comes prancing along with this bird of paradise, makin' us look like movie heroes. And what happens?

"The natural, of course. Most of these people are from the East; they are used to a hothouse atmosphere of stagnation, and we brought 'em a chance for fun and thrills. Can we blame them? Not us! Remember the tourist party that came to the ranch last year and the fun we had with 'em? We'd look fine blaming the other chap when the joke is on us!"

I argued the point with him.

"That ain't the way to size her up, Steve. Not a-tall! We're guests, and if these folks had the manners of Piute 'breeds, which they ain't, they'd try to overlook our rudeness and coarse upbringing. Instead of which, they aims to ride us. There ain't much to say for John Abbot letting 'em do it, neither, if he did have the grace—"

"He's in bad," says Steve. "I heard some gossip down to the rodeo, Pinky, about this place not making good. Don't remember just what it was; I didn't pay much attention at the time. The trouble with him is, he's too civilized—he's lost his point of view. He's been training with the wrong crowd, instead of being out riding his own fences, Pinky."

We worked for a while, getting our things stowed away in the bureau drawers and ridding ourselves of the layer of dust we had accumulated on the highway. All of a sudden Steve turns to me.

"You remember that knoll up behind the ranch house?"

"Where? Back on the H Bar L? Sure! What about it?"

"D'you suppose," he asks, "that I could build me a nice stucco bungalow on that knoll? We could run water down from the hill spring."

I stared at him. "Gosh sake, Steve! We got a good ranch house now, and what in time would we want with a bungalow?"

"You wouldn't," and he grinned at me. "I would. Maybe we'd have you in to dinner once or twice a week, if your boots were clean."

"We?" I said. "And who's this 'we' you've got on your brain?"

"Elizabeth Abbot and me," said Steve cheerfully. "I aim to take her brother's advice and stick around here—long enough to get married."

I fell back on the bed. Before I had let out the first laugh, Steve was on top of me with a pillow and knocked out my wind.

"I'll teach you to laugh!" says he. "Laugh your fool head off, cowboy, if you dare! And what's more, something's going to happen to your friend the Englishman one of these fine days."

"Don't call him my friend," I said weakly, pumping for new wind. "You durned fool, get off my stomach!"

"Will you help me to the limit?" he demanded, poising the pillow.

"Sure, Steve. Only the limit's liable to be the sky!"

"That's my object exactly," says he. "Paradise!"

CHAPTER III

PINKY LISTENS IN

UP UNTIL then, I guess, Courteney had just been amusing himself. But when morning came the bad blood really started.

Steve and I were up early, bathed and shaved, then dressed in all but our boots. When the bed was made, we lay down on

top of it and pulled a blanket over us. Along came Courteney
and a couple of other guys, as we had figured, to wake us up.

"Time to get up!" said some one, giggling. "Why didn't you
fellows get in bed?"

"Didn't want to get the sheets dirty," I says, sitting up and
yawning. "Hey, Steve!"

Steve pretended to wake up sudden, and let fly a bottle of
shoe polish. It took Courteney in the breastplate and dribbled
considerable, which spoiled his temper. He shot an oath at us,
and Steve sat up with a line of fancy swearing that took Courteney's breath away. Then everybody laughed and apologized,
but the Englishman went back to his room for a new outfit,
and I think he was vicious from that moment.

We ambled downstairs and out for a breath of air. Abbot
showed up, shook hands, and invited us to go coyote hunting
with the crowd that morning. Not for us. We hunted coyotes
at home for duty, and not for fun. About half the crowd was
going, but a few were staying for a game of bridge. Courteney
was one of the stayers.

Along came Miss Elizabeth and was introduced to her res-
cuers. Except for a bump on her forehead, she was looking fine,
and I could see that she had no knowledge of the little joke
that was going on. But she gave us a mighty queer look when
her brother introduced us as two cow-punchers.

"Oh!" she said as she shook hands. "I was in Salinas three
days ago, and saw the roping and riding contests. It was terribly
interesting!"

"Yes'm," I answered, Steve being too startled to speak. "We
was interested, too."

She looked me square in the eye, and I saw a laugh back in
her glance, but she said no more on the subject. We went in to
breakfast.

It did not take the girl very long to see that something queer
was going on, but she did not spot it, since her brother and
most of the crowd went off on their hunt. Courteney and three

other lads stayed home, and Steve intimated that he would like to learn bridge. He showed a roll of money, saying he'd won some prizes at the rodeo.

"If you'll play a few hands around to show me the game," says Steve, "I'll prob'ly catch on. I'm right handy at cards, gents."

Miss Betsy was going to register a protest, but I got her eye and led her outside to where the air was fresh. There was no use lying to that girl. She had spotted us.

"Now," I says, "don't waste no sympathy on Steve, miss. Every time that cowboy goes East to sell steers he boards at some society club in Chicago or Kansas City and pays for his keep by playin' auction at five cents a point. You seen us at the rodeo, did you?"

She tries to keep down the laugh, but it bubbled up in spite of her.

"Oh, you're a scream, Pinky!" she said, holding out her hand. "Shake! You and Steve own the H Bar L, don't you? I heard you introduced during the contests."

"Not around here," I said. "We're honest but ignorant punchers gettin' used to society ways."

"All right," she replied. "I'll play the game. Now, I have to go over to the ranch and see the foreman. Like to come along?"

You bet. I spent the whole morning riding about the ranch with her. Those vaqueros sure gave my outfit the merry smile, but that did not matter. The main thing was Miss Betsy and I got to be good pals. If her brother was half the man she showed herself, that ranch would have been the best on the coast.

When we got home, half an hour ahead of the hunting party, the auction game was on its last legs, and Steve was said to be a wizard at it. He cashed in for about two hundred bucks when the dinner gong sounded, and Courteney was still looking dazed.

"It ain't bad for a first time," says Steve apologetically. "But, say, gents, where I hit my real stride is the prime American game! Any time you want to set into a reg'lar session, draw, stud, or any other brand, just rise to it!"

Well, they started in at dinner—it was luncheon there—and Steve and me had our hands full to keep up with the stuff they pulled on us. I see Steve was looking rather peaked, and afterward I learned that he had overheard some remark which pointed to Miss Betsy and Courteney being about to be married or engaged.

I tired of acting the part so hard. After the meal I sneaks away. There was a library on the place, a nice, quiet room that nobody ever used, full of solid furniture and books. I pulls a big, soft leather chair up into a dark cubby-hole and stretched out there.

Since getting acquainted with Miss Betsy I had come to have a good opinion of Steve's judgment. None the less, it looked to me like Steve was up against pretty big odds, and both of us were riding to a fall. When Miss Betsy cottoned to the way we were being played for boobs, she would make a ruction, and our best play would be to say good-by and go home, unless we wanted to bust up a happy house party.

I was sleeping sound when a voice intrudes on me and brings me to.

"What's the full amount, Courteney?" said Abbot's voice.

"Thirty-three thousand." Courteney spoke mighty cool and confident. I could not see the two of them, and did not want to. "I bought up your I O U from Jack Repplier after that poker game at the Sierra Club, you know. Deuced glad to do it, old chap."

Abbot gave a groan. "Courteney, you're a prince! But, old man, I'll admit frankly I never suspected it was so much. I haven't the cash. The ranch has gone from bad to worse, and we're more or less up against it."

I got the idea, all right. Somebody had been stung hard, and Courteney had done the stinging. After this I could not very well expose myself, so I laid low and hoped they would go away. They did not.

"Say no more, old bean," retorted Courteney. "I'll tear up the bally paper."

"You won't!" snapped Abbot. That was the old man's blood in him speaking. "I'm off to San Francisco in the morning, and I'll be back with the cash. I'm ashamed of myself for neglecting a debt of honor this way, Courteney."

"Oh, I say! It's quite all right, you know—no hurry!" Courteney drawled his words. "Don't get the wind up over a bit of silly cash, old boy. Not worth it, really. Er—if it stays in the family, now—"

"Has Betsy promised to marry you?" snaps Abbot.

"Not in so many words, but I fancy she—"

"Well, I'm not going to slight a debt of honor on that score." Abbot scraped back a chair, as though rising. "The ranch is in my name and is good for twice that amount, so say no more. All good luck with Betsy, old man, and the quicker the better."

I heard Abbot leave the room, and the door slammed. Courteney's game puzzled me, for he seemed too slick an article to be out for cash alone, especially if he was doing his best to marry Betsy Abbot.

However, he had not left the library, and an instant later I heard him at the telephone, calling long distance. He put in a call for a San Francisco number and sat whistling a tune until the ring came. Then he answered pronto:

"Hello! Let me speak to Jack Repplier. Yes."

That gave me his game, and it was confirmed a moment later.

"Hello, Repplier? Courteney speaking. I say, Abbot is coming to the city to-morrow—he'll probably motor to Salinas or the junction and catch the express. You meet him at the station, without fail. He's coming to raise some money on the ranch, understand? Provide the money and get the mortgage."

He was silent for a moment, then chuckled. "Oh, a deed of trust, eh? Well, get a drink or so into him and I fancy he will do anything. Quite so. Ta-ta, old boy."

He hung up and left the room.

I sat thinking it over for a spell. Evidently he and some other chap, Repplier by name, were in cahoots. They swindled Abbot at cards and now meant to put up the money and get a deed of trust on the ranch. I knew what a deed of trust was—the same as a mortgage, only more so.

John Abbot was catching it coming and going. Courteney was out to grab the girl, the ranch, and all the money in sight, and unless some one stopped him he would get away with it.

So, making sure the door was shut, I went to the telephone and did a little talking for my own self. It was just as well that I got in my dirty work promptly, for when I left the library and went out to the veranda in search of the crowd, I found them gathered there. And I also found a deputy sheriff, who had just arrived, hunting me and Steve.

I don't know who was more painfully surprised, me or the deputy or the crowd. Steve was not in sight, and Abbot had been explaining to the deputy that the two desperadoes had drifted on their way—when I showed up.

"Where's your partner?" asked the deputy, amid the grieved silence.

"Him?" I returned, dutifully handing over my gun. "Why, he's about thirty miles from here now, I reckon. I rode back to get a toothbrush I'd left in my room."

John Abbot took the deputy to one side and tried to square him, but to no avail. While this was proceeding, I told Miss Betsy to let the matter ride, and I'd be back later. She quieted down the other folks, who were talking about what a shame it was and so forth. As the deputy was right set on taking me home with him and had a flivver to ride in, I was satisfied to take all the blame on my shoulders and leave Steve here with a free hand to play his game.

Steve, meantime, was hiding out.

The deputy was somewhat impressed by Abbot's statement that we were his guests and he would stand good for our fines, but as he insisted on giving me a free ride I waived all the argument. He swallowed the story about Steve having departed, however.

I shook hands with everybody except Courteney, who was on my blind side, and then started out. The deputy was decent enough to let me leave my angora chaps behind. He had no idea that I was anybody but a crazy puncher, so that was all right.

With a final wave to everybody, I climbed into the flivver and we started forth. On the way, which was a long way, the deputy let out that somebody had telephoned the sheriff that me and Steve were at Abbotsford. This message had come during the morning. I knew right away that this message had come from the Honorable Courteney.

"Thank fortune," I says to myself, "Courteney didn't have the nerve to stand up in front of the crowd and say that Steve was hiding upstairs! When I get back that hombre is going to have a powerful hard time of it."

Along late in the afternoon we hits the county seat. I was in a hurry to get the agony over with and be back with Steve, so when we got up before the justice I took all the blame and hauled out my check book. The justice was a sour-looking gent with no sense of humor at all.

"In order to impress upon the prisoner the felony of his behavior," says he, "I'll assess a fine of one hundred dollars and costs."

"Right," I assented. "Gimme a fountain pen."

"And three days," finishes the justice.

When I came to I was behind a nice, shiny steel grating. And I stayed there.

CHAPTER IV

TO FILL A FLUSH

THE SHERIFF had gone to San Quentin with a prisoner, and the deputies in charge would not let me write, telephone, or telegraph. So there I was, laid up, unable to let Steve know about Courteney's deviltry. Steve, on the other hand, never dreamed I was in jail, and went ahead playing a lone hand. That lets me out of the story for a spell.

After my departure, Steve provided quite a bit of fun for the crowd, but by this time Miss Betsy was next to the proceedings and she held her friends in check. She was interested in Steve, but could not quite figure him out. While she knew that he was no ranch hand, she was not certain just how far he was acting a part in pretending to be a boob. This was all right; when you get a girl puzzled, there's hope.

John Abbot was too busy with his own affairs to protect Steve. After dinner that night he called Miss Betsy into the library for a private conference. They excused themselves and left the crowd to trip the light fantastic, which was done to the joy of all concerned.

Abbot and Miss Betsy, in the library, were having a different kind of time. John Abbot, in whose name the estate was vested until his sister came of age and got her half, came out flat-footed and told her exactly what they were up against.

"I've been a fool," he said.

"Apparently," says Miss Betsy, taking it quite calm. "How deep?"

"Thirty-three thousand, and probably some odd, Betsy. The bank has my note for five thousand, which I got for running expenses until we ship those cattle to San Francisco. Most of that is gone now, however."

"I thought we were spending money pretty freely, John," she told him. "And this has gone for gambling?"

"Nearly all of it," he acknowledged. "Courteney is a good fellow. He wanted to tear up the I O U's and call it square."

"What prevented him, then?" asked Miss Betsy, level-eyed. John Abbot flushed.

"I did, of course! Do you think I'd back out like a cur?"

Miss Betsy shrugged her shoulders.

"Well, John, there's no use crying over spilled milk. You go ahead and raise this money. Bring back the cash, and bring back a deed transferring the ranch title to me. I'm going to take hold of this ranch and run it—and run everything connected with it. Do you understand?"

"Yes," he answered miserably. "Heaven knows you can't make any worse botch of it than I have, Betsy! The ranch has lost money for two years."

"I know it." She inspected him coolly. "And we turn over a new leaf immediately, John. No more entertaining; no more society. We'll sell the big cars and put in some flivvers. If you want to draw money at the bank, you can earn it. Any gambling will be done at other people's expense; not mine. Understand the program? Then be sure and bring back that transfer of title."

Abbot assented with that stricken penitence of a man who's pawned his shirt and socks and then draws the right card to fill a busted flush.

"I've been through hell this afternoon, sis," he said, pacing up and down the room. "You can't blame me any more than I blame my own folly."

"I'm as much to blame as you are," she put in calmly. "But now we've had our fun, and we'll get busy. You'll make a pretty good ranch foreman when you get rid of whiskey and cards and too many friends—and learn to take my orders."

"See here, Betsy!" Abbot halted and faced her. "Why don't you marry Courteney?"

A trace of red came into her cheeks.

"For one reason, John, he hasn't asked me."

"What! Do you mean—"

"Never mind, John; one reason is enough at a time. Now come along and forget your troubles! When this week's party is over we'll settle down to work."

She caught his arm and led him outside.

They found the gang around Steve, who was to all appearances thoroughly impregnated with sparkling fizz, and who was yodeling cowboy songs and telling range stories while everybody split their sides. Miss Betsy overheard some comments about him, and she went white with rage.

Abandoning her brother, she walked into the center of the crowd and took Steve by the wrist.

"Come out of this!" she exclaimed angrily. "You come with me!"

"Yes'm," says Steve, weaving to his feet.

Without a word more she led him out of the room into the garden that opened off the veranda. When they stood there in the moonlight, she let loose of Steve's wrist and gave him a scornful look.

"I'm ashamed of you!" she said. "A big, range-bred man like you, Steve Moran, letting these people turn you into a puppet and laugh at you behind your back!"

Steve looked mighty sober all of a sudden. Then he grinned.

"I'm having the time of my life, Miss Betsy!" he said in his natural voice. "It's a terrible waste of liquor, I will admit, and I doubt if the stuff will improve your carpets and potted plants—but think how your guests are being amused! Meeting a real cowboy for the first time!"

"So you're not drunk at all, eh?" She looked Steve up and down, and he was mortally astonished at the flare of anger in her eye. Then she turned loose on him.

"I suppose you and 'Pinky' Jenkins think pretty well of yourselves, don't you? Because you were able to help me, you take advantage of the fact to pose before us and before our guests as scatter-brain punchers. Because nobody seems to recognize you as the H Bar L owners, you pretend to be ignorant and uncouth—and you even go so far as to rob our guests at cards!"

This was a new and unexpected angle.

As a matter of fact, I had not told Miss Betsy enough and I had told her too much. She knew nothing of the fool bet that had sent us wandering her way. She naturally thought that we had chosen to act as poor cowboys on striking Abbotsford. She did blame the whole crowd, however, and because she was angry at the universe in general, she took it out on Steve and did not care how unjust she was about doing it.

Steve might have said a lot of things, but maybe he knew better than to argue with a woman, particularly one he intended to marry. He turned right white, and said nary a word. Miss Betsy went on, and when she had worn out her madness, she began to show traces of tears. She let slip two or three things which showed Steve that something desperate had happened to her entirely unconnected with us. He could put two and two together.

Well, they ended up nowhere. John Abbot came along to find them, and Miss Betsy was just as pleasant and cheerful as she had been depressed and angry a moment previously. Poor Steve was all up in the air.

Meantime, Courteney and two of his pals among those present were framing up a scheme.

The crowd was going out in the morning to watch the vaqueros round up some beef cattle that were to be shipped north. Without telling them all he planned, Courteney arranged for the two merry lads to dress up as bandits and hold the party up on the way home, giving their particular attention to Steve. So far as they knew, it was a lark, and they went in for it gladly.

They would have been a heap less eager had they known what Courteney was planning!

Well, Miss Betsy and Abbot and Steve came back to the main bunch and Abbot announced that he would be gone in the morning when they wakened. Somebody proposed a fare-well poker game, and there was general assent. Abbot excused himself to pack up, but not before he had a word or two with Courteney which seemed to cheer that gent a whole lot.

It was a queer sort of poker—the gents held cards and the ladies behind them did the betting. Wild? I'll say it was. Courteney had Miss Betsy behind him, and Steve had some gay young thing which thought two pair laid over a flush. Fortunately, Steve got one of his spurs tangled in his lady's gown, and about the time they concluded that when she bet Steve held nothing, Steve drew a pat hand. Then he pulled on his spur, and the lady got the signal, and after considerable handling of chips Steve hauled in the pot. That pot made good for all the rest.

Later the ladies retired and the game came down to earth. About one in the morning Steve sees Courteney getting too skillful with the cards, so he yawns and breaks up the game. Then he asks Courteney to step outside for a moment.

On the other side of the door, Steve looks at the Englishman.

"Next time," he says, "you want to inject the right card to fill a flush, you watch where that card comes from!"

"Eh?" Courteney pulls the single eyeglass on him. "What do you mean, my man?"

"Nothin' at all," returned Steve. "It's just a warning; savvy? I don't want to bust up the party. If you want to, just start something!"

Courteney concluded he did not want to, so it passed off that way. Of course, Steve miscued in not showing up Courteney, but he did not know that John Abbot was in so bad, and was honest enough in not wanting to make a row. Moreover, he was still up in the air over Miss Betsy, and his judgment was plumb spoiled temporarily.

With the next morning things opened up bright and fair. John Abbot had been gone since before daylight. About nine o'clock the folks began to assemble for breakfast. Steve was astonished by the warm greeting Miss Betsy handed him, and he made the best of it. After breakfast she took him aside.

"Now, Mr. Moran," she says real businesslike, "I want you to stop this affectation of being an ignorant ranch hand."

"With pleasure," returned Steve.

"I saw John off this morning," and she smiled at him suddenly. "He told me how it all started—and I don't blame you a bit. Why didn't you tell me last night?"

"Didn't dare," said Steve promptly.

"Dare?"

"No, ma'am. You looked too—well, you looked as though you needed somebody's shoulder to cry on, and I was aching to provide the shoulder," Steve explained. "Besides, I was hoping you might offer me a job as consulting expert. If you don't mind my saying it, there are a lot of things about this place that might be changed for the better."

"Oh!" Her tone was sarcastic. "You think your advice might be valuable?"

"To a ranch owner, yes."

"Very well." She nodded in a cool way. "Then you shall give me the benefit of it this morning."

"With all my heart," says Steve, and bowed. At this point Courteney interrupted, but Steve was satisfied that he had gotten off pretty well. He had almost spoken too fast for a minute.

Half an hour later they all rode off to watch the vaqueros at work. Courteney's two pals left the bunch on the way, but no one suspected anything.

## CHAPTER V

## RUCTIONS AND ROPES

WHEN THE two imitation bandits, dressed up to kill and with handkerchiefs hiding their faces, held up the party, Steve acted real prompt.

He thought his guns were loaded with blanks, of course. Therefore, he shot straight—and he discovered something was wrong. One of the bandits slid off his horse and lay quiet. The other clapped a hand to his arm and beat it in a hurry.

Five minutes later Steve realized what he was up against. The poor, innocent chap who had started to hold up the party for a joke had a bullet through him. Courteney was the first to spring the facts of the case, when the ladies got through screaming.

"You've murdered this man," he says to Steve, cold and deliberate.

"With blanks in my gun?" demanded Steve. He turned up the gun and looked at it. She was loaded—not a blank in sight.

This flabbergasted Steve. He could only stare at the gun in his hand and let his jaw drop, wondering how the gun that he had loaded with blanks now carried ball cartridges! This minute of stupefaction was a mighty bad thing for him.

The two other gents of the crowd, seeing one of their friends murdered and another wounded and lessening in the distance, lost their heads. All they could see was that poor Steve was a reckless desperado—a gunman! Perhaps Courteney had been doing some talking beforehand; I can't say as to this. At any rate, the two fellows jumped on Steve while he was staring at his gun. One of them got in a full-arm jolt under the ear that sent Steve staggering forward with his hands out.

Steve walked right into Courteney, and Courteney gave it to him square in the jaw. That put Steve down and out for the count, and the ladies screamed some more. Then Miss Betsy was out of the saddle and standing over Steve. She was white with fury.

"You cowards—to jump on him like that!" she sings out, facing the three. Courteney bowed slightly and smiled.

"Cowards, Miss Betsy? I say, now— He was armed, what? He has just murdered a man, perhaps two men; our friends. It's most regrettable and yet—"

Well, that was the absolute truth. Miss Betsy fought to hold back the tears, as she managed to take hold of the situation. The joke had turned out to be tragedy.

"You are right," she murmured, staring at Courteney, as the full horror of the thing flashed on her mind. "You are right. Emily! Girls! Ride on to the house and telephone to Doctor Smith at Santa Juana. Get him here right away!"

The other girls, including the chaperon of the party, were too paralyzed to move until Miss Betsy quirted their horses into action. Then they moved quick enough.

"Is he dead?" Miss Betsy went to Courteney, who was leaning above the fake bandit. The other two were tying up poor Steve.

"Shot through the lung, I believe," and Courteney rose.

When Steve came to life, he was locked in an empty room over the garage, and outside the door a greaser vaquero with a gun at his hip stood guard.

The vaquero had orders not to talk, and he obeyed them. Steve got the makin's off him, however, and settled down to figure things out. He saw that he was up against a mighty bad proposition when it came to facing a jury decision.

Of course, bandits are still known in California, and there would be extenuating features to the case. On the other hand, no jury on earth would understand, or care to understand, just why Steve had been prancing around Abbotsford playing bad man and cowboy. Back of that would come the complaint from the two gents who had got "shot up" on the highway.

"It's bad," says Steve to himself. "The best I can hope for will be manslaughter. No jury in these parts are going to have any sympathy for an imitation bad man. And the first thing they'll ask will be why I shot at all, if I thought the gun was loaded only with blanks? If I tell the truth and say I was a plain damn' fool, then they'll say I ought to be behind the bars—and they'll send me there."

How had his cartridges been exchanged? That was what paralyzed Steve. The more he thought about it, the less he could understand it. He had been certain the previous night that the loads were blanks.

Feeling pretty well disgusted, he got rid of all the cowboy paraphernalia, stripped to shirt and pants and boots, and kicked the gaudy junk into a corner. He had just done this when the door opens. Into the room comes Courteney, with the vaquero behind him.

"What news?" demanded Steve quickly. "Was that fool killed?"

Courteney inspects him like he was some insect.

"The doctor has not yet arrived," he answered at last. "Dick Jones has a broken arm. Poor Thornton, I believe, was shot through the lung, but he is still alive."

"What made you cursed fools jump on me like this?" snapped Steve. "How was I to know those fellows were putting up a game?"

Courteney fingered his mustache and smiled.

"My good man," says he, "you are in no position to bandy words, really! You have taken advantage of our indulgence—"

"See here!" exclaimed Steve, getting red. "See here, what d'you know about my guns being loaded with ball cartridge? Hey?"

Courteney started, then chuckled.

"Oh, come! 'Pon my word, Moran, don't try to come that over us! It won't do. Not a bit. Sorry, you know, that we have to keep you under restraint until—"

"You may well be sorry." Steve was losing his temper good and proper by this time. "I'm going to walk out of here, understand? You've got no right to keep me here."

"My dear fellow, don't grow rash!" says Courteney smoothly. "I have every right in the world to handle your case, as Miss Abbot's fiancé."

That was a plain lie, but Steve did not know it.

"I've got you figured, you tinhorn card sharp!" says Steve, the last of his temper going bang. "You've been doing some tall winning in this crowd of suckers, haven't you? And I'll bet two cents you know something about those guns of mine."

Courteney smiled in his supercilious way, and that was the last straw. This here smile of his got Steve like a red umbrella does a locoed steer.

"You were darned ready to use your mitts a while back," he says. "Use 'em now!"

With that he took two steps across the room and grabbed Courteney. The vaquero, whom Steve had clear forgotten, tries to interfere, and Steve kicks him into the corner. At this the poor greaser figures that Steve has gone loco, and he lets loose with the gun in his belt.

Being a greaser, he sends two shots into the ceiling. The third bullet nicks Steve over the ear—a fraction of an inch closer and it would have done the work. Then Steve gets the vaquero in both hands, twists the gun away, and slaps the poor devil with it over the skull. He kicks him out the doorway, with blood running down his face, and then turns back to finish with Courteney.

"Use 'em!" he says, stuffing the gun into his hip pocket.

To give the Englishman his due, he was no slouch with his fists. He did all that Steve told him to, and then some, and for a while he had some chance of winning. Steve was still feeling pretty groggy, while the blood from his scalp, where the vaquero's bullet had nicked him, ran into his eyes and blinded him. But Courteney tried to finish matters with a kick and then Steve really got mad and went for him.

Now, owing to that morning's ructions, men being shot and so forth, the cattle work had been abandoned and the vaqueros had come in to the big house, hoping for more excitement. They were all greasers, and, although they were not dressed up in movie style, those boys were business from the ground up.

The doctor from Santa Juana had just arrived, and everybody was busy inside the house where the vaquero in the garage began shooting. Then he came forth minus his gun, with blood running over his face from where Steve had raked his skull with the gun sight, and he sought out his compañeros.

"Help!" he sings out when he reaches them. "The desperado has killed me and is now murdering Señor Courteney!"

Then he went down in a heap, and they thought he was dead sure enough.

That was all those vaqueros needed. They milled around for a moment or two, then the lynching bee was in full progress. They all had guns, and they started to get Steve and string him up. They came a-smoking, too. If you want to see a real, earnest lynching party, you stir up a bunch of greasers!

Steve had finished putting Courteney to sleep and was heading for the house when the dozen vaqueros came bearing down upon him, some mounted and others running. They started shooting when they sighted him, and Steve saw he would never make the house. So he ducked back for the stables, got out the gun he had captured, and whanged away with it.

He got to the barn with bullets spattering all around him and his gun empty. About this time Steve began to wish he was back on the H Bar L; it sure is remarkable how a mess of trouble will make a man long for his own country! To Steve it looked as though everybody here was either crooked or crazy, except himself—and he was not right certain in regard to himself.

Once inside the barn, Steve looks around for a weapon. All he can find is an old-fashioned blacksnake whip, so he grabs this and crawls out of sight. Then that crowd of greasers hit the barn like a cyclone and tore through it.

Steve lets them go past, and edges outside. Two vaqueros were just dismounting to join the party, and Steve went for them. There was more shooting and some yelling, but Steve managed to lay out both the vaqueros with his whip, and then climbed into the first saddle he saw.

"Home, James!" says he, and lit out.

He got about a hundred yards in the lead before the lynching party was mounted again and after him, ropes swinging and guns barking. That is a pretty safe lead when greasers are shooting, however, and Steve yipped that bronc into more exertion than the poor brute had experienced in months.

He was thankful when Abbotsford faded out behind and he was heading for the highway and civilization, with the greasers strung out behind. Even greasers are bound to do some damage with unlimited bullets, however. Steve had no more than begun to feel real grateful to Providence than he felt the bronc shiver and gasp.

Then they went down in a heap. When Steve got through plowing up the dirt, two ropes had settled over his shoulders. They had him.

## CHAPTER VI

### ENTER BROADWAY DUKE

THE HOURS of my enforced incarceration ran their due course. Along about noon of the following day the deputy informed me that the sheriff had come home and wanted to see me. I came forth and was escorted to the sheriff's office. Lo and behold, it was no other than old Mike McKelly, who had been raised with me on Silver Creek!

"Pinky Jenkins, you r'arin' fool!" He lets out a yell of laughter. "Pinky, I'm a heap joyful over seein' you here! I'd ha' give ten dollars to been here yesterday and see the jedge plaster it on you!"

"Well, I ain't suffered much," I says, shaking hands. "When do I get turned loose?"

"Here and now, Pinky. Come home with me for some grub. My land! That's a gaudy shirt you have on!"

I got off the subject of clothes and went home with Mike. Mrs. McKelly had a late dinner waiting, and we set into a great old meal and enjoyed the general talk. Mike was a heap interested in hearing about our adventures, and we were right in the middle of things when the sheriff was called to the telephone.

He came back looking mighty glum.

"There's trouble afoot, Pinky! Steve Moran has shot up two men over to Abbot's. Doc Smith is just lighting out for there. Says one of 'em is dead. If this here joke turns out thataway, Pinky, it's going to be bad med'cine! I sure hate to go take in Steve for murder. You'd better come along."

"Murder!" I choked at that. "Good gosh, Mike! It can't be! Steve had nothin' but blanks in his gun."

"Well, let's crank up the old flivver and go," says Mike. "We can't beat the doc there, but we can run him pretty hard. I'll deputize you. Here's a gun."

We piled into the sheriff's flivver and set forth.

We did little talking on the way. Mike was driving too fast to permit it, and I was thinking too hard. What had happened, I could not imagine, unless Steve had gone after Courteney and had done him in.

On the way we passed an Elite limousine, the same which Steve and I had pulled out of the ditch. John Abbot was driving it, and he was headed for home instead of being in San Francisco. We went by him like a bat out of purgatory, for Mike was stepping on the tail of that flivver, and Abbot seemed to be in no hurry. He had not heard the news, evidently.

At any other time I would have been glad to see Abbot, since it was evident my little scheme via the telephone had worked, and he had not gone to San Francisco, after all. Just now, however, I was too much taken up with what lay ahead of us.

Presently we drew in toward Abbotsford. When we rounded a bend in the road we were suddenly aware of a lot of commotion ahead. A crowd of vaqueros were gathered about some inanimate object underneath a live oak, and it looked to me considerable like somebody had located a horse thief.

"Lynchin' bee, Mike!" I yelled.

"Abbot's punchers, too," says he, and gave her more gas.

Our arrival disarranged proceedings a heap. When I saw who was at the wrong end of the rope and recognized Steve's red hair and cheerful grin, I starts in to make trouble. Those greasers were cooling off a bit by this time, however, and when Mike and I had heard what they had to say, we looked to Steve for confirmation.

Steve was rubbing his wrists and making sure no bones were broken.

"It's all true, more or less," he said. "Much obliged to you for coming along so handy, boys!"

"My land, Steve!" says Mike, staring at him. "Did you go loco, like they say? Did you kill one of 'em and murder Courteney and—"

"Mike, give me a chance to breathe, will you?" Steve grinned. "I sure did kick up a little trouble back yonder, but so far as I know there's nobody dead."

"Well, hop in here and we'll go see."

Steve climbed into the flivver. The vaqueros knew Mike well enough to give up any more thoughts of lynching, and we starts for the Abbot place. As we went along, Steve told us all that had taken place, and by the time we reached Abbotsford the sheriff had Steve's story well in his mind.

"There's Doc Smith getting ready to leave," says Mike, "so Thornton is either dead or alive by this time. Hey, Doc!"

Miss Betsy and the others came piling out of the house to meet us. The doctor was first on hand, however, and he gave us joyful news. Thornton, the imitation bandit, was not dead and was not going to die. This immediately put a new light on things.

"Your neck is safe, Steve," says the sheriff, clapping him on the back. "Nobody can kick on you laying out a couple of bandits, so go ahead and act cheerful. Who is this coming to join the party?"

This proved to be Honorable Felton Courteney, making his way from the garage, where he had been lying dead to the world. It was a silent crowd that greeted him, for he was one sight to behold. As he came closer Mike stepped out and took a good look at him.

"Well, well!" spoke out the sheriff. "This here is the luckiest day in the year for me, ain't it, now? I'm plumb glad to meet up with you, Mister Broadway Duke!"

Courteney straightened up and tried to see through two black eyes.

"What's that?" he said.

"Me speaking, the sheriff of Pacific County," and Mike jingled the handcuffs he had produced. "Broadway Duke, alias English Bob, alias—"

"I say, there is some mistake here!" spoke up Courteney. "Miss Abbot—"

"There certainly is a mistake," and Miss Betsy joined us. "This gentleman is one of our guests, Mr. McKelly. He is—"

"I brought back a full description of him from the big city, Miss Abbot," and Mike McKelly grinned at us. "I know more about him than you can tell, believe me! Mighty sorry if it discommodes you, ma'am, but this here gent is worth five hundred dollars—"

Courteney makes a motion to his pocket, but Mike had him ironed in a jiffy. While this was going on, John Abbot arrived on the scene.

Poor Abbot was completely taken off his feet. Mike explained that Courteney was wanted for some fine-art swindling in several cities and had probably forged the English credentials which had put him in good with the Abbots and others. Then I took John by the arm and led him aside.

"You didn't go to Frisco," I says, "so it's probably the case that old Bill Hastings met you at the station and loaned you some money. Ain't it so?"

Abbot gave a gasp and stared at me. "How—how did you know?"

"I fixed it that way," I told him. "I was asleep in the library yesterday when you had your talk with Courteney. When you had gone, he telephoned a gent named Repplier in San Francisco. They had it framed for Repplier to meet you and get a mortgage on the ranch, savvy? So I telephoned Bill Hastings at Salinas and told him to meet you before you got started. He made out the papers in my name, didn't he?"

"What?" Abbot choked. "Are you the T. Jasper Jenkins who had given Bill Hastings some loose money to invest?"

"That's me," I said, and turned. "Oh, Mike! Introduce me and Steve, will you?"

So Mike performed the introductions, and when the crowd learned that we were not punchers at all, but owned a whale of a good ranch, they had mighty little to say. I tells Abbot to tear up the mortgage papers and return the money, which he did. There was no more talk about paying his debts to Courteney, him being a card sharp of the first water.

Mike put Courteney in the flivver, so I allowed I would go back to town with him and from there home to the H Bar L. Abbot and Miss Betsy were right set on having me stop over a spell, but I was homesick. As for the bet about riding back in the rainbow outfit, that was all off so far as I was concerned.

Steve elected to stay at Abbotsford another day or two.

I said good-by all around and got into the flivver. I figured on sending one of the boys after the two broncs, but Abbot promised to ship them home for us. As we were getting ready to pull out, Steve comes up and gets my ear.

"See here, Pinky, when you get home pack up those evening clothes of mine and ship 'em by express to me, will you?"

"You go plumb to Jericho," I said, settling back in the car. "If you can't win that girl without soup and fish, let her go! Beat it, Mike!"

So we beat it, and that was all there was to the story.

A STRANGER AND TOOK IN

# CHAPTER I

## THE EIGHTEENTH AMENDMENT

IF I had used any horse sense, of course, I might have applied to Dolan, him being one of the San Francisco supervisors as well as a cattle buyer. Presumably he was wise to prohibition. Not having any sense, I set out to find me a drink on my own responsibility. Not that I cared for liquor particularly, but I sure hated not being able to have it in case of emergency.

I had come up from the H Bar L, which same is my private registered brand, with a bunch of cattle. These were safely turned over to Pat Dolan, and his check turned in to the bank. I bought me a new suit of clothes. That started the trouble. While they were being altered to fit, I had a couple of days to kill in San Francisco.

So, as I was saying, I got thirsty. Funny thing! I was never thirsty before it became illegal to be thirsty. Besides, I was a heap lonesome in San Francisco, not knowing a soul except Pat Dolan. He was too busy running his own business and the city government to bother much with a down-state cattleman. My pardner, Steve Moran, had supplied me with letters to some of his high-toned college clubs, but there was too much formality about them places. Besides, I wasn't dressed the part, exactly.

In fact I must have needed that new suit of clothes. When I comes into the hotel—and it was a quiet joint at that, no fancy place—there was a simultaneous forward move on the part of two bellhops and a bouncer. After some word had been said, the proprietor comes to the front, and I hollers for help.

"Don't worry about my looks," I says. "I don't aim to set in the front window and attract custom, pardner. When it comes to that, I'll bet you five hundred even that I could buy out this hotel and still have money in the bank!"

That tavern keeper was a wise man. He declined to bet. He soothed me down and told me the house belonged to me. However, I took the hint and ordered me a suit of clothes. If I had not had to wait for them, there would have been no story at all.

After ordering the suit, I got my boots shined and my pants brushed, which concession to life in a great city made me feel quite respectable. I sure hated to part with those old clothes. They had come from a Seattle mail-order house three years before the war, and were still going strong; too strong, maybe! This reflection made me feel sorrowful, and that made me want to break the law. So we get back to where we had started—getting the drink.

Not having been in San Francisco much in late years, I was considerable of a stranger to local customs. So I waited on the corner until I saw a man who looked like he might cough up some information, and I approached him.

"Pardner," I says with a real confidential air, "could you direct me to where I might locate a shot of old-fashioned hooch?"

He looks me over with a cold and hostile eye.

"Stranger," says he, "that information cost me two hundred bucks and ten days, the last fellow I gave it to. You go foller your nose!"

He walked off. However, I patted myself on the back, for it was now certain that the said information was to be had. If I had approached him otherwise, he might have coughed up; I could see that he was suspicious of me. Maybe it was a natural feeling.

Presently I saw a plump, prosperous, smiling fellow wearing a long ulster. He was waiting for a truck to pass and let him cross the street. I came up to him, and this time I made no mistakes.

"Pardner," I says, "don't get me wrong. I'm Tom Jenkins of the H Bar L. I got about seven thousand head o' cattle on the hoof, considerable coin in the bank, and I'm a stranger here. If you're suspicious, I can prove them statements. Now, then, can you tell me where I can go and spend a little money breakin' the eighteenth amendment?"

He chuckled, took my arm, and drew me in to the curb.

"I'm a stranger in the city myself, Mr. Jenkins," he said, "so I can't tell you. But I can advise you."

"Do so," I urged him. He chuckled again.

"I saw in this morning's paper that Chinatown has just received a large consignment of Chinese liquors; they are native medicines, so the government does not interfere. If I were you, Mr. Jenkins, I'd go take a walk through Chinatown."

"Pardner, I'll do it!" I grabs his hand for a hearty shake. "Tell me where you hang out, and I'll slip around with a flask—"

"I'm from Alaska, Mr. Jenkins," he broke in. "I'm afraid we'd better dispense with gratitude. Good luck to you!"

Well, looking back on it now, I can see that maybe he was kidding me about Chinatown. At the time it did not occur to me. I had always intended to see how the chinks lived, so I wandered off in that general direction.

After climbing a mighty steep hill, I found myself in Chinatown. When I had shook off several licensed and patented guides with long whiskers, I went down the line inspecting the windows. The first ones were mighty pretty, and I lingered. Presently the gathering shades of night reminded me that I was more hungry than thirsty, so I went on.

Then I came to some drug stores. After I had looked in their windows and seen coiled rattlers and Gila monsters and lizards waiting to be mixed up, not to mention dried things that looked

a heap like scalps, I concluded that my thirst could wait quite some time. In fact I was not thirsty at all any more. So I kept on going until I struck a civilized eating place, and got me a set up of ham and eggs, medium.

When I came out of there, it was dark. Now all of this is what they call prelude. It goes to show how one thing leads up to another. I came out of the hash house and stood there on the curb, rolling me a cigarette and wishing I knew somebody in town—and right then it happened!

That street is narrow, about as narrow as the alley behind the hotel in San Juan Batista. Where I was standing, the curbing was only a matter of opinion. Automobiles were numbersome, but I naturally supposed that a citizen had some rights, so I paid them no attention. I had just got that cigarette nicely rolled and licked, and was fishing for a match in my vest, when—biff! Something bumped me on the off hind ham and tried to knock down an iron telephone pole with me. I realized dimly that an automobile without any lights was standing over me and daring me to get up. Then, as the books say, I knew no more.

I'll tell the world, it was true! I didn't know. As to what immediately followed, I learned afterward.

Two gents were driving the car. Having also encountered the iron pole, the car had halted temporarily. The two gents threw me into the tonneau, claiming they would rush me to the hospital. In that way they got off before the police got wise. The car was not much damaged, and I was not hurt to speak of.

That was how I came to be somewhere else again when I woke up.

"He's a tough-looking nut," I heard somebody say. "Some tramp who was hanging around to panhandle a tourist. Give him a swig, Ike."

Ike obeyed, and so I come to get the drink I had craved. Part of my features had come into contact with something harder, with the natural result that my nose was skinned, my cheek bruised, and my left eye was like a greaser with four bits in his pants—all swelled up. Not that looks have ever troubled me to speak of, but I sure hate to lose what I got.

"Bruised up, that's all," said a new voice. This was Ike, and that voice brought me around in a hurry. I recognized it, and I hoped that Ike would not recognize me. So I laid back and heaved a sigh and pretended to sleep.

From the feel of things I gathered that I was laying on a hard floor. There was a queer smell in the air that reminded me of those Chinatown stores, but I did not investigate it. For the present, I was in no condition to rise up and go to shooting—which same I would have to do pronto, if Ike Kramer realized that I was Tom Jenkins.

"Here's a gat in his hip pocket," said Ike, who was exploring my person, "and a couple o' dollars in small change. What in thunder did ye want to bring him here for, Spuds?"

"He's just the guy I want," said Spuds, whoever he might be. "He ain't no panhandler, Ike! Feel his muscle! He's a bindle stiff just in from workin' the fruit country, and spent his coin already. He'll be ready to talk turkey. Leave me to handle him. You take the car in to town and get that front axle straightened out. Telephone Ginger to be out here day after to-morrow with the boys, that I'll have everything in shape for the Las Rosas Ranch deal, and that we got to pull that off and then scatter quick.

Tell him to stay on the Frisco side of the bay until then. We don't want no dicks investigatin' this here ranch."

"Right," says Ike, and stomped away.

This conversation, added to my knowledge of Ike Kramer, made me conclude that the longer I stayed dead, the better off I'd be. Evidently, these gents had carted me across the bay somewhere, to one of the chicken coops they call ranches in these parts. Also, Spuds and Ike and Ginger and "the boys" were not what you might call on speaking terms with the police. That fitted in pretty well with what I knew of Ike Kramer.

This Ike Kramer, about three months previous, had been drawing pay checks from the H Bar L. He was no cowman, but more or less of a mechanic, and Steve had hired him to turn out some concrete piping for a patch of alfalfa land we were fixing to irrigate. That was all right; only Ike Kramer was no account.

One night I comes into the bunk house and finds him trimming the boys with a pack of cards that was sure made to order. When I busted up the proceedings, Ike Kramer unlimbered a little pearl-handled gat and missed me three times before I got him. The result was that I took a quirt and laid into that gent from heels to neck. After quirting him to a frazzle, I kicks him off the place. Exit Ike Kramer.

Fortunately I had enough sense not to claim his acquaintance right now, and he failed a plenty to recognize me. Nobody would have recognized me either, what with the left side of my face looking like a map of Flanders in wartime. I breathed freer when the door slammed behind Ike, and I was alone with the other man.

Opening my one good eye I looked around.

A dim electric bulb was burning, and as far I could see, this was some kind of a storehouse, stacked high with bales and barrels and kegs. What interested me however was the handsome gent sittin' on a keg rolling him a cigarette. Handsome? This here Spuds was all that the Venus Apollo ain't, if you get me! He had a bullet head, a cauliflower ear, a broken nose, eyebrows that had been knocked into one smear, and fists on him like hams. Prize fighter, and no mistake.

"Hullo!" he says, looking at me over his cigarette. "Woke up, have you?"

"More or less," I says. "Where am I?"

He grinned nastily. "Where guys don't ask no questions, see? Mebbe you want to pick up some easy coin—ten bucks a day and keep your mouth shut."

"If it was like my left eye," I says, "I wouldn't have to keep it shut. It'd stay that way. What's the idea?"

"Spill it, bo," he says. "Who are you?"

I sat up. "My name's Jasper. I been workin' on a ranch down south. What hit me?"

"A car run you down and I brung you here," he speaks up, watching me close. "Want that job or not?"

"Sure," I told him pronto. "Sure. Oh, sure! You bet I want it."


CHAPTER II

PARDNERS

"ALL RIGHT," he says. "I'm 'Spuds' Brosky, see? This is my ranch and trainin' quarters. You do what I say, and you pull down ten a day and found. Suit you?"

"Sure," I says.

"Git up, then, an' come along."

I weaves to my feet and manages to amble a bit. My gun was gone, but I was right cheerful to know that Ike had failed to locate my money. I had about five hundred tucked away under my left knee. It interfered some with sittin' on my heels; still, I never interfered none with the processes of nature by sittin' that way, bein' built to sit otherwise.

Spuds Brosky opened a door that led into an adjoining chamber, and I followed him. This was a little room, with another dim electric bulb, a bunk, and a washstand for furniture.

"This is yours, Jasper," says Brosky. "Hop to the hay. I'll see you in the mornin'."

He went out and closed the door. Listening real hard I heard a bolt slip home. So I sets on the cot and fabricates a smoke.

The presence of Ike Kramer, who appeared to be serving as chauffeur, was more than enough to tell me that I was in bad. Then the conversation I had overheard made things pretty clear. Clear enough, that is, to show me that Tom J. Jenkins had to step wide and handsome if he ever wanted to see his hotel and his new suit of clothes again.

This was the rendezvous of a gang, and no mistake. Pugs and gunmen from San Francisco. It was over across the bay, and was probably a lonely place. My cigarette got me that far, then I turned out the lamp and settled down on the cot. I was not fool enough to make any breaks. Besides I had been on my feet all day, and the asphalt made my legs sore. Like a wise gent, I lets slumber woo me with remarkable success.

Daylight wakened me. When I had pulled on my boots, I went to a cracked mirror hanging over the washstand, and inspected what I saw. If I was lookin' for any disguise, I sure had it good and plenty! My own pardner would never have knowed me again. The left side of my face was a swell affair, as the toothache advertisement says, and the right side showed pressing need of a razor.

"Mr. Jenkins," I says, "you are some hard-lookin' citizen and no mistake! Added to which, your old suit of clothes certainly got the worst of it when that automobile embraced you! I guess Ike Kramer won't know you again if he does see you. Just what game is Brosky putting over, anyhow? Well, you got loads of time to find out."

The door swung open, and Brosky summoned me forth. Seen by daylight, he was less impressive than ever from the standpoint of beauty. He gives me the once over, and a sneer.

"Fifty years old, ain't you? Fifty years old, and nothin' but a bindle stiff! Well, come along and we'll lay out your work. Any objection to bachin' it? No cook here."

"Suits me," I says briefly.

We went outside. The place where I had bunked was a long, large building something like a barn; Brosky said it had been built to store prunes in. Besides this, there was a bungalow and a garage. No other buildings in sight. The ranch was set out to prunes, but I judged the trees had not been touched for two years.

A fine rain was falling. A fair dirt road came up to the house and ended, so it was a branch off some highway. Hills all around. An automobile was out in front, the engine purring away merrily, and a figure was in the front seat waiting for Brosky.

"I've got to beat it," he says as he leads me toward the bungalow. "You camp out in the shack here. There's a stiff locked in the main room, and it's your job to keep an eye on him. I'll be back in a couple o' days."

He grabbed me suddenly by the shoulder, swung me around, and put his ugly face close to mine.

"Listen here, bo!" he says to me sternly. "If that guy breaks away, I'll smash you up and then frame you into San Quentin! Get me? You're here to watch him and nothin' else. Get me?"

I had to work hard to keep from getting him with my right, but remembered in time what I was supposed to be.

"Sure," I responds, meek and gentle. "Suits me, pardner."

We went into the bungalow, and he showed me a fine layout of groceries and eatables in the kitchen. Passing on, the two bedrooms and sun parlor were sure a sight—a dirtier hole I had never seen before! To judge from the pictures on the walls, this gang of Brosky's must be a fine young lot of penitentiary material. Brosky told me to clean up a bit, then unlocked the door of the main room.

We looked in on a gent who reposed on a sofa, his face to the wall and a dark streak showing on his cheek. He looked to be sleeping. Brosky cursed him and locked the door, handing me the key.

"This here ain't nothin' illegal, is it?" I asked.

"Illegal?" Brosky grinned as he spoke. "Not much, Jasper—not much! That gink in there is Gentleman John, and we're holdin' him for the cops, see? Broke out o' San Quentin last year. A lifer. You mind your step with him!"

"Naturally I will," I assented.

"If a truck comes in," he went on, "don't you pay no attention to what it does, savvy? Keep your eyes shut, both of 'em! That's all. So long."

"So long," I says.

I watched him depart. He got into the auto and she turned around. Ike Kramer was at the wheel, but I took good care that Ike did not have a good look at me. The car streaked away through the rain, and I was monarch of all I surveyed.

If I was a gay young man like Steve Moran, for instance, I would doubtless have waded through that gang like a movie hero. But I ain't. I'm slow and cautious, and I was in a plumb strange country. For that matter, I knew nothing about my whereabouts, and I still felt mighty shaky from my bruised head.

However, what had captured my wandering fancy was the smell in that warehouse where I had come to myself the previous night—the smell that reminded me of Chinatown. It was not prunes, unless my prune education had been a whole lot neglected. Whatever it was, that smell might explain the activities of Brosky's little bunch of pets, so as soon as I was alone on the place I started to explore the warehouse.

I was not bothering about Gentleman John—he was locked up and safe.

At the warehouse I found myself balked good and plenty. Every door was not only locked and hasped, but barricaded. I might have got in with an ax, but that wasn't on the program. So I went back to the house, lighted the oil stove, and began to rustle up breakfast. A bottle of liniment turned up, so I gave my injuries a dose of this. The bottle must have been laying around that bungalow several years, for it was thick and smelled like all the spices of Araby that had been spoiled for the last three hundred years—however, the stuff was strong, and took hold right away. It cheered me up a heap.

After laying away the best breakfast I had eaten since leaving the H Bar L, I began to feel sorry for Gentleman John. A search of the place showed no weapon in sight. Arming myself with a flatiron and the bottle of liniment, I went to look at the prisoner. When I opened the door, I found him sitting on the sofa holding his head.

"I'll ease you some breakfast right quick," I sung out, shutting the door again.

On the second trip I brought what grub was left. He was sitting as before, but lifted his head to look up at me. To my surprise, he was a decent-appearing young chap.

"Something smells powerful strong," he says, sniffing the air.

"Liniment, pardner," I told him. "Want some? I brung the bottle—"

"No, thanks," he says, and uttered a groan. "Gimme some coffee! Where am I?"

"Search me. Here's your coffee. Mean to tell me you don't know where you're at?"

He grabbed the cup and poured the coffee down his throat.

"How should I know?" he demanded, wiping his lips. "Gosh, that makes me feel good! Who are you, anyhow? What hit me?"

He fingered a bump over his ear, looking dazed and a heap bewildered.

"Don't start anything, now!" I warned him. "I know you're Gentleman John, and that you've done busted out of San

Quentin, and I'm sure heeled for trouble. Otherwise, you're all right."

"San Quentin!" he repeated, staring hard at me. "Gentleman John! Say, which of us is crazy?"

I did not answer him, but begun to roll me a cigarette. When I licked her, I bit off the twisted end. Quite a trick to that—it was a habit I had picked up off Steve Moran. Seeing me do it, the prisoner opened his eyes wider.

"Good land!" he exclaimed. "I never knew but one man to do that stunt! Where did a one-eyed tramp like you ever know Steve Moran?"

The cigarette fell out of my fingers.

"Now look what you done!" I says. "See here, do you know Steve?"

"Do I know him?" he repeated. "Great Scott, man! Is he anywheres around here? Go tell him Jim Bailey wants to see him—"

He could have knocked me down with a feather at that. I had often heard Steve speak of this Bailey gent, who according to him was one white man and a bosom friend.

"Quit it!" I says, sparring for time. "You ain't Jim Bailey! You're an escaped lifer from the penitentiary."

He stared at me like I was a six-legged boarhound.

"I was Jim Bailey last night," he says thoughtfully after a spell of silence. "Up to nine o'clock, that is. Then Kramer brought home the car and I fired him, and something happened to—"

He began to finger his wounded head once more. The name of Kramer, however, fetched me around in a hurry. I began to think that somebody had lied a heap to me.

"Got anything to prove that you're Bailey?" I says.

He fished some papers out of his pocket. They were addressed to Jim Bailey at the Las Rosas Ranch. This last name started my brain to working all regular.

"All right, pardner," and I handed back the papers. "You win! You're Bailey."

"Much obliged." He grinned cheerfully. "And who the deuce are you?"

"Tom Jenkins."

"Steve Moran's pardner—oh, come off!" Poor Bailey looked staggered. "Why, Jenkins is an old-time rancher, a cowman! You're a drunken stiff with a hangover."

I pulled out my watch, opened her up, and handed her over. Steve give me that watch one time early in our acquaintance, after I had taken a bunch of steers overland on the old Utah trail, on a fool bet. There was quite an inscription in the back of the watch. Bailey, he scratches his head and looks me over again.

"Where'd you rob Jenkins?" he asks.

"Durn it, you pesky fool, *I* am Jenkins!" I tells him. "There's somethin' mighty queer in all this here business, and I want to find out what it is. D'you know the guy who owns this place—a pug named Brosky?"

"Never heard of him."

"Well, listen."

I started in and told him all about how I had come here. After a while I began to impress him that I was telling the truth. The name of Ike Kramer reached him, likewise.

"Why," he says, "Kramer was my chauffeur until last night! I found out that he was a sneak thief and fired him. He must have hit me—"

"Him or an earthquake," I agreed.

He sat back, looked me over again, and then come to his feet with a grin on his face and his hand out.

"Upon my soul, I believe you're Tom Jenkins!" he said. "Shake!"

We shook, and then got down to business.

## CHAPTER III

### FILING UP EVIDENCE

JIM BAILEY was a quiet young chap with a keen eye and a good jaw on him. The more I saw of him, the better I liked him.

He informs me that quite a spell back, he had got tired of leadin' a gay life in the city, where his only excitement was dancing, bucking the stock market with his surplus coin, and dodging holdup men in high society. So he had bought him a ranch in the hills across the bay, the Las Rosas. I judged a girl had something to do with it, and I was right, as usual.

The Las Rosas, it seemed, was sixty acres set out to prunes, surrounding an elegant house that had cost a fortune. Jim Bailey bought the works cheap enough, and set in to make a name for himself. When the yearly round-up took place, he expected to clean up several thousand off his prunes.

"Fine!" I tells him. "Are we anywhere near home?"

"Search me!" he says with a grin. "I know as much where we are as you do."

"That ain't all I don't know," I said. "What has this here Brosky and his gang got to do with you? Or with your ranch?"

Bailey gave a low whistle, and frowned.

"Looks bad!" he said after a while. "For one thing that house was pretty well stocked up with booze when I bought her. Probably Kramer got his job with me to work from the inside. The gang means to loot my place."

"If that's all," I says, "let 'em loot! I got no sympathy with young fellows like you who think they must stock up on the hard stuff or else hold a lodge of sorrow all their lives."

"Oh!" says he, and looks at me with a twinkle in his eye. "Is this the hardboiled cattle raiser who wanted to turn San Francisco upside down to find him a drink of hooch?"

He had me there, all right.

"However," he went on, seriously enough, "it ain't the liquor I care about, Jenkins. They can loot the whole works; I bought it for my future guests, that's all."

Something was troubling him—something worse than liquor, I could see. So I urged him to come clean. He was just about to do so, when we caught the rumble and bang of a truck coming along at good speed. We both jumped for the windows.

Sure enough, there was a truck and a big one, coming up the road at full speed. Seeing four men standing in her, behind the driver's seat, I knew that this must be the arrival of which Brosky had spoken, and that they must be going to do something to the contents of the warehouse.

"Duck," I says to Bailey. "I'll set out on the back stoop and watch proceedin's, but you keep out o' sight. Lay down and play dead! Thank fortune, Kramer ain't in the crowd."

"Find out where we are, if you can," he returned.

I took up the flatiron and went to the kitchen, locking the door of the dungeon cell behind me in case anybody took a look at the prisoner. I did miss the old forty-five a heap, but a flatiron ain't so bad in a pinch. I found that out one time when a chink laundryman had an argument with T.J. Jenkins and laid said Jenkins out cold. After which occasion, said Jenkins bought him a flatiron and practiced up until he was right handy with the tool.

Gaining the back stoop, I set down on the steps, laid the flatiron beside me, and went to work on a cigarette. The big truck rolled up and rolled on, while the men in her looked me over pretty hard. She rolls on to the warehouse. One of the men, which disembarked there, attacked the locks on the doors, while another of them came strolling over to me.

I'm here to tell you that citizen was tough! Not the brutal Brosky type, but cool and deadly; the kind that shoots first and asks for money later. He packed as vicious an eye as I've ever seen outside a moving picture. He had seen better days, too—

looked like he had once been a gentleman. I ain't never been one myself, so I ain't a good judge.

"Hullo!" he says, stopping and looking me over. "Who the devil are you?"

"Modesty forbids me mentionin' the fact," I returned, lighting my cigarette. "Leavin' modesty out of the deal, Brosky has likewise recommended silence. When it comes to takin' advice, stranger, I'm plumb gentle and reconciled."

"Oh! You're the fellow Brosky ran over!" He gave a nasty chuckle, and smiled that thin-lipped smile of his. It was like a piece of ice. The fact begun to percolate to my brain that this man was no mere gangster. He confirmed the suspicion immediately.

"Brosky," he told me coolly, "takes his orders from me. Savvy that? You talk like a cattleman. Ever play stud?"

"I have dallied with the fickle pasteboards once or twice in my life," I confessed.

"All right," he says. "You tell Brosky that he's to stay here to-morrow. I'm going to take you to the Las Rosas in his place. Any news from Ginger?"

"Stranger," I says, "you're in over my depth. I don't know Ginger, nor you neither. I don't even know where I am! If you got any message for Brosky, write her out and I'll deliver it."

He nodded assent. "Right," he admitted. "I'll do it."

He unbuttoned a long coat he was wearing. Underneath this, I saw a right good outfit of clothes, and a jeweled scarfpin. He fetched out a gold pencil, and scribbled a note on a bit of an old envelope from his pocket.

"This will fix it up with Spuds," he said, as he gave me the note. "Now you tell him this: He's to stay here to-morrow and watch Bailey. He's not to come over to the Las Rosas at all. Ginger will bring the boys there, and after the clean-up I'll bring everybody here for the split and the get-away. Savvy?"

"Plenty," and I nodded. He turned away and went to join the others.

I sat and smoked, thinking hard. Why he wanted me at the Las Rosas, I had no notion. It was plain that he had been out of touch with Brosky, but had heard of me joining the gang from somebody else. Thus, he did not know the lie Brosky had told me about Jim Bailey being an escaped convict.

In the course of a long and mostly misspent existence, I have learned that it pays to keep cool and waste a little time on education. So I tucked away the note and went on resting my feet, hoping to learn more.

Having opened up the warehouse, the four men and the driver began to load up their truck. The load consisted of nothing but kegs and barrels, which presumably contained hard liquor. In this event, it was not hard to see that the one truck-load before me represented a very tidy fortune.

When the liquor was aboard, the gang piled some of the matting bundles around, above, and behind, so that the kegs were invisible. Then they locked up the warehouse again, piled on the truck, and the leader waved his hand to me.

"I'll send for you to-morrow," he sings out.

I watched the truck rumble away, down the road and out of sight, then I rejoined Bailey.

While he hears what had taken place, he listens with a slight frown on his face; then his keen eyes lighted up suddenly, and he reached for the note. We opened her out and found only a brief message telling Murphy to stay at the bungalow and wait for orders. The note was signed "Scranton."

"Whew!" Jim Bailey let out a whistle. "I've got it! Was this chap a tall, slender devil, with a smile on him like hard ice?"

"You've said it," I responds.

"He's the man, then!" Bailey sits up. "This guy Scranton comes of a good family, Jenkins."

"Come quite a ways, I reckon. But go ahead."

"He ran through a lot of money, and about six months ago was expelled from one or two clubs to which I belong for some crooked work. I never met him personally. But he's the man higher up in this gang—no doubt about that!"

"Spill it," I ordered. "Unbosom. Elucidate! My cards is down."

"Plain enough." Bailey had the thing by the tail, to judge by his looks. He was real excited. "You know how the whisky thing is worked around here?"

"If I knowed, would I be here?"

He explained. It seemed that without a permit from the Federal director, no truck driver could move any liquor. Hence and, naturally, forged permits had come into existence. Like everything else, San Francisco had witnessed a lot of liquor robberies. It was clear, then, that this gang had pulled off a lot of those robberies, moved the stuff across the bay with forged permits, and that over on this side Scranton was disposing of the liquor. It was on this end that the real brains were needed. Brosky and his toughs could handle little things like robberies without any help.

"Well," I said, "we had already figured most of that before the truck came. What was it you was about to get off your chest? Why does Scranton want me at the Las Rosas Ranch tomorrow? What's the game there?"

Jim Bailey grinned at me, a trifle sheepish.

"Well, you see, I'm to be married next week," he explained. "So I had invited a few of my old friends out to the ranch tomorrow night, for a farewell bachelor party. Nobody there but the chink who cooks for me, savvy?"

"Oh, I savvies plenty!" I told him. "And I should think you'd had more sense—"

He grew red. "See here, none of that! It's to be a gentleman's party, Jenkins—no rough stuff whatever. A little wine served, of course; that's all. A rousing good game of stud, and an old-fashioned barbecue."

I takes back my hard thoughts. This chap was all right, and any friends of his were sure to be all right. And, of course, Steve was a friend of his.

"I tried to get Steve to come," he went on, like he was reading my thoughts, "but he was pretty busy at the ranch, he said."

I had to grin at this because Steve had only been married about four months. He was as hard to pry away from home as a gent down with smallpox. It just couldn't be done.

"Now, as I figure it," he pursued with new animation, "here's the game Scranton and his friends have in mind! You see, the six fellows who are coming over will all bring a wad along for the stud game; they can all afford to lose a good bit, and so can I. What's more, I keep a little money in the house—"

"How much is a little?" I puts in.

"A couple of thousand. Don't interrupt. Kramer, of course, knew that the party was coming off. I had arranged for him to take the big car to town and bring the boys from the ferry. So he put Scranton's gang wise, and Scranton planned a clean-up. When I fired Kramer last night, Kramer hit me over the old bean and cleared me out of the place."

"Oh, I see!" At this, light began to break over me. "Scranton plans some sort of a con game, which will end by cleaning out your booze, and your friends likewise! If the whole crowd runs accordin' to your form, Jim, I suppose there'll be six or eight thousand in the party. A nice little wad, by gosh!"

"Well, we have to spoil this game somehow," said Jim Bailey, looking worried. "I can't let my friends come out to my place and be robbed!"

I nodded. Here was a fine chance for Scranton to make a haul off a party of young plutocrats with more money than sense. However, it was up to us to prevent the deal if we could.

"If we leaves here now and immediate," I referred to Jim, "we'll stave off the raid but we won't catch the raiders. They'll vanish. Now, let's you and me set right here. Brosky comes back sometime to-day, prob'ly alone. To-morrow morning, Scranton sends for me. Chances is, he'll send Kramer. I owe Brosky considerable for what his car done to me last night, so I'll take care of Brosky. You owe Ike Kramer for that jolt he give you, so you can take care of Ike. Then you and me takes Kramer's car and goes to the party. What say?"

"Fine!" he exclaimed. "Fine! But there are details to settle—"

"Settle 'em when the time comes," I says, and gets up. "Let's go take a look at the inside o' that warehouse, Jim. I'm curious about that Chinese smell."

CHAPTER IV

THE SURPRISE PARTY

WE LEFT the house, after indulging in a bath and a general clean-up, which made us both feel considerable better.

In the garage we located a few tools lying around, and advanced in force on the long shed. This was roughly built with battens over the planks. In no time at all we removed a couple of battens, pried out a plank, and crawled inside.

The kegs were gone of course, and the piles of stuff were largely depleted. A good many of the bales remained, however. Jim Bailey looked at the matting around them, and showed me the stencils in English or Chinese.

"One of the transpacific mail steamers was looted a couple of weeks ago, here in port," he said. "Or rather, her warehouse was looted. Here's some of the stuff—silk and other things. This is a sweet gang we're up against, Jenkins!"

"Nope," I said. "You look at it plumb wrong, Jim."

"Eh?" He gave me a puzzled look. "How so?"

"It's the other way round—that there gang is up against us. Savvy? Got any money?"

"Kramer cleaned me out. Why?"

"Well, I'll lend you a hundred off my private roll."

"What for?" he asks.

"So's we can keep busy. There's some old decks of cards back at the house. Let's go get interested in a seven-up game."

"Then you don't aim to tip off the police about this place?"

"Sure," I says. "All in good time. What we got to do is to aim at a general round-up, ain't it? We can't do that until we learn just what Scranton's game is at your ranch. Do any of these gents know you by sight?"

"Kramer does. None of the rest, I imagine. I never met Scranton."

"Well," I tells him, "crawl out and begin to wish you turn up a jack every deal, because I sure aim to trim you at seven-up! Come on."

We left the shed, replaced what we had displaced, and went our ways to the house. There we cleaned up a bit and got things so we could forget the dirt, and finally, after lunch, settled down to an old-time session at seven-up. There ain't no better game for two hands or four, and we managed to enjoy ourselves considerable, at two bits a corner.

We were surprised when evening came, with no sign of Spuds Brosky or his crowd, although I kept a sharp watch out for him. We sailed into supper, and nearly got caught at it; we were just washing up the dishes, when the sound of an engine reached us from outside. Jim Bailey made a dive for his room, and when the door opened up I was wiping the dishes and singing "Old Dan Tucker" in a carefree manner.

Brosky came in, alone, and I heard the car departing.

"How's everything?" he says.

"Fine. Had supper?"

"Yep. That guy all right?"

"I guess so," I said. "I ain't troubled him none, and he ain't sung out for no grub. I was afraid to get too close to him, you see, him bein' a desperate man and all."

Brosky gives me a sneer and stamped off to look at Bailey. Pretty soon he comes back, and I hands him the note Scranton had left.

He was an ugly cuss and no mistake, and his cussing was ugly likewise. When he asked for particulars, I told him what Scranton had said. At this he cussed some more, but this time admiringly. He seemed to think a lot of Scranton.

"Bo, if you had as much nerve as that guy, you'd be livin' on Nob Hill!" he says. "Kramer will meet him to-night. Let's see, now! He'll have his three ginks, you, an' Kramer—six all together. I guess that'll be a cinch! Ginger will bring two more with him."

"What's the lay?" I asked, hopin' to get some information. Instead of which, he only turned on me with a snarl and a curse.

"Scranton has pulled you into it—go ask him!" he said. "You git to askin' questions, and somethin' will happen to you real sudden!"

"What?" I says.

He reached for his coat pocket, and I let him have the flatiron, which same I had been fondling the while. Poor Brosky! I almost felt sorry for him. Flatirons ain't usually reckoned among the deadly weapons, and there's quite a knack to throwing them; but when they hit, they sure do make some impression.

For a fraction of a second Brosky knowed something had connected with him, then he was down for the count, with a fall that shook the house. Jim Bailey came on the jump. He stood in the doorway, lookin' from me to Brosky.

"What's the matter?" he says.

"Nothin' at all, Jim. Brosky, here, he done tried to flirt with a flatiron. It ain't done in the best society. Now look at his face, would you? I reckon we're even."

"Great gosh!" exclaimed Jim. "Was that why you brought that flatiron into my room this morning? Do you toss those things about for amusement?"

"Correct." I kneeled over Brosky and discovered that aside from a heap of damage to his facial ornaments, which were already off center, he had not suffered much damage.

We went through him and collected an automatic out of one pocket, another out of another, and a pair of brass knuckles from elsewhere. Besides these, a wad of money which I pocketed for future use. This wad seemed to be all brand-new fifties.

"Chuck him in the guardhouse," I told Bailey. "This gent don't deserve any pity to mention, Jim, so repress them arguments I see creeping up your spine. Wait till I get through with him, and we'll lock him in a bedroom."

When I got through with him, Spuds Brosky was one harmless person. I done roped his hands, feet and mouth with a clothesline I found behind the back door, and we carried him into one of the bedrooms. There I roped him to the bed, good and tight.

"Now what?" asked Bailey. "Are we agreed that our future plans will depend upon Mr. Scranton and his project of tomorrow night?"

"Sure," I assented.

"But how are we to know what said project might be? He may kidnap my friends and hold them to ransom, or he may rob and assault them, or he may merely murder them."

"We'll make this gent talk, right pronto," and I indicated Brosky. To my surprise Jim Bailey laughed.

"Don't! Have a heart now. Let's play out the game like sports—what say? Supposing Kramer comes after you in the morning, alone; I'll attend to him, and we'll leave him here to keep Brosky company. Get the cops after them, if you like. Then I'll drive you to the ranch, and you can tell Scranton that Kramer sent you back alone in the car—account for his absence in any way you like. I'll hide out around the ranch house, and we'll see what turns up and meet it according. What say?"

"It's sporty, no denying that," I told him. "But, me bein' a gray-haired old man with one foot in the grave and one side of my face black and tan, I ain't much set on bein' sporty, Jim! That's a fact."

"You're a liar," he shot back. "I've heard too much about you from Steve Moran. How about the time you and Bill Cook went down to Arizona, and you tells everybody he was the detective sent down to handle the mining men, and then you got drunk and started to shoot up the place and they tried to lynch Bill—"

"Have mercy!" I holds up both hands, grinning. "Conceded, Jim, conceded! You wins your point. Say no more. Let's go finish that game of seven-up, and then get a good night's sleep. Are you willin' or not?"

"Suits me," he assented.

And we done so.

Morning came in due course, like mornings usually do, and found us much refreshed. It found me looking considerable worse than the day before, because the left side of my face had lost its raw look, and from that angle I appeared somewhat like a greaser what had been stung by cholla cactus and then painted himself with iodine. However, we had each of us a gun. Not that I am set much on these automatics, but they make fine hitting weapons if you hold 'em the natural way and strike out with the front sight.

About Spuds Brosky, neither me nor Jim Bailey bothered our heads. A day or so without food or water or action would be just the thing for him, we figured. Of course, we were layin' our bets on the chance that Kramer would come to get me, and would come alone.

By nine in the morning nobody had showed up, and we were getting nervous. Shortly thereafter, however, we made out a car approaching up the road, so we laid low. We watched from the windows as she arrived; sure enough it was Kramer, and alone. He turned around at the gate, left his engine running, and started in on foot for the house. Naturally we let him come.

He walked right in on the surprise party. Man, oh, man! I was never so tickled in all my life as when Jim Bailey received him! I shut the door behind him, and that no-account skunk tried to pull a gun until I took a hand. His artillery gone, we just naturally let nature take its course between him and Bailey.

About ten minutes later, we sewed Ike Kramer up alongside Spuds Brosky. Jim allowed that he was feeling a heap better.

So, with no man pursuing, we climbs into the car and starts for nowhere.


CHAPTER V

CLEARED FOR ACTION

NATURALLY, IT was no trick at all for me and Jim Bailey to get our bearings. The first house we struck Jim went in and got directions.

It proved that we were about forty miles from the Las Rosas Ranch, all on the highway. That means about an hour and a quarter in California, or less, depending on the car you got and what make of motor cycle the speed cops use.

Not being in any special hurry, we ambles along until we come to San Leandro, the little town outside of which lay Jim's rancho. There we dropped in to a hash house and got us a good feed. I tried to argue Jim into telephoning his San Francisco friends and calling off the party, but he vetoed it right off.

"All right," I says. "It's your funeral, not mine. What's your program?"

"Leave me here, and go ahead alone to the ranch," says he promptly. "I'll sneak in after dark and see what happens. You wise up the boys when they come, and be prepared for trouble. With you and Kramer out of it, Scranton will have seven men instead of nine. There'll be eight of us, so we can handle it."

I could see he was wild for the general excitement indicated by his scheme, and would not listen to tipping off the cops, so I shut up. We shook hands by the curb and parted.

Left alone with the car, I drove down the street a ways and then stopped at a drug store. In the telephone booth, I calls the chief of police in San Francisco long distance.

"Listen here!" I says, when somebody answered. "You got a fine gang of crooks over on this side of the bay, and you'd better come get 'em. Never mind who this is! Fellow named Spuds Brosky has a ranch thirty miles south of San Leandro. He's there now, tied up, and he's got a shed full of looted liquor and stuff stolen from the China Mail steamers. His gang is staging a stag party at the Las Rosas Ranch, ten miles north of San Leandro, to-night. Drop in there toward the shank of the evening, and get there before the ranch is plumb looted. So long!"

I rang off, and my conscience felt a heap better as I drove out of town.

Being provided with plenty of directions by Jim Bailey, I had no trouble finding the Las Rosas Ranch. When I left the highway behind and found the place, I was astonished; the house was a big stucco affair, big as three barns, and fixed up something scrumptious. A man came down the steps, wearing a regular waiter's soup and fish—and then I recognized him for one of the men that had been in the truck with Scranton.

"Oh, it's you!" he says. "Beat it inside here, you boob—don't let that old chink see you! He ain't wise yet, and we're going to keep him from suspectin'. Come along."

I followed him into the house. I always thought we had some ranch house down to the H Bar L, but this place laid over any I ever saw. Waxed floors, Oriental rugs, big mirrors, and all kinds of doolinks scattered around. Jim Bailey had probably been fixing up for his bride, and he sure had a pretty nest, I'll say! Real elegant, too.

Well, Scranton met me inside. That gent was fixed up so I had hard work recognizing him again—wearing clothes that set him off fine, and a big pair of these owl specks hugging his face. He stood and grinned at me. Behind him I seen a couple more of his gang, wearing the same soup-and-fish outfit as the first one.

"Well," he says, shaking hands with me real hearty, "this is sure a surprise, Mr. Jenkins! How'd you leave everything at the H Bar L?"

His icy smile turned me cold inside. All I could do was to reach for my gun and back into a corner, naturally supposing that somehow he had discovered who I was. Instead of staging any fireworks, however, my action made the whole crowd laugh.

"Come, come!" exclaimed Scranton. "Put up the gun. Here's the lay, now: You're to pretend that you're a cattleman named Jenkins, savvy? He's a great friend of the chap who owns this place, or at least he ought to be. You've come up from down State to attend this festive gathering, understand? Didn't Kramer tell you about it?"

Gradually I got the stiffness out of my neck. So this was it! Ike Kramer had told them about Jenkins, and finding that I was a cowman, Scranton had the notion of me posing as Jenkins. Wouldn't that tickle a feather duster?

"Why," I says, "why, that's all right with me, pardner! But what's the idea?"

"Where's Kramer?" he asked sharply.

"Back at the ranch," I says. "Brosky was took sick this morning. Kramer sent me along with the car and said he'd be here later."

"All right," said Scranton, and nodded. "There's to be a party here late this afternoon, and you're to play stud, get me? Now come along, and I'll start you off on the road to being a gentleman. One of you boys take Kramer's place, and go meet that crowd with the car! They are coming over on the three o'clock ferry, understand? Rush 'em here. Get here by four, and remember you're a chauffeur and be polite. That's all. Come on, Mr. Jenkins!"

We came on.

Scranton showed me the house, exactly as if he'd been the owner and me his guest, callin' me "Mr. Jenkins" and introducing me as such to his grinning gang. And all the time, so far as Scranton knew, I was just an old bindle stiff! There was deviltry in that gent, and I seen that he was laying for Jim Bailey's friends with some deep game.

He showed me the guest rooms upstairs, settled me in one of them, and called in his gang. He intended to use them as valets and waiters and what not on Bailey's friends, and told them to practice up on me. That was all right for a time, but pretty soon I kicked.

I got my gun, which Scranton did not object to me having, and backed away.

"Gents," I said, "I don't object to nothing in reason, but I been shaving and bathing myself, off and on, for fifty year and I aim to keep it up. Savvy that?"

Scranton grinned and called 'em off. "Go ahead, Mr. Jenkins, the house is yours!" Then he added: "All, that is, except the liquor. Heaven help the first one of you that touches a drop until I give the word!"

Finding myself alone at last, I waded in and enjoyed a general clean-up and shave. That face of mine certainly was a sight! My left profile looked like the back of a rainbow.

A complete outfit of Jim Bailey's clothes had been laid out for me, and I hopped into it with great eclaw, as Frenchy Dubois used to say. I was beginning to enjoy myself fine, especially the notion of me posing as Tom Jenkins, which same I was. What was Scranton's game? That stuck me; naturally, I could not guess it. He might have held up the party and robbed them, without all this fooling around.

When I rejoined Scranton downstairs, he took me out and introduced me to the chink cook, who was fixing up the barbecue pits in the back yard, and tending the fires. Then we went inside again, and settled down in the library with a box of Bailey's cigars. Scranton called up a number, and pretty soon was talking with Ginger, whoever that gent was. I gathered that Ginger and his gang was to arrive with the truck.

"When you come," says Scranton, "tie up the chink and go right to work. We'll keep the party occupied. When the truck is loaded, and not until, is the time to cash in."

He rang off. I glanced at him over my cigar.

"What kind of a stud game are you goin' to perpetrate? Cold decks or what?"

To my surprise, he gives me a deadly look and shook his head.

"None of that, my man!" he ordered."This game is on the level, understand? Here's a stake. We'll settle up afterward, when we reach Brosky's place."

He slips me a roll of bills, which same I pockets. This remark of his, together with what I could judge of the man, gave me the clew to his game.

Believe it or not, Scranton was taking big risks. For what? Nothing else than to sit once more in a game with a party of real gents! He had been a gentleman once, remember, and he was unable to forget it. Bad as he was, he had a hankering inside of him for a touch of decency, and he was going to get it. Then he would rob the whole party and blow.

Queer mix-up, eh? Such were the facts, however. Of course he could afford to play the game square, because he would end up by getting all the money in the party; just the same it was a queer kind of human nature.

Well, the time slipped on. The library was cleared for action, the table and chips laid out, and a buffet table loaded with wines. Four o'clock came and went. Scranton had plundered the wall safe which held Jim Bailey's valuables, so he was well stocked with cash. Then one of the gang jumps in with word the party was coming.

Scranton dragged me out to the front porch to welcome them. Jim's big Twin Eight slipped up to the door, and out tumbled six gents who lighted with yells and started forward.

Then they stopped at sight of us. Most of them recognized my companion.

"Scranton!" said somebody.

"Exactly." Scranton smiled at them. "Gentlemen, Mr. Bailey has put me in charge of his ranch and insisted that I should join in the events of the evening. Unfortunately, he was called to San Francisco half an hour ago—his fiancee was injured in an accident to-day. He just called up from the ferry to advise me that he would be back this evening, and to go ahead with the party."

This was blamed clever. These gents knew Scranton, knew he had gone bad. They naturally judged that he was trying to live on the square and that Jim Bailey was helping him. It was up to them to accept him as the gentleman he had been, under Bailey's roof—and they done it. Yes, sir! I'll say that crowd was a bunch of real sports.

They came up and shook hands with Scranton, who introduced me. Several of them knowed Steve Moran, and they were tickled to death to meet me. Scranton looked kind of puzzled at the way I played my part, answering questions about Steve and so forth, but of course he could not dream that I was the real Tom Jenkins. As we followed the others inside, he grinned.

"Good work!" he murmurs to me. "You're all right. Keep it up."

"Thanks," I says. "I aim to."

If Scranton had been anything but the cold-hearted devil he was, the way those gents took him at his word and made him one of themselves would have stung him deep. But not him!

There was considerable talk for a while. The boys had brung along a present for Jim Bailey, a big silver trophy cup with an inscription about him having copped the finest girl in them parts, and a bunch of mourning wreaths and floral offerings with "Gone Home" on them. We got these things fixed up in the dining room to surprise Jim when he came, and then adjourned to the scene of action.

When Bailey's bunch unlimbered their rolls—oh, boy! Nothing but yellow chips went on that board. I reached down to my first national bank and got my private roll; added to what Brosky and Scranton had provided, it made a fair showing and got me a small stack. Preliminaries over with, we cut for deal and settled down to the serious business of the day.

I have sat in some wild games of stud, hither and yon, but never with a bunch like that. One was a banker, two were stockbrokers, and the other three were just spenders. Knowing the game was on the level, I used my judgment and set in to win, which same I done. In an hour there was a stack four deep in front of me and more coming.

At this point one of the waiters called me to the telephone. I went out with him.

"Listen, bo!" he says, outside the library. "When the punch comes in, you lay off it, savvy? It's fixed."

I savvied and went back to the game, giving out that Jim Bailey had been on the wire with word that he was coming back. At this Scranton gives me a look of approval.

There was more or less wine consumed, but Scranton did not touch it. So things went on until about eight o'clock, when I heard a truck roll up. No word yet from Jim Bailey, and I was nervous. Pretty soon the chink showed up with word that the barbecue was ready, so we cashed in and prepared to move. After the grub the game would be taken up again.

Just here, two of the waiters brought in a steaming bowl of punch. Everybody but me and Scranton laid into it heavy, and that ended the festivities so far as they were concerned. Whoever had doped that stuff, sure knew his business!

CHAPTER VI

PANIC

HERE WAS something that Jim Bailey had not counted on! Those six friends of his went limp as soon as the punch hit their insides. The stuff must have held a large-sized dose of chloral, for those gents went out of action swift and sure.

This showed me Scranton's game. By the time these boys woke up and figured out that it was no joke at all but a real robbery, Scranton and Brosky's gang would have scattered to the four winds and would be safe. I might have warned these gents, but to what good? Scranton would have downed me, held them up, and beat it before they had understood the proceedings.

The waiters come in to grin at the six sleepers. Ginger and his gang hopped along also, to share in the looting that started pronto. All told, the party was rough and tough; as sweet a crowd of city gangsters as you ever dreamed of!

"All right," says Scranton. "Go through the place, boys; take everything that can be turned into quick money, but don't destroy stuff."

"We ain't finished with the cellar yet," spoke up Ginger, a red-headed mick.

"Everybody to the cellar, then," says Scranton.

Everybody piled toward the cellar door, which opened out of the kitchen. I got lost in the confusion and stayed behind for a look around, with half a notion that I could telephone to the San Leandro police.

I went to the side door, however, for a look. Outside was standing the truck, partly loaded with bottled goods. Beside it, the cellar doors were flung back. As I stood there I saw something move to one side, and jerked for my gun. Jim Bailey's voice reached me.

"That you, Jenkins?"

"It's me, so come on," I sung out cautious.

Bailey ran across the drive and joined me. He had some queer contraption on his back, like a big tank, that strapped across his shoulders.

"How's everything?" he said.

"Pretty punk," I told him. "Those gents who come to see you are stripped and doped. They'll wake up about to-morrow night. Scranton's gang is down cellar."

"Lordy! That's great!" he says. "You go back and lock the kitchen door to the cellar. Do it quick! Then come here and watch the fun."

"What's that thing on your back?" I said.

He jabbed me in the ribs, then shrunk into the doorway beside me as two of the gang come up to the truck with a case of liquor. Judging that he had some sort of fool scheme to put across, and figuring that we might as well catch the gang down cellar, I went back to the kitchen to close that door.

As I steps into the kitchen, the red-head Ginger comes up from the cellar.

"Hey, you!" he sings at me. "Beat it down here! We got to clean this stuff out."

"All right," I says, and steps to the door.

Poor old Ginger never knew what hit him. I swiped him over the empty place that should have held brains, and the front sight of that automatic bit into him deep. Ginger never let out a yip, but tumbled over and went to sleep underneath the stove.

I jumps to the door, shut it, and locked it, then rolled a big white refrigerator up against it for good measure. This done, I went back to join Bailey, wondering what he had up his sleeve.

"Done?" he asks.

"Done, pardner. That gent Ginger is done likewise. Now, what's the idea?"

"Chemicals," he says, and switched a nozzle and hose out of the contraption on his back. "This is a spray, and she sprays like a house afire! She's pumped up to high pressure, and here goes for results. Stand by!"

Before I could stop him, the cheerful fool gets down by the open cellar doors, points his nozzle into the opening, and lets fly.

Two of the gang were on the way up with a case. One of them let out a howl, and there came a crash as the liquor dropped. Then there came some more howls. I got a whiff of the stuff, which same looked a heap like steam, and it near tumbled me over.

"Gosh, don't kill 'em all!" I says.

"No danger!" Bailey grinned at me as he responded.

A gun barked, and a bullet tore past us. From inside came a noise of pounding, and I knew they were tackling the door up to the kitchen. Bailey switched off his stuff and climbed out from under the tank. He gives me the hose.

"Catch 'em as they come up," he says, "but don't try to make 'em go back. Give me a chance for work, now!"

I held down on the doorway, and just in time. Two of the gang were on the way up, and I let 'em have the stuff fair and square. One of them came through alive, and Bailey caught him as he emerged—caught him with a sweet right and left that knocked that gent out for fair.

"Next!" he says.

Three came all at once, and they came a-smoking. I got to them with the spray, but all of a sudden the tank give a "whoom!" as a bullet went through it. Them three gents emerged, staggering but game, and Jim Bailey dropped one of them. A cloud of choking spray-smoke was all around us from the busted tank, and I paused for no more experiments but used my gun on those gents with telling effect.

When I had shot one of them in the leg and put a bullet through the other's gun hand, they quit work and joined the boys Jim had knocked out. I slammed the cellar doors, then groped my way out of the smoke.

"Durn it!" I tells Jim, who was coughing his head off beside me. "This was a fine fool trick! Get a gun, you blamed idiot, and quit using your fists!"

Bailey seen the sense to that, and groped after one of the guns dropped by the gang.

At this juncture a tremendous crash echoed from inside the house. The door into the kitchen was down, and the refrigerator with it to judge from the sound. Now we had no chance whatever to round up the gang.

"This is the last time I ever do police work!" I says to Jim. "They'll be swarming over us in a minute. It's going to be a gangster finish—everybody shootin', with poison gas throwed in for good measure! Hop into that truck, and do it lively!"

We hopped into the truck, both of us, and got down among the cases and barrels that had been moved out of Jim's cellar.

I seen a gangster battle once in New York, when I was doin' trick riding in Madison Square Garden with a circus. It was many years ago, but memory has abode with me strong. So has a wild bullet I got in my innards. So, as we crouched, I took Jim by the neck and swore to throttle him if he got reckless with his gun before I give the word. I had no intention of giving the word, but did not mention the fact.

In a fraction of a minute Scranton and his crowd were turnin' the moonlight blue all around us. They gathered that the gang had started a scrap, until one of the gassed gents recovers enough to holler something about the dicks. At that the crowd came aboard the truck with a simultaneous yell. Scranton tried to hold 'em back, but those gents were anxious to get away in a hurry. So finally Scranton laughed and followed them.

They crowded in to the back end. Me and Jim were up forward under the driver's seat, behind a barricade of cases, so we passed unobserved. Somebody cranked up, and the truck began to throb. At that minute, looking out over the stern, I seen a flash of light down the road that might have come from a car's headlights.

"Hold steady!" I tells Jim.

"Where's that guy Jenkins?" yells somebody. "He ain't here, Scranton!"

"To thunder with him!" exclaimed Scranton. "Everybody in? Where's Ginger?"

The sentiment was unanimous that Ginger could fish for himself, and the truck began to move. That gang was panic-stricken. Scranton tried to argue with them, and somebody took a shot at him.

With that, blazes cut loose. Scranton pulled a gun and began to shoot, cursing them for the cowards they were.

## CHAPTER VII

### PERFECT PEACE

WHEN SCRANTON lost his temper and his head at the same time, the truck had got turned around and was headed for the open sea of moonlight.

When he started shooting, the gang went into him with all guns out. Bullets hummed all around, hither and yon. One of them went over my head, there was a tremendous crash, and the driver let out a last yell as he smashed down.

"She's runnin' wild!" I says to Jim Bailey. "Good night to your booze now, pardner!"

"Curse the booze!" he answered, and rose up with his gun smoking.

Then I'll say there was something doing!

Scranton was down on top of the gassed gents who had been throwed in. Some of the gang were scrambling forward to reach the driver's seat, others were fighting among themselves like a pack of dogs. Meantime, the truck was rumbling and roaring among the prune trees with nobody at the helm.

Bing! went a tree, and bang! went Jim's gun. Fortunately, the old ship was rearing like a sunfishin' broncho in that plowed ground, what with trees and rocks underfoot. I went down on top of Jim, and the bullets missed us.

The gang was yelling at one another to run and shoot us and beat it and what not—clear out of their heads. A bullet smashed a bottle of wine in my face as I rose up, and I got the gent that fired it—got him proper, too. Looking back, I could see a string of figures behind us. Every time the truck rose up and climbed a tree somebody got shook off like a ripe prune.

Then—*bam!* We come up all standing against something solid, which later turned out to be a concrete well house.

The sudden halt was unexpected by all hands. The truck upended on her nose a little, then settled back and began to trickle red juice from busted bottles. Seventeen cases of rich wines, all busted, were slung on top of me and Jim, with several gangsters in the pile likewise. For as much as three minutes, I reckon, we lay there counting stars and wondering how much damage the earthquake had done.

First thing I heard was Jim Bailey gulping and muttering by my ear.

"Gulp! That was champagne," he murmurs dreamily. "Gulp! That was burgundy with a dash of port. Gulp! That was riesling flavored with gin. Gulp! That was—"

I left him to gulp in peace, and struggled up. When I had picked broken glass out of my system and shoved back a few cases and barrels, it dawned upon me that day must have broken some hours ahead of time, by the light around us.

Instead of day, however, it was light from a car standing close by. As I waited I caught a shot, then another; then some yells. All of a sudden a husky gent climbed the pile of débris on the truck and waved a gun at me.

"Hands up!" he says. "Oh, sergeant! Here's more on the truck!"

"Thank the Lord! The cops are here!" I remarked, and elevated my hands. "Come on, Jim!"

Jim rose up, with a part of a champagne bottle in his hair, and two cops hauled us off the truck. A big touring car was standing near by, and from the sights and sounds I concluded that half a dozen policemen had come along to investigate our private riot.

"Put 'em with the others!" said the sergeant, but Jim halted him.

"Hold on, officer! I'm the owner of this place—Bailey."

"You the guy that telephoned San Francisco?" demanded the cop.

"No, he ain't," I speaks up. "I'm the guilty party."

"You look it," says the sergeant. "Take 'em all to the house, boys."

Ten minutes later everybody was corraled in the kitchen of the house. It was a sick-looking gang. I'll tell the world! Scranton was dead, and so were two or three others—I did not stop to count heads. Ginger was placed amid the rest.

The police sergeant came into the kitchen tearing his hair.

"Six men doped in there!" he hollered. "A chink tied up outside—hey! Haul that chink in here and see if he identifies that guy as Bailey!"

Jim grinned at this. The poor chink was dragged in, and he identified Jim all right. After that things settled down. Jim identified me pronto—and you should have seen the eyes of those gangsters bulge when they found I really was Tom Jenkins!

It appeared that my telephone message had stirred something. Brosky and Kramer had been found, and the shed had been inspected. Then the cops had headed for here with the results aforesaid.

In half an hour I was once more alone with Jim and the chink cook, partaking of a cigar and wondering if all had been a dream.

We wanders into the library and inspects those six happy sleepers around the poker table. Jim looked at them and grinned.

"Tell you what let's do!" he says to me. "Suppose we leave
these poor boobs right here. They'll wake up to-morrow some
time. We'll be back from court by then, and we'll take up the
party where she left off—tell these chaps they got drunk and
fell asleep, savvy? They'll lose a day out of life and—"

"Jim," I says, "you're on! But not me. I got important business
elsewhere."

"Here!" he exclaimed. "You've got to stay and see this
through!"

"Not me. I've swore off peaceful country life in these parts.
Besides, as I say, I got to be in San Francisco to-morrow sure,
without fail."

"What for?" he says.

"A suit of clothes," and I rolls a cigarette.

WHERE THE RAILROAD ENDED

CHAPTER I

WE BEGIN OUR JOURNEY

WELL, WHEN me and Steve Moran done sold out the H Bar L for a quarter of a million cash, it was considerable of a surprise to all concerned. But when a gent comes along and offers twice what your ranch is worth, what are you aiming to do, I'm asking?

I held out the old brand, which was registered in my name. I spent thirty years with the H Bar L, and I meant to keep her with me. After the deed was done and the crime committed, I felt real sorrowful. However, it had to be did. Steve's wife, she was goin' home to visit her folks for a few months on business of an interestin' nature, as the newspapers say; and while Steve was waiting around to be told he was a proud father, he figured on going somewheres with me and looking for a new place to start in life.

On our last night in the old shack I was moaning around about having no place to go and wanting to find a quiet, retired spot to end my days away from crowds. The gent named Sloan, who had bought us out, gives me a grin.

"If you want quiet," he says, "go up to Simplex County!"

"Where's that?" says Steve. "I never heard of that county."

"Nobody else did; that's why I left there," and Sloan laughs fit to kill. "I still own a few hundred acres there. She's a hundred miles north of San Francisco, without a railroad or even a store."

"But ain't Simplex County progressive at all?"

"Progressive?" Sloan waved his cigar helplessly. "Listen, now—listen! Up to a year or so ago they were still using six-hoss stages in them parts! Can you 'magine it? There's a hill several miles long—the north side of St. Helena Mountain—and full of curves so that a car can't hardly go down slow enough. These natives—listen, now!— they'd take them six-hoss stages down at a gallop—at a gallop, mind you!"

"How many died doin' of it?" I inquired.

"Nary a one. Sometimes a hoss would get run over, I hear, but that's all. There's a man up around them parts yet, an old pilgrim with three-foot whiskers, named 'Shorty' Jones. He's the only man ever drove an eight-hoss team down St. Helena, they say, only he'd come lashing 'em all the way. Gosh! But speakin' of Simplex County, gents, she's opening up and land prices are booming. Some day my acres there will be worth money."

Steve looks at me, and I seen trouble coming by the light in his wild eye. He was a reckless young devil, was Steve.

" 'Pinky,' " he says, addressing me by my usual handle, "Pinky, I'll bet you five thousand dollars you ain't got the nerve to drive a six-hoss outfit down that mountain!"

"You don't need to bet," I says. "I admits it here and now. What's more, you ain't going to drive one down, neither! I aims to protect your family if you don't."

"Want to run up there in our Elite tourster?" says Steve. "We might look over this uncivilized section of land, Pinky."

"I'm agreeable," I responds. "It's one of the sections of California I ain't never seen. But I ain't mentioning any land deal, Steve. If we goes, we goes as pilgrims, not investors. There may be no civilization up there, but I bet there's real-estate sharks!"

"Plenty," says Sloan to us, nodding assent. "Plenty. But if you gents will accept a letter to a friend of mine, you'll be treated white and no questions asked."

We could not ask anything fairer than that.

Later on, while we were alone, I had quite an argument with
Steve along the lines of curbing his reckless instincts for the
sake of his family. I gives him quite a lecture about it, too.

"Now you're a rich man, Steve," I concludes. "Rich, that is,
from a common-sense viewpoint. It's up to you to give your
family the best in life. Stick close to a city."

"Are you figuring on shakin' me, Pinky?" he says with a cold
air.

"Not me. But I'm too old to change my ways, Steve. I wouldn't
feel happy if I didn't have a few head o' cattle to keep me worried,
and all the family I got is the H Bar L brand. It's different with
you. You can't afford to be so dog-goned reckless at your age—"

Steve grinned.

"Wait a minute, Pinky! When you was my age what was you
doing? I didn't see it, but I've heard about it. You had won a
reputation in the Panhandle country that would shock a blind
mule. You had a ten-year sentence suspended on you in Montana
for your share in the sheep war. Two sheriffs in this section of
California had warned you to shoot on sight. You had been
indicted—"

I felt myself getting red.

"Quit it!" I tells him. "Times has changed since them days,
so don't be a fool."

"And listen here," he went on, giving me the cold eye. "I know
blamed well why you jumped at the notion of going to Simplex
County! I've heard you tell about your old pal who was up there
somewhere—old John Parker, who was in the Injun wars with
you! When we get there, you two old idiots will sit around a
fire all day tellin' how you scouted for Gen'ral Howard and made
Gen'ral Miles the man he was and all in all saved the entire
United States from disaster. All you doddering old men are
alike—"

That was enough. I hauled off with the boot I had just
removed and caught Steve above the ear. He come back with
the water pitcher, which missed me but splintered the door and

busted. Then we closed. Fortunately, I still had one boot on, while Steve had both off, so I stepped hard on his foot with my heel. That give me enough advantage so that in another minute I went to the floor with him, only I was on top.

Just then Sloan comes poking his head into the room.

"For the land's sake, have a heart!" he cries. "Have you gents forgot that I own these premises? Look at that door! Look at that window! Good gosh, can't you fellows be friends any more, now that you got some cash in the bank?"

I looked up at him, keepin' my hold on Steve.

"See here, pilgrim," I says, "maybe you'll agree with this here young water-sprout that I'm an old and wore-out animal, good for nothin' but a home for the aged? If so, speak up! I'd admire to argue the matter here and now."

"Lord forbid!" says Sloan. "Spare him for his wife's sake, Jenkins!"

"Do it," adds Steve, from underneath. "Do it, Pinky! I retracts all them sentiments."

So I done it, and we retires for the night.

Next day we got our personal effects toted off in a truck, oiled up the big Elite tourster—guaranteed to do ninety-five miles an hour—and says farewell to the old ranch. Before we went, Sloan has a last talk with us and hands over the letter of introduction. It was to a man Lon Shawl, who had a place somewhere up in Simplex County.

"You ain't going right off?" said Sloan.

"We aims to spend three days with Mis' Moran and her folks," I told him. "One day to get welcomed, one to play the phonygraph, and one to pack up and move on. Why?"

"Well, don't take too much loose cash with you," he said, regarding us earnestly. "I don't mind saying that the roads up in that country are lonesome, and holdups do occur. I got robbed six months ago. They been having trouble with automobile bandits, too, and I hear a number of cars have been stole. So keep your eyes open. If you meet that Shorty Jones, step wide to one side."

"Who, him?" I says. "The gent that drove an eight-hoss team? What's the idea?"

"He has a notion of picking on tourists," said Sloan, and grinned. "He don't like 'em, and wants to keep 'em out of the county. He's what you might call a bad man, I guess. They say he never drove the stage unless he was drunk, and there wasn't a sober man in the country could handle an eight-hoss team with him, drunk or sober. Once he—but never mind. Here's hoping you gents don't meet him."

"Amen—for his sake," says Steve Moran, giving me a wicked glance. "Ain't there any law up there, Sloan?"

"None to speak of, and that's the truth!" Sloan replies fervently. "There's no revenue officer north of Santa Rosa, and that's over on the coast. So everybody in Simplex County has their own still, and no questions asked. If you meet Shorty Jones, and he's drunk, you hit him first or there'll be a rare old fight!"

"Thanks for the warning," I tell him. "This here is a plumb peaceable expedition, and we'll sure steer clear of trouble with the natives up beyond."

Thus we departed. To tell the truth, I did hanker to see old John Parker again; him and me had scouted for Howard's outfit, and had sojourned down in the Jornada in the Apache troubles.

So that night I wrote him a letter, telling him to meet us if he wasn't too crippled up with old age and rheumatism.

## CHAPTER II

### TROUBLE

SOMEHOW, IT looks like every time me and Steve Moran go somewheres, trouble dogs us.

This time was no exception. We avoids San Francisco, coming up the inside way via Oakland and points north. As we were heading for St. Helena, this involved ferrying over to Vallejo. Which same we done with results.

It was raining hard when we hit the Vallejo ferry, or had been raining most of the day. Owing to a mudhole and a detour we had shipped some mud. When I got the ferry tickets, I noticed that our license plates were plastered over with mud, and I aimed to clean them off, but luckily forgot it.

Well, we got first aboard the ferry, which meant first off on the other side of the bay. I noticed a fellow standing on the lower deck, watching the cars; he had a long, slick nose that run to a sharp point.

"Steve," I says, "stick with the car. Somethin' tells me that Sharpnose back yonder is a rumbound. Let's hope it ain't so, but take no chances."

Steve gave a grunt of disgust. Neither of us is a drinking man any more, owing to his respect for his wife and mine for my stomach. Just the same, we had two quarts of twenty-year-old stowed away in the car, which same I was carrying north as a present for old John Parker. So we was breaking the law, you might say, and it weighed some on our conscience—some, but not a whole lot.

"If your intuition is sure," said Steve, "we'd better pitch those bottles overboard, Pinky. I'd sure hate to have this twin eight confiscated!"

"Pitch 'em overboard?" I says. "Not yet, pardner—not yet! Old John Parker fought for his country, and, by gosh, I'll fight to help his rheumatism! You climb into the back of this here cloverleaf, and lay low."

"Now, Pinky, don't get reckless," he says with a wicked grin. "They can catch us sure, either at Napa or St. Helena with speed cops. There are no cops north of St. Helena, but—"

"None north of Napa either," I reminds him, "owing to highway construction. I been going over these road bulletins, pardner, and I've got the trails in my head, so shut up."

I climbs out and wanders down past the line of crowded cars and trucks. Pretty, soon my suspicions were confirmed. I had a glimpse of Sharpnose rummaging a light truck containing two dagoes, who were looking a heap pained and uneasy. Also, somebody had give the alarm and the gents with bottles in their cars were sneaking to the windows. I turned around and worked my way back to Steve.

"It's a race against time," I told him. "We got ten minutes more before docking. If he gets to us, you take the car out and wait for me. I'll come a-running. And stay hid, now!"

He stayed hid in the back seat, chortling to himself like an idiot.

I waited, watching the approaching shores with what the books call agonized impatience. The Vallejo cliffs came in close, then we came opposite the big flour mills, and I heard the flivvers begin to pop as different fellows cranked up. Just as we slowed down for the dock, however, I felt a tap on my arm and turned around to see Sharpnose at my elbow.

"You own this car?" he asked.

"Yep," I says. "What of it?"

"Nothin' much. Only I want to take a look through her for booze."

I clapped my hand to my hip with a surprised look, and Sharpnose grinned.

"Oh!" he says. "You're carrying it on your person, are you? I'll have to take a look—"

"Hold on, hold on!" I said, excited-like. "Not here in public!"

He nodded, caught my arm, and led me to a room for the crew. When the door had closed behind us, I noticed with gratification that the place was empty.

"Listen!" I says to him. "Suppose I was to slip you a thousand-dollar bribe?"

With that, I hauled my roll into view. His mouth begun to water—and I stuck the roll back into my pocket.

"I was just supposin', stranger," I told him. "I wouldn't do nothing of the kind, of course. You want to search me?"

He allowed he did, so I put my arms in the air.

He leans forward and reaches for my hip. My left hand descends and catches him by the neck. My right descends like-wise, only to arise again with a jolt on the end of it. It took that gent plumb in the jaw, and he just went limp. At that instant we hit the dock.

Taking his handkerchief and mine, I tied his wrists and gagged him, then locked the door. When I got out, the gang plank was down and Steve was starting. I made the running board with a jump, and scrambled inside as the car went forward.

"All right, take it easy," I says. "He won't be able to get the officers after us until the boat gets back across the bay. We got an hour's start, easy."

"We can't make St. Helena in an hour," says Steve.

"We should worry. Our license plates are an inch thick with mud. All the cops can look for is an Elite tourster. What more do you want than an even break, cowboy?"

Well, I proved to be in Class A when it came to prophecy. We went through one little burg after another, and not a sign of trouble. It was about five in the evening when we struck the town of St. Helena, and we pulled right into an open-air station for gas and oil. It was growing dark by this time.

I thought the service station man looked us over pretty hard. When I was paying our bill, he took me aside.

"I don't want to butt in," he says, "but about half an hour ago the sheriff was here. He's lookin' for a car of your make and model to come through from the south; seems, like there was some trouble on the Vallejo ferryboat. I don't know if it would interest you, but—"

"It interests me this much, stranger," I says, laying a five-dollar bill in his hand, "And we're sure obliged. I reckon we won't stop here for supper."

Steve agreed with me when I broke the news. We ducked through the back streets, struck the bridge at the north end of town, and sailed north. An hour later we were reposing in a hostelry in the little town of Kildare, where the railroad ended, and we were safe for the night anyhow.

Ahead of us lay Simplex County. To get into it, we had to climb St. Helena Mountain—a long climb of several miles. This was the place Sloan had told us about, but I was interested in it for another reason. Some gent named Stevenson, that wrote stories, had once lived up on this mountain. The hotel proprietor tells me that he had knowed him well, and that this gent used to get hundred-dollar checks and spend his money regardless. When I found that he had moved away, however, I lost interest.

Kildare was a right pretty little place, with some hot springs and geysers that tourists came to see, and was the jumping-off place for Simplex County. Not that the county was close by— that is, the civilized part of it. After finishing with St. Helena Mountain, there come Bottleglass Mountain and Corncob Mountain, all long ones with narrow roads that curved like the neck of a goose.

After breakfast, Steve and me paid our bill and walked over to the garage where we had laid up the car. As we were getting her out, a man rose up and halted us.

"You boys goin' north?" he hails. "Could you give me a lift up the mountain?"

I looked that gent over with growing alarm, for which there was excuse. He was six feet and a half tall, and about four wide; no fat on him, neither! He had gray whiskers that come to his belt, it was a cinch he had not renewed his acquaintance with soap and water since his mammy bathed him last, and from his clothes he might have been sleeping in the woods for a year or so. He smelt like a bottle of gin had busted in his pocket.

He was not pretty to look at, but Steve never refuses to give a man a lift.

"Sure," he says. "Hop in! Pinky, let him in the back."

Not me. Old John Parker's whisky was in the back, and I preferred to keep it company my ownself. I retires into the cloverleaf, and the big gent climbs in. The old Elite sure knowed she had him aboard, too; when he comes over the rail she shivers and grunts from radiator to tail light.

"My name's Moran," says Steve, holding out his hand with his usual friendly smile.

"Jones is mine," says the passenger, folding Steve's hand away in one fist. "Shorty Jones. You ain't got a drink about you, old-timer?"

Steve looks at him and gulps twice. Me, I begins to un-buckle my grip, where I had a gun stored away. So this was Shorty Jones! Steve introduces me, and I gets to his hand first with a warm grip. Shorty looks me in the eyes, takes all I can give him, and grins back at me. Then he squeezes my hand, real gentle, and I hollers for help.

"Glad to meet you, gents," he says. "Mighty kind of you to lift me up the mountain."

"Are you the fellow," asks Steve feebly, "who used to drive a stage?"

"I'm him," says Shorty.

Steve could not help himself, naturally. We had taken this gent aboard, and it was now our funeral. So we starts out of town, not feeling half as merry as we acted. I feels mighty thankful when I gets my gun out of the grip. She was my old forty-five—another thing to be thankful for. Nothing less than her would have any effect on that human gorilla in the front seat.

Before we gets well started climbing the mountain, this here Shorty Jones, who hid half the scenery from my enraptured gaze, lifts a flask out of his pocket and puts away half of it in one gulp. He offers it to me and Steve, and when we refused, he downed the other half and tossed the flask away. Steve glanced at him, kind of startledlike.

"Ain't you afraid of wholesaling booze that way, Shorty?"

"Who me?" Shorty started to laugh. The laugh come up out of him like thunder, a regular bellowing wave of it. "Why, stranger, when I drove an eight-hoss team over these hills, I never done it on less'n two quarts of licker! Never. Heard of Shorty Jones, ain't ye? Most folks have in these parts!"

"Is the road on the other side anything like this?" asked Steve, pointing at the road. She was just wide enough for two cars to pass and she twisted like a corkscrew.

"This? Like this?" Shorty Jones gave a sniff that nearly lifted the top off the car. "Why, compared to the downgrade this here is a boulevard, stranger! A boulevard! Over yonder, ye got to circle on two wheels at every turn!"

"And you used to drive down at a gallop, eh?" said Steve. "How'd you brake the stage?"

"Brake her?" Shorty grunts. "A touch of the brake and she goes over, certain! Nope, nobody was ever fool enough to brake one of them stages and do it twice!"

"But supposing you met somebody on the way up?"

Shorty chuckles. "Everybody but strangers kep' off them hills when we was coming down," he says. "If they didn't, we went through 'em! Why, the last month I was drivin', all I had aboard was three chinks. We got down about to the double-loop turn, and there was a fool pilgrim with a team, square in the road!

"I yells to him to jump, which he done. But them fool chinks thought I meant for them to jump. They done it likewise. We went through that team and over 'em, and after gettin' down the mountain I sends back for the chinks. But they was dead, poor critters!"

Shorty shook his head and looked sorrowful. Then he asked:

"What you two pilgroms doin' up here?"

"Looking around," said Steve carelessly. "We might settle, if we like it."

"Oh!" says Shorty Jones, with a black look. "I don't guess you're goin' to like it, then."

"Why not?" asked Steve.

"Climate ain't healthy," replied Shorty, and fell silent. I ain't a phrenologist, but from the back of his head I could tell that this gent was going to make us trouble.

## CHAPTER III

### A DOUBLE HOLDUP

WELL, WE ambled along up that mountain, which was the most mountainous mountain the Elite had ever experienced, I reckon. Twice we had to stop and cool off, what with running in low all the time.

Shorty Jones had relapsed into a sullen, ugly silence. However, he began to talk again, and seemed presently to throw off his bad humor. He told several stories of the old days and made himself right pleasant. If he hadn't been such a disreputable old skate we might have enjoyed him.

When we got toward the top of the mountain he begged Steve to stop the car.

"You gents have treated me white," he says. "Now, we ain't got far to climb—the toll gate is at the top of the hill. I want to git past that there toll house without bein' observed, savvy? If you gents would let me in back, out o' sight, I'd be a heap obliged."

Steve gave me a look, and I nodded. Why not? It was our play to humor this gent and get rid of him if we could. He went on to tell us that he wanted to get out at the first bend the other side of the toll gate. It is a heap easier to swallow your feelings and slide out of trouble than it is to provoke a fuss sometimes.

So we changed places, letting Shorty in behind. Having already packed the whisky inside my grip, I felt reasonably safe about it. That human gorilla filled in the cloverleaf seat for all it would hold, and tells us to go ahead.

"There's some of the old stages settin' up alongside the toll house," he says, when we came in sight of the gate.

Then he ducked down out of sight and said no more. We rolled up to the gate and honked. Beside the house were half a dozen stages, which sure took me back to the old days! High springs, box and all, the real article.

An old lady come out and took our money. She had a right nimble tongue and started in to ride us, like mountain folks do to city visitors, until Steve smiled at her. Then she warmed up a trifle.

"When you folks git to Centertown," she says, "leave word at the stage office that somebody stole one of these here old stages last night, will you? Run it down the hill, most like, only we ain't found it."

"We sure will, ma'am," I says. "But what would anybody steal one of them things for?"

"My land, how do I know?" she asked. "They been laid up here for two years and ain't been bothered since."

She said farewell, and we shoves ahead, starting downhill almost at once. There was about a quarter mile of fair road before reaching the first bend. Shorty Jones tells us that right here he always used to whip up his hosses, so as to get some real speed before striking the steep grades that went on for several miles.

The country all this while had been wild. Except the toll house, we had seen only one or two houses since leaving Kildare.

Nothing but mountain and forest all around, without even a telephone wire to speak of modern improvements. As pretty a place for a holdup as any I had ever seen. The trees came down right close to the road.

We came to the first bend, which was a short and sharp one. As we turned, Steve threw in the brakes—luckily, he had slowed down to let our unwelcome guest alight, and he could stop in a hurry.

The road was blocked, and blocked a-plenty! One half of it was taken up by a monstrous big Spangler car, brand new, and painted a bright yellow. Steve and me had speculated on getting us a Spangler before we bought the Elite, but the Spangler would set us back about ten thousand, so we got the other instead. But that canary yellow Spangler sure was some car for looks, I'll tell the world!

There were other things to draw our attention, however. Alongside the Spangler car was drawn up one of those old-time stages, hitched up with an eight-hoss team, and three mighty tough-looking citizens standing around. The stage was empty, but from their looks the three gents were full. All of them were rough, bearded, and carried shotguns.

"Hello!" I says, not suspecting anything wrong, as Steve brought the car to a halt. "Here's the stage that was stole!"

"You bet," came the voice of Shorty Jones from behind us. "And here's the gent that stole her! You two pilgrims alight, and keep your hands in the air."

I looks around and exchanged glances with a pistol about half as big as Shorty. At the same time, the three gents advanced on us with guns ready.

"There's no argument a-tall," I says, and climbed out.

"What is this—a holdup?" asks Steve, as he followed me.

"You might call it such." Shorty Jones climbed out of the car. "Line up!"

Steve and me lined up. Shorty turned to the three guests, who grinned at him.

"Hello, boys! I see you got a tourist, eh? Where is he?"

One of the three shook his head, regretfullike.

"He didn't cotton to the notion, Shorty," he says. "He done tried to run away, so we had to impress him with a load of facts. He's under them bushes."

He pointed to a pile of brush alongside the road, and I seen a pair of boots sticking out. This begun to look like business.

"You confounded thugs!" exclaimed Steve, his eyes shining. "You'll have the law climbing you for this—you murderers!"

The four bandits laughed. They were all of Shorty's type—big burly gents, more or less elderly.

"Any money on him?" asked Shorty.

"Couple of hundred," says one of the three. "And a good gold watch. She's a fine car, too, only there can't none of us run her. Too many doodads and things. Too darned bad we had to shoot that tourist so quick—he could have showed us a heap of things about her! But these here friends of yours is lookin' plumb anxious, Shorty. Let's relieve 'em."

We were surrounded and relieved. Fortunately, I always carry most of my wad under my left knee. They missed that, but got all we had in our pockets, which was enough. Shorty pulls out my gun and gives a loud guffaw.

"Here's a bad guy, boys!" says he. "Durned if he ain't an old-timer—look at what he totes! Real man's gun, ain't it?" And he slung the old gun into the bushes.

"Durn your measly hide, you'll pay for that!" I tells him.

Shorty grinned, poked his own gun in my waistband, and ordered me to climb into the stage coach. I done so. After me, Steve got in—both of us on the driver's seat. Shorty tells one of his men to keep a gun cocked in our direction, which was done.

"Now," he says to his friends, "I'll take these two pilgrims off to my place, savvy? I'll guarantee to keep 'em there a week. By that time you boys can have these cars repainted and drove out of the county. Sell 'em in the city, as usual."

"But we can't drive this durned yeller bird!" says one.

They all drifts over to the Spangler and begins to work over the instrument board. Shorty stood around and scratched his head. It was plain to see that when it came to driving that high-priced and complicated piece of mechanism, he was as far away from home as the others.

"Gosh!" I said. "Them ignorant fools will plumb ruin our car."

"They'll plumb ruin us, likewise," said Steve gloomily, "if we don't talk low. Look at that poor chap under those bushes!"

"Can't see only his boots," I said. "That's all I want to see, if they done used one of them ten-gauge shotguns on him. Well, it sure looks like old John Parker had lost his licker! Say, Steve! D'you reckon this here Shorty is goin' to drive us in this wagon?"

Steve gave a start.

"Why—sure!" he remarks.

It was clear that he relished the notion just as much as I did. This gang seemed to have a right good program laid out. When they caught a car, Shorty Jones would take the owner to some ranch off in the hills and hold him there until the car was sold. Why nobody had laid information against Shorty it was hard to say—we would probably find out in time. Most likely Shorty had some way of making his victims shut up.

"What I can't understand," I went on, "is why old John Parker didn't show up! I wrote him to meet us at this here toll house, if he could. However, it don't matter now. We'll have one fine ride down this hill, Steve."

Steve grunted. "You let me get a chance to get my hands on that ruffian!"

He got his wish in a hurry. Just then Shorty Jones comes swaggering over to us with a proposal to make.

"Can either o' you pilgrims drive that there yeller car?" he asks. "If you'll drive her for us, I'll let up a whole lot on you."

Steve rises up.

"Drive her for you crooks and murderers?" he sings out. "Why, you gorilla-faced imitation of humanity, I'll see you hanged first! Here's what I think of you and your gang—"

Just what Steve said would hardly do to repeat, but he said a-plenty. The sight of that poor fellow's boots sticking out from them bushes must have riled Steve up considerable. He don't cuss much as a rule, but when he gets real warmed up he can sure create an atmospheric disturbance.

He done so now, in a real and earnest fashion. At first Shorty listens as though amused; but pretty soon the three other gents begins to grin and pass comments on Steve's jaw work. A slow flush creeps up above the rim of Shorty's beard, and when Steve reached his ancestry and presumably simian relatives, this here Jones man was some mad. He shoves away his gun and shakes his fist at us.

"That's enough!" he shouted. "Any more of that there talk, and I comes for you!"

"Come on, you several kinds of a rat!" says Steve.

Shorty started forward and reached up for Steve. But Steve was already on the way down, and he laid into Shorty with both fists before he reached the ground.

Bein' seated in the stage, I was up higher than the others. Just here I noted a disturbance among the bushes where the road curved out of sight below! What it was I did not see, and did not care at the moment.

"Durn your hide!" sung out Shorty, when Steve biffed him in the whiskers. "I'll—"

Steve landed again, with a cheerful chortle, and Shorty went for him. If Steve had been able to keep away, he might have done something; but Shorty grabbed him first. Once inside them gorilla arms, no man alive could have managed to do much damage. Shorty folded himself over Steve and begun to hug him like a bear.

Steve was gone. He had no more chance than a fly, but kept on doing what he could. I was a heap relieved when the other bandits gave no signs of shooting, but watched the scrap with joyful faces.

By a lucky stagger and a quick back-heel, Steve threw Shorty off his balance. Them two touched the ground with a crash that shook the trees. Shorty was underneath, but he just gave one shake of his big frame, and whirled himself up in the air. "Woof!" says Steve, and come down under two hundred pounds of Jones meat.

"Now," says Shorty, raising up with both fists locked in Steve's throat, "now whine, ye polecat!"

Instead of whining, Steve caught them flowing whiskers in both hands—and yanked. Shorty emitted a wild howl. In the midst of this pleasing scene, there intruded a voice; a quiet, cold sort of voice which sort of went right through everybody like an icy breeze. All it said was three words.

"Hands up, gents!"

## CHAPTER IV

### RACE FOR FREEDOM

NOW I observed what had caused the disturbance in them bushes.

A lone stranger had been riding up the road, had seen the fracas, and had withdrew to hide his features. He had done so with a red bandanna, over which his eyes surveyed us real cool. He set in his saddle, and each hand held a forty-five which covered all and sundry.

"Pronto!" he says, when nobody moved. *"Los manos arriba!"*

One of his guns belched, and the bullet knocked the shotgun out of the hands of the bandit next me. Those three bad guys stuck up their arms in a hurry. Shorty tugged himself loose, rose, and looked into the stranger's guns. His arms went up likewise.

"You on the ground," says the stranger to Steve, "go git their guns!"

Oh, but Tom Jenkins was one happy man, I'll tell the world! And for why! Because when this here stranger give out his orders in Spanish, his identity was disclosed likewise. I knowed right off that this was old John Parker—yes, sir! Why he had bothered to hide his face was more than I could say, but I gathered he did not want to be recognized, so I played the card as she laid, and said nothing.

"Hello!" says Steve, getting up and staring. "Who are you? What in time did you butt in for when I had him licked?"

"Had me licked?" cried Shorty Jones. "Consarn ye—"

"Shet up!" says John Parker, hitching up his guns. "You, young feller, disarm 'em!"

Steve collected himself, and went to work. Pretty soon he had a pile of shotguns and pistols laying in the road.

"Hey, Steve!" I says. "Go get that old gun of mine out of them bushes, if the stranger don't object."

"Go to it," says the stranger. "But hand her to me first."

Steve was plumb astonished over all this, but went hunting my gun. Shorty Jones and his pals stared at old John Parker, looking like the devil had suddenly appeared before them. Steve found my gun and handed it to Parker. He looked her over and returned her.

"That's her," he says. "Same old gun. Gents, what's happened here?"

"Enough and plenty," I told him, holding the gun in my lap. "These four desperadoes has murdered a poor pilgrim. There's his boots sticking out of them bushes—"

"Leave him be—he's dead and happy," says the stranger. "You gents was sure lucky that I come along! These coyotes sure are bad med'cine. Look at that big skunk, Jones! He's known for a hoss thief, he's yeller clear through—"

"You're a liar!" cries Shorty, his face mighty red. "Who in time are you?"

"Shet up." Old John Parker pressed the trigger, and Shorty jumps up in the air as the bullet cut his whiskers. "That's me, savvy? You, young feller!" This was to Steve. "Go through them gents and let's see how much dinero they pack."

At this, all four of them bandits put up a squawk. It did not last long. Old John Parker, he fired once from each gun. One bullet grazed one of the bandit's trousers, and the other one knocked off Shorty's disreputable old hat. After this they kept mighty still.

Steve went through them. He not only produced our money, but he produced a heap more. If it all come from the dead man lying in the bushes, that poor pilgrim must have been a millionaire.

"Keep what's yours," says old John Parker, "and give me the rest."

Steve looks at me, sort of dubious.

"Do it," I says. "This here bandit is on the square, which same them murderers ain't."

So Steve hands over the most of the money, and old John pockets it. Me, I was setting back having the time of my life watching Parker go through them four bandits. I hoped he would do a little fancy shooting, him having a reputation in the old days; but he seemed plumb satisfied with what he had done already.

When he had shoved the money into his pockets, Parker leans over and says something in Steve's ear. Now, I might have been wise enough to look out for trouble, only I wasn't. Old John Parker would sooner put over a joke on his friends than eat, but this was no time for jokes and he should have known it.

"Are you willin' to guard these gents?" says old John to me.

"You bet I am!" I said, thumbing my gun.

"All right." He turns and sends another bullet through them whiskers of Shorty Jones. "You, Jones! Hop up there beside that victim of your'n! Move lively!"

Shorty, sputtering oaths, climbed up beside me. "Watch out for that gun," he says with a sour look. "She's cocked, you galoot!"

"She won't be cocked no more if you start anything," I tells him prompt.

"All right!" Old John Parker fired again, and the bullet cut through the whiskers of another gent. "You three p'izen skunks, climb inside that there stage! Pronto!"

They were so anxious to please him by this time that they fought one another to get in first. Old John Parker turns his hoss with his knees, and waves both guns.

"All right!" he sings out. "They're your meat, Pinky—take 'em!"

With that, the fool shot over the head of each leader.

Blam! First thing I knowed, that stage was shooting down the mountainside, the hosses plunging and rearing and the brake grinding away underneath. My gun went off and the bullet flew wild.

Shorty Jones let out a scream. Then he leaned over, grabbed the wrapped reins, threw off the brake, and sent a stream of cuss words into the air. I had a notion to jump, but just then we went around the curve on two wheels and all I could do was to hang on. Shorty stood up, caught out the whip, and laid her on. After that, to jump would have been sheer suicide.

I never did hear any yelling to beat what them there bandits uttered from inside the coach. Yell? They simply perforated the air! Shorty Jones, standing up and lashing them poor brutes, had us going downhill at a mile-a-minute gait. The old stage rocked from side to side like she would go off the springs. Every time we hit a rock she went up ten feet in the air and come down with a crash.

"Whoopee!" yelled Shorty, his whiskers streaming over his shoulders. "Go to it, gals! Hit 'er up, thar! Dogged if this ain't like old times! Set quiet, pilgrim, set quiet!"

I set quiet, all right, and prayed.

Before us, that cussed mountain road just dropped out of sight. She was narrow, and she was winding; them two terms are comprehensive. We took the next curve, sideswung, hesitated in the air, and decided to jolt back to all four wheels. One of them bandits was half in and half out the window, trying to jump but lacking nerve.

"Knock that durned fool inside!" orders Shorty to me.

I leans back and taps the gent with my gun, and he went back inside. We went faster and faster, until I begins to think we'd run over the trailers any minute. Still and all, Shorty handled the lines like a veteran. He had the hosses under control, all right, but I was not worrying about the hosses. It was the stage that worried me.

Woof! Down and around a curve, then another, in a double horseshoe. The old stage creaked and slid, first on two wheels then on the other two. Nothing could stop us now, short of an earthquake; all six hosses were galloping full speed, and we thundered down that road to beat the band. If I shot one of the leaders, we would pile up something awful, I figured, so I held my hand and watched for a soft spot.

Curve after curve, drop after drop—that road went on for miles! The three inside had yelled themselves out. One was prayin' and the other two were groanin'. Shorty Jones, however, stood up there and enjoyed himself. If it hadn't been for the dead man up the road, I could have admired this old rascal for the way he conducted the procession.

Suddenly I heard Shorty begin to swear something awful. I looked, and on a curve that jumped into sight ahead, perhaps a hundred feet below us, appeared a flivver with one man in her, coming up the hill.

"Shoot, for the lord's sake!" yells Shorty to me.

I emptied the gun in the air, which same made the animals jump ahead. When we would hit that poor fool in the flivver there was no telling; the road curved so much that he might be half a mile away, or a hundred yards. He was so far below us when we had sighted him, that we were sure to be going considerable faster when we did hit him.

All of a sudden we hit a fairly long open stretch, and come into it with a yell. At the same instant, the flivver appeared at the other end of it. That driver took just one look at what was coming, and even at the distance I seen him turn green.

"Jump!" Shorty's voice must have carried a mile. "Jump, ye durned fool!"

The gent turned his flivver to the side of the road and vanished. I never did see what became of him, but I judge he run into the brush and stayed there. Next minute we were on a hairpin turn.

"Over we goes!" yelled Shorty, and we went over. "Back again!" he yells, and back we come sure enough.

I rose up, seeing a good stretch ahead, and got my lips to the ear of the old scoundrel.

"I ain't no deputy!" I shouted. "Get me through safe, and I'll turn ye loose!"

He grinned and gave the gallopers his lash, and I set down again. Murder or no murder, I was a heap more concerned with saving my life than I was with getting justice done. And by the way things looked, I had a faint notion that Shorty Jones might pull us through alive yet, if his luck held.

We swung and lurched on down that mountain road. Every time we hit a curve I looked to see if anybody was coming up; tragedies were imminent, only nobody showed up. Every time we slued over on two wheels, I prayed hard, but my praying and Shorty's reins done the work pretty well. That big gorilla was a wonder. Each time we laid another curve behind us and struck on all four wheels, I forgave him in full, all over again.

He had a voice on him like a fog horn. "Hit 'er up!" he would yell, and crack his long whip like a pistol. "Git on, thar! Move lively or we'll run ye down—git ap!" What with his yelling, and the whip cracking and the pounding of hooves, not to mention the rattling bang and crash every time the old stage struck a high spot, you could have heard us coming half a mile away.

Luckily for themselves, some tourists heard us. There was a halfway spot down the hill, where a watering place was located. We went past that like a cyclone, and I had a glimpse of two automobiles trying to hide behind the trees.

Right after that we lurched around a sharp corner and tore off one window and half the rear top seat on a tree. Shorty Jones looks down at me and grins.

"Keep your word, pilgrim?" he shouts.

"Sure!" I says. "Get me safe to land, and you can go."

"I'll do it," he yelled. "I'll do it if we die a-doing it! Whoopee!"

From inside the coach there suddenly rose an awful chorus of yells. I'll say those gents were frightened clear down to their boots! Next thing was a crash, and the old stage begun to wobble.

"She's splittin' apart!" screamed one of the bandits. "Stop her, Shorty!"

"Stop a prairie fire!" says Shorty. "Hold tight, pilgrim—I'll pull ye through."

*Cr-r-runch!* I found myself leaning on air, and like to fell backward. When I recovers I finds the front seat in place, over the two front wheels, and nothing more. I looks back to see the rest of the stage rolling and smashing into the trees, while the three bandits turned somersaults with it.

"Glory be! Git ap!" yelled Shorty, standing and lashing the team.

With most of the load gone, the six horses sure went down that mountain fast! The front seat was dancing a jig under us, and I seen plain that she was not going to last more than sixty seconds. So did Shorty.

"Now's your time!" he sung out, when we swung into an open stretch, with a bridge at the end of it. "When we hit the creek, jump! If she don't last that long, we lose."

I prayed hard that she would hang together, and won out again. When we hit that bridge, I judge we were going two miles a minute. I started to jump, but what was left of the front end beat me to it, and I went headfirst into the air.

As I come down, I had a glimpse of Shorty, likewise in the air, dancing on one ear. Then the water hit me.


## CHAPTER V

## THE BANDIT'S RETURN

LUCKILY FOR me, the recent rains had filled that creek plumb full.

As it was, I burrowed in the mud for a spell, then crawled ashore and found a dry spot. When I had clawed the mud out of my hair and felt myself all over without finding anything busted, I felt a heap relieved. Then I hears a voice.

"Peace, perfect peace, in this dark world of sin!" it orates.

I stood up and took a squint around the bridge. There on the other side sat Shorty Jones. The six-hoss team had clear vanished. Shorty was rocking himself back and forth, looking sort of dazed and talking about nothing in particular. His head and whiskers were just one big mass of red mud.

Somebody had been executing bridge repairs lately, and had been reckless enough to leave a length of two-by-four lying near by. I appropriated it and walked in on Shorty. Having witnessed him in action, I wasted no time on preliminaries, but hauled off and whaled him over the ear.

He fell backward into the water, then picked himself up and waded ashore.

"Want any more?" I says, heaving up the timber.

He turns around and wades across the creek to the other bank.

"Not me, pilgrim, not me!" he returns. "I'm plumb satisfied. Ain't it a beautiful day! Hear the little birds sing and see the pretty stars—my gosh, you got a hard fist! So long."

He climbed up the bank, hit the road, and wandered thence after the vanished team. As long as I could see him, he was staggering from one side of the road to the other, talking to himself and combing the mud out of his whiskers with his fingers. Pretty soon he was gone, and I set down on the bridge to confer with myself.

It was not exactly a happy conference. I figures out that Steve and old John Parker would come along before long, and I aims to execute justice on old John. However, he had rescued us from the bandits, and I had an uneasy notion that we would be traced north and the Simplex County sheriff set after us by the prohibition folks. In which event, we might have to depend on old John to get out of the trouble involved. So all in all, I lays aside the timber with a sigh of regret, and abandons my revenge.

While I was resting my heels, I examines the old forty-five, and concludes that she ain't damaged. I dried the cartridges and dried her as well as I could. This labor of love was just about completed, when I observed a small but popular make of car, as the newspapers call it, coming toward me from the direction in which the team and Shorty Jones had vanished.

The man driving her wore a wide-brimmed Stetson, and had a face like a successful financier. Seeing which, I lays the gun in my lap and waited. He halted his car on the bridge, leaving the engine running and stared at me. I stared back at him.

"What you doin' here?" he says.

"Recovering, mostly," I tells him. "Did you meet a gent down the road with mud in his hair?"

"Didn't meet nobody," he says. "But the remains of six hosses come into Centertown. Where'd they come from?"

"The other way, most likely."

"Look here!" he said angrily. "You gimme straight answers, feller! Seen anything of a big Spangler car, bright yeller, on the grade?"

"Uh-huh." I points up the hill. "She's lay in' up the road a ways—quite a ways. So is her owner. All I seen was his boots, but that was plenty. I don't hanker to examine a gent that's connected with a ten-gauge shotgun at close quarters."

His mouth opened and he turned pale.

"Wh-what!" he stammers. "Good heavens! It ain't possible he's dead?"

"Dead is the best word for it, I reckon," I says.

I was watching him close enough, and when I seen his eyes change from a startled look to an angry one, I was ready. He starts his hand toward his pocket, and I covered him.

"Don't do it!" I says. "Don't even think o' doing it, stranger! Instead, climb down out o' that car, and climb quick."

He looked dazed, then slowly got out of the car. I rose up and started forward.

"Hold on—you're makin' a mistake!" he said. "I'm the sheriff of this county. You look like a powerful disreputable character to me! If what you're telling me is true—"

"Listen, you!" I cut in. "Sheriff or no sheriff, I don't stand bein' called a liar by no man, savvy? You shut your mouth and keep it shut. I'm goin' to borrow your car and ride into Center-town, and I'll leave her there for you."

He opened his mouth to speak. I pulled back the hammer with my thumb and he shut his mouth again in a hurry.

Meantime, I was thinking fast. This was the sheriff and no mistake, because he had throwed open his coat and showed a star. Chances were he was looking for me and Steve, but he would soon forget that when he got busy with the murder and the bandits.

Now, I owed John Parker something for the trick he had played sending me down the mountain in that durned stage. The sheriff seemed to know the gent who had owned that yellow car, and it was a cinch he would know old John Parker. I hankered to pay old John back heavy, and I also hankered to get clear away from here and rest in peace for a spell.

"Now, sheriff," I says, "I'm a stranger in this here country, but I come well recommended and well heeled. Shut your trap! I'm talkin'. My name's Jenkins, and I got letters to a gent by the name o' Lon Shawl, which same will answer for me at all times."

The sheriff's eyes widened out, so I judged he was acquainted with Sloan's friend, Lon Shawl. He got real red in the face, and looked like he ached to say something, but that hammer of mine was back and he didn't dare utter a word.

"I know what you want," I says. "You aim to deputize me and force me along. You ain't going to do it, savvy? First word from you, I shoots. Now, my advice to you is to turn around and walk up the mountain. You're due to find considerable excitement ahead, so you can keep your gun in case of need.

"I dunno the name of the gent who owned that yellow car, but he's layin' up yonder under a pile of brush, and his boots is protruding. You'll meet my pardner, Steve Moran, coming down in a big Elite tourster. Deputize him, and he'll take you back to the place. The fellow who done the shooting was there when I left, and you'll find him mighty bad medicine. Parker, they called him, old John Parker. That's all I know, so I'm sayin' farewell until later. Not a word, mind you! I ain't servin' as no deputy."

When I mentioned Parker's name, I thought the sheriff would bust from compressed air. Then, the next minute, he turns around and heads up the mountain fast as he could go.

"Thank fortune!" I says to myself, as I climbs into his flivver. "I've got myself nicely extricated from a heap of bad medicine. What's more, I've paid out old John Parker for his funny work! By the time the sheriff gets to the truth of what's happened up yonder, and goes on the trail of Shorty Jones and the bandits, I'll have a breathin' spell. Then if Steve comes along, we'll hop into the Elite and beat it away from this durned county."

I backed the flivver off the bridge, turned her around, and headed for Centertown, which, according to a road sign, was five miles away.

That five miles was all good road, and I hummed along at a good clip. On the way, I kept my eyes open for Shorty, but he was not to be seen, and I judged he had dived into the timber somewheres.

Centertown was a collection of houses that had not changed in fifty years by the look, except for a big hotel and garage. Out in front of this the whole population was assembled around the six-hoss team, which same must have created some excitement. Seeing that Shorty Jones was not here, I drove up and hailed the garage man. Everybody surrounded me and demanded to know what had happened.

"I don't know nothing a-tall," I says, and turned to the garage man. "Sheriff done lent me his car, and I want to leave it here for him. You know a gent that lives somewheres near here, name of John Parker?"

"Parker?" he says. "You mean old Colonel Parker, the Injun fighter?"

"That's him."

"Why, he lives out of town two or three mile, sure."

"Well, s'pose you hop in and drive me out there, and then bring the sheriff's car back. I'll pay you for your trouble."

"Sure!" he says, and climbed in.

We got out of town without any trouble. That garage man, however, was curious.

"What in thunder has been goin' on up the mountain?" he asks me. "I wisht I knew!"

"If you did, you'd wish you didn't," I says. "Don't ask no question, feller, but drive!"

He drove. In less than half an hour we reached a mighty pretty little ranch laying on a hillside. The house was small, but mighty handsome.

"Parker ain't married, is he?" I says.

"Not that anybody knows of," and the fellow grinned. "I guess a dollar will fix it up. Thanks."

He departs with the car, and I leads Tom Jenkins into the house. A Chinaman shows up, and when I says that I'm an old friend of Parkers, the chink makes me at home. The main room had a big fire in it, before which I dries myself out, and the chink fetches me a hot drink or two.

I'm bound to admit that old John had done well in the world, according to his location. There was a big fruit orchard around the house, and inside she was fixed up scrumptious, with no end of guns and pelts on the walls, and pictures. John had framed up all his militia commissions and letters from the generals we had known, and he had a big picture of me that had been took in Broken Bow in '89, mounted in a gilt frame. When I looked back at myself that way, I had to admit that in the old days I was a good-looking kid.

Well, after locating John's tobacco and rolling a few, I feels hungry. So I wanders into the adjoining room, which was old John's bedroom. Leaving the door ajar an inch or so, I took off my boots and stretched out comfortable on the bed. Right above me was a double-barrel shotgun and a box of shells on a shelf. I was still looking at the gun when slumber overpowers me and I drops off.

When I waked up, I perceived that I must have been asleep for quite some time, because I had an empty feeling inside of me, and by the light I could tell the afternoon was drawing on apace, as the books say.

All of a sudden, a voice woke me up immediate—fetched me up all standing, in fact. It was a powerful, roaring big voice, and it came from the next room. Other voices mixed in; there was a heap of laughing and talking going on, but that one voice was like an electric shock to me.

It was the voice of Shorty Jones!

CHAPTER VI

THE LANE WITH A TURNING

INSIDE OF five seconds I was standing at the crack in the door and looking over a scene that would have staggered anybody, knowing what I did.

The fire in the big fireplace was roaring away full blast and the room was well lighted. Around the center table were sitting five men. One of them, facing me, was Shorty Jones. He looked a heap different from what he done when we had parted, however. Then he had been just a tramp; now he was dressed up fit to kill, with a boiled shirt and white collar, and a big diamond in his necktie. Dressed this way, he was better looking than before, but he had a big raw bump over his ear which had come from my hand. Seeing it made me feel better.

Beside him sat no other than the sheriff himself. Lined up around the table were the other three bandits. They were like-wise dressed up to some extent, but it was plain that they had suffered from their somersaults when the stage split in two. They were bunged up and scratched, and one of them had his arm in a sling.

There was nobody else in the room—no sign of Steve or old John Parker. On the table before these gents, however, there was a big pile of money; and with it, the two identical bottles of whisky which I had brought along for old John.

"So Parker handed over the money without a fuss, eh?" says one of the bandits. The sheriff laughed and waved his hand at the table.

"There it is, boys. By gosh, when I flashed that murder story on old John, he nigh threw a fit!"

"I'd ha' give a hundred dollars to see his face!" exclaimed Shorty Jones. Then the whole gang broke out laughing, so loudly that it like to raised the roof.

I steps back from the door. It was plain enough to me what had happened. The sheriff was in with the gang, of course! He had fixed things somehow, probably by clapping Steve in jail and old John with him, on the charge of murdering that tourist in the yellow car. Now the whole gang had come here to divide the loot.

"Well," thinks I, "it's better to be born lucky than rich! They never even looked in on me—and here I am! And here's old John's gun, by gosh!"

I moved quick and easy. I got that double-barreled shotgun down from the wall. She was an old-timer, single action, but spick and span. The shells in the box fitted her, you bet. I threw in a couple, then went to the door.

Shorty Jones was ordering the chink to bring a corkscrew and some hot water, and he examined one of the whisky bottles with a loving eye. So, to top all, this gang meant to bury that whisky! It was too much.

I stood there at the door with the gun up, and let the door swing open real gentle. Nobody observed me. The bandits begun to count out and divide the money on the table. In the midst of this momentary silence, I cocks both barrels of that shotgun.

Everybody jumped like they'd been shot. Shorty Jones looks up and sees me. His mouth opens, and he sets the whisky bottle on the table.

"Set steady," I warns him. "Don't bust them bottles! Now, gents, elevate all around, and do it durned sudden."

They done it, twisting their heads to see where I was.

"I got you gents cold," I says. "You're a fine sheriff, you with the star! By gosh, you wait till—"

At this minute the outside door opens. Into the room came Steve Moran, with old John Parker beside him.

They looked at the five gents reaching for the ceiling, then they looked at me. Steve got red in the face and choked over something. Old John stared at me like I was a ghost.

"Where'd you come from?" he asked.

"I been right here, asleep," I tells him. "Get them skunks' artillery, John!"

Steve lets out a yell and doubles up. Then Shorty Jones he begun to laugh and every one else chimes in. I never in all my life seen men who could give way to laughter like these parties! One and all bent over and straightened up, and you could have heard the "haw-haw" for a mile.

"Come out of your hole, Pinky!" hollers old John, wiping the tears from his eyes. "Lay down that gun before you hurt somebody!"

"I aims to hurt somebody," I says, feeling anything but humorous. "You, Steve! Have you gone crazy?"

"Not me, Pinky," and Steve wipes his cheeks. "But—oh, lord! This is rich—haw-haw!"

"I'll haw-haw you!" I says, and lets go one barrel at the ceiling.

When the smoke clears away, I was reclining gracefully on the carpet and seven gents were draped over me.

"You got me down," I says from the bottom of the pile. "I'm satisfied."

Shorty Jones hauls me up.

"By glory, I'm glad to meet you!" he says, still laughing. "Here, let me introduce my friends, old-timer!"

He brought up the three bandits, who grinned and tried to shake hands. Last of all come the sheriff, and Shorty claps him on the shoulder.

"This here is my friend the sheriff, Lon Shawl," he says. "You see, Jenkins, Sloan wrote us you and Steve were on the way, and for us to receive you fittingly, which same we tried hard to do—oh, by glory, look at his face! Haw-haw!"

They were at it again, and Steve rolled around the floor laughing. I begun to think that somebody had made a mistake after all. Lon Shawl—the sheriff! And Sloan had written these gents to meet me and Steve—

"Come on in out of the rain, Pinky!" cried Steve, coming to his feet and hanging on to the table for support. "The holdup was all framed!"

"All framed, was it?" I says. "How about the murder? How about that tourist in the yellow Spangler?"

"That there is my own car, Pinky," says Shorty Jones, wiping the tears off his whiskers. "She's standing outside this blessed minute! What wasn't on the program was old John Parker coming along when he did."

"Whoop!" Old John let out an Injun yell. He was plumb tickled to death with himself. "I seen what was up, and acted according, Pinky. It was all a—"

"See here!" I said. "I seen that there tourist—"

"You seen his boots!" Steve had another relapse. "You seen a pair of boots, you poor simp! And when Parker set you goin' down the mountain, the joke was on the other foot, I'll say."

I sinks down into a chair. Pretty soon I began to get things straight in my head, and then I looks around.

"Dog-gone it!" I exclaimed and managed to grin. "Shorty, I sure apologizes for that there wrack over the ear! But you had it comin'. Say, sheriff, is anybody looking for us down below?"

The sheriff unwraps himself from his chair and stops laughing long enough to answer. "They were, Pinky, they were!" he says. "But I sent out word that them two desperate criminals had gone on north to Seattle. Now are you satisfied?"

"The drinks are on me," I says, and indicated the bottles. "Go to it, gents!"

And that was how our trip ended.

FAST WORK IN HIGH VALLEY

# CHAPTER I

## ONE HUNDRED
## THOUSAND TO INVEST

I USED TO think that, if I ever got a wad of money in the bank, I'd kiss the cow country good-by and be a sailor on the ocean. I done it, too, once—but never mind about that. The memory still hurts. What I started to tell about was me and Simplex County, which is in California.

I was visiting there with old John Parker. Probably you've heard of him—Colonel Parker? I expect so. Chief scout in all the late Injun wars, and the squarest man ever born. It was him prevented that uprising in Walla Walla, back in '79; but what I started to say was about what happened to me.

Steve Moran and I sold out the H Bar L, down South, only I kept the brand my ownself. Then Steve come up North with me, looking for a place to locate fresh. We got there, but Steve heard that he was a proud father, so he beat it for home and mother.

"The wad is yours, Pinky," he tells me before blowing. "You go ahead and invest for both of us. Don't buy too durned much land, savvy? And watch out for the land sharks."

Old John Parker grinned at us. John sure loved to have a joke!

"Tom Jenkins is a born sucker, Steve," he says confidential. "It ain't safe for you to leave him all that there cash. No, sir! I've knowed him about forty year, and I never seen a surer sucker than him."

Steve thought that Parker meant it and flared up a mite.

"You think Pinky's a sucker, do you?" he said.

"I do," asserted old John, winking at me. "Why, let me tell you something! Him and me was over in the Tetons once, lookin' for a silver mine—"

"Never mind that," cuts in Steve, "Do you honestly think anybody in this dog-goned backward, ignorant neck of the woods can stick Pinky?"

"Anybody can do it," says old John. "Anybody! He'll get shook down proper."

"Bet you five thousand," Steve comes back snappy, "that it ain't done by next month—and no strings on Pinky, neither! Put up or shut up."

That riled the colonel, and he put up in a hurry. Too much of a hurry, maybe.

After Steve had departed, taking our car with him, old John sets in to rub my fur the right way. It was none of my funeral, however. I knowed all the time that he was joking, and if he got caught for a bet of five thousand he could stand it. He had money to burn.

Old John was the whitest man ever lived, only he liked a joke. He liked a scrap, too. If you think he was too old to fight, think again! Well, John figures on steering me about the county and advising me on a place—only that night he gets down with a spell of rheumatism. A real bad spell, too.

Then he allows to have some old-timers take me in charge. At that I sunfishes.

"Forget it!" I tells him. "I ain't going to have a passel o' friends treatin' me like a cripple, savin' my breath for me, watchin' out I don't bust my fool head! Am I a baby or a man? Sufferin' caterpillars! Durn your hide, ain't I cut my eyeteeth? To hear you talk a body would think Tom Jenkins was in his dotage! He ain't, and I aim to demonstrate it."

"All right, Pinky, all right," says John. He groaned and felt of his back where I had rubbed in horse liniment. "Dang this rheumatiz! It's awful. Stay here and help me."

"You fought Injuns for fifty year or so," I says, "and I reckon you can fight the rheumatiz a spell. Besides, you got a chink cook around. You're all right."

"Where you goin' to start in?" queries John. "What kind o' land you want?"

"Anything that'll raise beef. Range. Up here, I expect, a small valley would be O.K. You see, Steve and me ain't lookin' for a big thing. I want something to keep me busy and keep the H Bar L on the map. A hundred thousand will likely provide the whole works. The rest of our dough we'll leave in the bank."

Old John turns and earnest face to me.

"Look-a-here, Pinky!" he says, real solemn. "If it gits out that you got a hundred thousand to spend these here Simplex County land agents will hold a massacree! You bet! They'll shake you down to the limit! Now, I got your best interests at heart, and I ain't goin' to see you git skunked."

"All right, John," I tells him. "I'm goin' to buy me a flivver and beat it up to them two towns on the lake. Bartlett, where the pears come from, and Simplex City, the county seat. S'pose you give me a line on them land agents."

"I'm s'prised at you, Pinky! But go ahead, it's your funeral! If you go, go heeled."

"I aim to," I says. "But what about them sharks? Who's the worst?"

"Ain't no worst, Pinky. The county seat's got three—Ma Germain, which she's a woman; Elbow P. Greaser, what runs for Congress and hopes for a miracle; and Herbert S. Sweetsir, Esquire, what come from England and ain't forgot it yet."

"The layout don't sound good, especially the lady. John, you remember that time in Reno, when they had a lady lookout and you caught 'em with a cold deck, and there was considerable ruction?"

"And nobody dast shoot the lady," he says real sorrowful. "Same here, Pinky."

"Well, what about Bartlett?" I inquires. "That's a pear and fruit district I hear. I ain't partial to county seats, anyhow; but this here Bartlett—"

"She's live, all right," and John rubs his back some more. "There's two sharks there, Pinky. One is John Q. Potentate, which has considerable rep as a fighter, or leastways he had. Ag'in him is Joel X. Williams, which he is a man of mystery, nobody havin' found what his middle name stands for. It was him sold me this place."

"Oh!" I says. "Then—"

"Don't say it," says John. "Wait! Williams is doin' all the business in the county. But lay off him! That's all I got to say. If you want a line on him go ask Tom Renfrew, what runs the pear sheds."

"By gosh I ain't askin' nobody!" I busts out, feeling like I'd et some locoweed. "I'm plumb tangled up. I'm goin' to buy chips and play a lone hand, savvy?"

"And for gosh sake keep your fool mouth shet!" says John. "Once you let 'em know what's on your mind and in your jeans, they'll hold ghost dances and git your scalp. Any gent with a hundred thousand in his pockets sure has got to step wide an' handsome! And, Pinky—don't sign nothin'. Not a thing! Dang it, wait a couple o' days, and mebbe I can hit the saddle."

"I ain't hittin' any saddle," I says. "I'm hittin' a flivver."

Which same I done.

I went out that same day to Centertown, near which we was domiciled, and bought me a flivver. I bought her under the name of Tom Jasper and seen to it that the license tag under the windshield was all fixed up in that name. You see, old John's advice about keepin' quiet had sure got my goat. It was blamed good advice. I could see plenty of ructions ahead if Simplex County found out that I was Tom J. Jenkins of the H Bar L, with a wad that would choke a steer. And I had no notion of getting shook down.

I arranged with John to write me under the name of Jasper, at Bartlett, if anything turned up. Then, next day, I started out.

Up to Bartlett she was about a good half day's drive, barring all trouble; through the mountains the whole way until we hit the valley where the lake and civilization was. And I'll say she was a pretty country. Fruit trees in bloom and all that, and pear orchards everywhere. Along late in the afternoon I come into Bartlett and headed for the hotel.

That hotel was run by a Swede, and the Swede was run by his wife. I got all due respect for a lady; so the less I say about that hotel the better. Anyhow, I got supper and went out to see the town.

Right off everybody in sight was a heap interested in me. The town wasn't much to view. I gathered that she existed for the sake of the pear sheds, where everybody worked three months in the year and lived on their earnings the remaining nine months. The chief industry was landing suckers to buy land, for the country was just opening up.

The metropolis was not very big for a fact. There was a picture show that ran one night a week and every twenty-ninth of February; two garages; the usual miscellaneous buildings, and a pool room. The pool room was the village club. Out on the stoop in front were perched most of the solid citizens, evidently waiting for something to happen. The others were inside, settled around some card tables. Quite a few drummers were in town because it was too late to flivver out.

Well, I got a slant at Williams, who was standing outside his real-estate office talking to some bosom friend he called Ike. This Joel X. gent looked all right to me, bein' large in size and husky, and by the way he talked I liked him. But old John had warned me, so I strolls on.

At the hotel I got me some county maps and set down to puzzle out the lay of the land. There was a lake two-three mile off, and high land around the end. I figures out that some little valleys over there would suit fine. Havin' talked things over previous with John I decides to go look at a place called High Valley, next morning. We had figured that by the time we got some stock on the hoof and had created a real ranch, the State would build a highway into the county, or a railroad would be run in. Anyhow this was the time to locate here, before the boom came along.

I got talkin' at the supper table with a drummer who peddled candy. He was a good sort, and we took a shine to each other. After supper I went up to his room, and we had a drink.

"I know this town like a book," he said. "S'pose we set into a game, Jasper? If you ain't too wild in your habits and could see a two-bit game, we can sure find it."

"You said somethin', pilgrim!" I tells him. "Lead on!"

We meanders down to the pool room, which at that early hour was about empty. In behind the screen we found a couple of gents runnin' cards at a table. The drummer gets greeted joyful and introduces me.

"Meet my friend Jasper," he says. "Jasper, this here is John Q. Potentate, and this here is Tom Renfrew runs the pear sheds hereabouts. What say to a two-bit ante?"

We were suited. Potentate was a big guy with stooped shoulders and a bull-moose nose. Renfrew was a husky six feet and a half tall, and built to suit. He had a bad eye and a good grin, and I liked him fine.

So the game starts in.

## CHAPTER II

## IN HIGH VALLEY

**B**EFORE THAT game was half an hour old several things happened. A couple more gents sits in, and I begins to watch John Q. Potentate on the deal; also the place begins to fill up, and questions begins to circle around my head.

There was considerable curiosity about Tom Jasper. I lets on that I was bound for Seattle and had stopped off to see the country. This did not altogether satisfy, but it eased things down a bit.

Along about the time the first straight flush come up I noticed a little old man with long whiskers standin' behind Potentate and lookin' hard at me. All of a sudden, during the deal, he speaks up.

"Say!" he pipes at me, "you ever been over Trinidad way?"

"Not real recent," I responds. I had been to Trinidad fifteen years back, but I hadn't any proud memories of the visit. "Why?"

"You're the livin' double of a feller I seen there when I was deputy sheriff quite a spell back! Yep, the livin' double! Ain't it strange how ye meet folks in Californy?"

"Sometimes," I says, giving him the cold eye, "it's too durned strange, pilgrim. I hope this gent who resembled me was respectable?"

"Not yet," says the old granddad. "His name was Jenkins. Huh! He was a gunman, an' he shot one o' the finest gamblers in Colorado, and he raised particular Ned! Yep. He was run out o' Trinidad as a menace to the community."

"Well," I says, reaching across the table and grabbing the left fist of John Q. Potentate, "if he was here now he'd sure be smoking! Partner, shake out them two aces you jest slipped—"

You should have heard that bull-nosed gent roar! Before he had got to his feet he was lookin' into my gun. He looked hard, swallowed twice, and showed up the two aces.

"Now," I says, "you beat it quick! If you crave action, feller, produce a gun."

However, it seemed that this line of action was not exactly suited to the civilized notions of Simplex County. John Q. took his foot in his hand and vanished hurriedly. I cashed in and drew out of the game, bein' advised by all and sundry that anybody who toted a gun was not popular in them precincts.

When I went outside this Tom Renfrew come after me.

"Hold on, Jasper!" he says. "You done exactly right with that skunk Potentate, and I aims to shake hands with you."

We shook, and he walks back to the hotel with me. That drummer had vanished.

"If you stick around these parts," said Renfrew, "watch out for Potentate. He's liable to skin you alive if he gits the chance. You ain't lookin' for a job?"

"Not hardly," I says. "I did aim to look up a piece o' land for a man, but I guess things is too durned civilized around here. By the way, do you know a gent here name o' Williams, what handles land?"

Renfrew took me by the arm.

"Jasper," he says, real earnest, "I like you. I'll tell you the sober truth—keep away from Williams! That man would skin a jack rabbit's tail to git the pelt!"

"I seen him on the street to-day," I says, "and he looked square to my notion."

"Don't trust to looks," says Renfrew. "What kind o' land you after?"

"None. Feller asked me to take a squint around for him."

"Hm!" says Renfrew. "How much cash has he?"

"About five hundred."

"Oh! Well, tell him I'll sell him my half interest in the meat market for that."

"He ain't on that end of the cow," I says.

"All right. I'll sell him my half o' the garage, then."

"He don't need it. He runs a flivver."

"Half o' the jewelry store, then—"

"Look here," I says. "Do you own this here burg?"

"Half of it," he informs me with a grin. And, come to find out, he did!

Well, he was a first-rate sort of chap, and we collaborates for quite some while on the hotel porch. I gradually sheers off the question of my five-hundred-dollar friend, and we talks general. Renfrew, it seems, had put up ready money for most of the town and kept a half interest in the business end, so he was not worrying about his next meal.

In the course of our palaver I mentions that some day I might settle down in this part of the country, and we talked land. High Valley was mentioned. Renfrew says he has a shack up there where he goes during the hot weather, and he tells me a lot about the valley. I see right off it is just the place I've been looking for.

We parts with mutual admiration and respect, and I goes up to my room and goes to sleep. When daybreak come I snuck out of the place to where the flivver was parked in the back yard. I had grub in the car for me and her both, so I delayed for nothing but cranked up and went. We slid out of town before sunup, and not a soul was early enough to see us depart.

As quick as the town dropped behind I felt considerable more like myself. I had got in bad by showing a gun durin' that poker game—I could see plain that these citizens looked down on me as a roughneck cattle hand—and besides which, Renfrew was the only real man in the crowd I had met. Then, maybe, that drink with the drummer had caused me to act a little sudden. And above all that whiskered gent, what had recognized me, made the town look unpleasant to my tastes.

Right over the town there towered Uncle Sam Mountain—a real he-hill, too. My road took me hither and yon—mostly yon. It was a good road, but the gent what laid out had figured on visiting every ranch for a drink en route, and the result was like an angle-worm.

High Valley was forty miles from town, around the end of the lake in the hills. The road took me through a couple of villages, but I did no pausing. It was not easy to navigate them roads, however, and so it was about nine o'clock when I finally hit High Valley and begun a tour of investigation.

This particular valley, as I had previously learned, had played in hard luck. One gent had burned out there, another had washed out durin' the rains, and the only remaining settler had lost his family from the flu. I figures there is nothin' else left to hit except lightning, and I'm always willing to gamble on that.

The road into High Valley was not a highway; it ended somewheres in the valley. That road was thick with coveys of mountain quail, and I scared off two deer coming in. It was not legal season for either one, and I always believe in drawin' the line at breaking the game laws. So I drew the line when the next bunch of quail showed up, knocked the heads off two birds with the old six-gun, and rested content.

Right there I got me a combination breakfast-dinner, left the car underneath the trees, and set off to explore afoot. The main thing was to get the general lay of the land and to see how the water situation was. I wasn't expecting to market cattle, you see; what I wanted was a quiet, retired ranch where I could do what I liked, keep the old H Bar L on the map, and maybe do some fancy breeding. Not being near any shipping point did not worry me.

It wasn't long before I become plumb joyful. No doubt whatever about it; this here place was exactly the thing I had been hoping for! There was water in plenty, hot and cold springs both, while the feed situation would never bother in a country like this, where there was hardly enough frost to kill bean bushes.

Then the valley itself was just to my mind. It was like a box cañon in shape, only fairly large. About a thousand acres down at this end; the upper flat, where the only settler lived, looked to have twice as much more.

I settled down on a knoll and looked that valley over real careful from every angle with my binoculars. In half an hour of speculatin' I had the whole thing in my mind—just where I'd build the house, just where the corral and bunk house and barns would go, and so forth. She was the prettiest layout you ever saw, too! On a small scale, of course, but I was not hankering for any outlandish-sized ranch to keep me busy in my old age. Most of the valley was brush land, but a patch of alfalfa on the upper flat showed there were possibilities and then some.

Presently, along toward noon, I came back toward my car feeling pretty well satisfied with things. When I drew close I saw that another flivver stood near it, and a single gent was regarding me in a stern and unhandsome fashion. He was a stranger to me, but from the look in his eye I judged there was trouble in the air.

"Howdy, stranger," he says. "Is this here your car?"

"Nope," I retorts. "Leastways it's hired for the occasion, but she belongs to a gent name o' Jasper. Might I inquire as to your curiosity?"

"You et lunch here, didn't you?"

"Dog-gone it, pilgrim, you got the inquiringest mind I ever see!" I tells him. "What in purgatory has my business got to do with yours?"

"Did you ever see a deppity game warden's badge?" he says, and shows one. "Where did them quail feathers come from?"

"Far's I know, from a quail. Why?"

"Stranger, this ain't a jokin' matter, and if—"

"Conceded," I assents. "Further, I ain't jokin'. S'pose you find that gent Jasper what drove me up here! He'll prob'ly be the one done the shootin'. I ain't got any shot—"

"What might your name be?" he inquires, sharp and sudden.

"Jenkins," I says. "Tom Jenkins."

Just then another gent shows up from the brush.

"Not a sign of any one," he sings out. Then he sees me. "Hullo! Found him, have you?"

"Not him but another," says the deputy. "This one says his name's Jenkins. Know him?"

I stares at the other man, who was no less than Joel X. Williams, the land agent. He knowed well enough I was Jasper, from havin' heard of me in town and seen me around the day previous.

"Sure," he says right hearty. "How are ye, Jenkins? Where's that Jasper guy?"

"Prob'ly ducked out," I says and grinned.

I am not defending myself, of course. There are times when a man will do the durndest fool things just from plain cussedness; this was one of the times. Ordinary I hate the skunk who'll break the game laws—but I shot them quail none the less. And ate 'em. And enjoyed 'em. It's only human to be a blamed fool, most likely.

Besides, that fool deputy had never asked if I had shot the quail or not, had he?


CHAPTER III

ALL BUT EIGHTY ACRES

THE DEPUTY struck out on the back trail to find Jasper. It proved that Williams had met the deputy and had given him a ride. When he was gone the land agent looked at me and grinned. More than ever I liked his looks.

"Jasper," he says, "or Jenkins, you'd better beat it quick!"

"Not me," I says. "I'm a heap obliged to you. Reckon I'll take my medicine after a bit, though. I was just a plain fool. Hello! You got a flat tire?"

"Yep. That's how come we happened to stop and find your quail feathers." He grinned. "Well I got to work a while. See you later."

I cranked up the flivver and started up the valley. This Williams looked good to me, and I couldn't understand why old John had warned me off him. Still, John knew a heap better than I did.

Following the road that led up the valley I came pretty soon to the home site of the sole survivor. It was a site, sure enough, and not much more, being a home-made cabin patched together from tin cans and barrel staves. The proprietor came forth to greet me. He was an elderly rascal by the name of Simcoe, and he didn't know the Civil War was settled yet.

We got to talking about one thing and another.

"I was in the Trinidad expedition when I was a kid," he says, "and I went with old Josiah Gregg to Clear Lake, when he died. Mebbe you recall him. He writ books. So do I. I've writ a book about Quantrill's raiders, and if I ever git enough money, by gosh, I'll print it up! She'll make folks set up, I tell ye."

"How much land you got here?" I asks.

"All in sight. Hull quarter section."

"How much you want for it?"

The old snoozer got real excited at this. He takes me out back of the house to where he had a still set up and was brewin' Missouri moonshine, and we had a drink. One was plenty for me—plenty! I have experienced considerable warfare in the way of putting down booze, but this here brand of rattler antidote would have made a tarantula turn pale at one whiff.

There was no mortgage on old Simcoe's place, for a wonder; the old geezer had homesteaded it years ago and had been too lazy to borrow on it. However, he had been in the notion of selling it lately and had all the papers—abstract of title and all. I had a couple of blank deeds in my own pocket, so we were all set to talk swap.

Come to find out, except when his family were killed off by the flu old Simcoe had not been to town in ten years. He knew nothing about land values having increased. In fact he had a mighty slender stock of knowledge about anything later than Quantrell's raiders. So when he mentioned a thousand cash for his quarter section he was plumb apologetic.

"Time o' the funerals," he says, "I got these here papers. One o' them land agents, he said to have 'em. He allowed he'd sell the place some day, mebbe. But he ain't done it."

"Well," I says, after finding that his land took in the whole upper flat, "I don't aim to skin no man, Simcoe. You got this land cleared. It ain't worth a cent lessn' five thousand—likely more. I'll give you five thousand cash. What say?"

He like to fainted. Presently he got his tongue back, and we signed up.

While we were doing so I looks up sudden to see two birds strolling along. One looked like a Cornish chicken, but the other was the most startlin' bit of bird color I've seen in a long while—long head and tail, and plumb handsome. Reminded me of "Shorty" Nesbit, down on the Running F in Arizona, when he got all dolled up for town.

"Good gosh!" I says. "What kind of fancy peacocks are you raising?"

"Raising nothin'!" says Simcoe, rolling his eye. "Them's some kind o' Chiny birds that's been let run in these hills till they're the most pestiferous nuisance you ever seen. But eatin'—yum! They lay over any kind o' eatin' you ever struck! Got cawn-fed hawg beat a mile—"

"Well let's get them papers signed," I cuts in, and we returns to business.

Probably half an hour had served to do the whole thing, and this here upper part of the valley was mine. Simcoe did not know who owned the lower part; said it had changed hands more or less. So, this portion of the affair being concluded, I retires to the Lizzie and ambles back to where I had come from.

"If old John Parker could see me now," I says, "he'd feel considerable easier about the cash in my pocket! Or, rather, the check book. Hello—what's this?"

Right here the road was mighty narrow, with brush close on each side. I comes around a bend, and another car came likewise, but going the wrong way. We stops with a margin of two inches between the radiators, and I see John Q. Potentate sitting under the other steering wheel and regarding me.

"Git out o' the road!" I says.

"Git yourself!" returns John Q. He alights out of his car and shakes a skinny fist at me. "Ye durned skunk, git off'n my land!"

"Your land?" I says, also comin' to earth. "Where d'ye git that stuff? It's mine, and I got the papers to prove it!"

Potentate turns green and shakes his fist again.

"So that's what you been doin' up here!" he yells. "You and that yeller dog Williams have been fixin' to put it over on me! Did Simcoe sell you that land? Did he dast do it?"

"He sure did, pilgrim," I says, feelin' a heap satisfied.

"It's a swindle!" hollers John Q. "The sale won't hold—he's signed up with me! Nobody but me can sell his land—and I ain't selling! I want it my ownself."

I surveys him with a grin of pure delight.

"You got to go a ways to get it, then—a durned long ways! A man can't sell his own land, hey? Sounds likely. And let me tell you, go easy with them names! Thought you could buy Simcoe's land for a thousand and cheat him cool, did you? Nix! That there plum is in my own pocket."

There was something to this that I didn't know, but it was not worrying me. I was looking for a chance to land on Potentate's bull-moose nose, and he was about to give me the chance when Joel X. Williams come strolling along and intervened.

"What's all this?" he says.

Potentate turned, gave him one look, then whirled and began to leg it toward Simcoe's shack, leaving his car where she lay. Williams looked after him, then at me.

"What's the idea?" he asks. "Is he crazy?"

"If he ain't, I am," I says. "He seems right sore about me buyin' Simcoe's place."

"Have you bought it?" asks Williams.

"Signed, sealed, an' delivered. Got any objections?"

"Nope." He grinned then broke into a real hearty laugh. "Gosh, but this is rich! I'll bet he's ready to go up like a balloon! Don't you know about this here place?"

"I'm ignorant and proud of it," says I. "Where's your car?"

"Where she was. Blowout and no extry shoe." He begins to roll a cigarette. "Let's set down, and I'll spill the story. You sure have dropped a monkey-wrench in the works!"

We reclines in the shade, and he orates. I likes this gent, as I've said, and the more he talks the more I like him. He seemed to think it was a good joke that I'd bought the Simcoe place, even if the joke did spoil his hopes. He sure took it like a gent.

It seemed this here entire High Valley was divided into three parts, as the feller said about Gaul in the medical book. Simcoe owned the upper part. John Q. Potentate owned a strip of eighty acres in the middle. Williams had an option on the whole lower section, and the option expired in two days more.

There was the makings of a fine feud here, more particular on account of the bad business blood between Williams and Potentate. Each one wanted Simcoe's land, and wanted it bad. Potentate had signed up Simcoe to sell it, but had been trying to screw him down to a price of five hundred. Williams refused to buy it through Potentate and give the latter gent the com-mission—even if Potentate would have sold it to him, which was unlikely.

And now a complete and total stranger, which same was Tom J. Jenkins, had stepped in and snapped up the Simcoe ranch! It was enough to bust up all the happy schemes of both land agents. Likewise I could see where all the plans of T.J. Jenkins were going to be upset unless somebody turned a jack at the next deal.

And it was my deal.

"Now," I says, "understand at the start that I ain't sellin' that land; I stands pat. If any war starts up I ain't interested unless drug in. Where three is concerned I am out."

"But supposin' only two was concerned?" queries Williams.

"Now you're talkin', pilgrim," I says prompt. "Want to sell that option?"

He rolls another cigarette, slants his eye at the hills, and talks.

"This here," he opines, "would make a swell little cattle range. That's all national forest reserve on them hills back yonder; can be had for the asking. Why, no, Mr. Jasper or Jenkins, I don't rightly *want* to sell that there option. It gives me the whole lower part o' this valley for ten thousand, ye see."

"I don't need no specs to see that," I says. "Brush land, uncleared—huh! You mean you'll sell it to me for ten thousand—and make right smart on the deal!"

"I'll sell you the land for ten thousand and charge an extry thousand on account of the option," he says real cool. "I'm makin' money, you know—that's my business! I don't aim to operate at no loss; not yet! But," and he gives me a good look, "I ain't holdin' you up, none whatever. I figures, for instance, that you want the land, and you'd likely go as high as thirty thousand to get it, just to satisfy a stubborn nature. But I ain't a robber."

I had to grin at this, because that gent had me sized up exactly right. Putting it the way he did, his proposition was fair. Fair enough, that is.

"If I buy your land, then," I says, "there's an eighty-acre strip belonging to John Q. that runs right through my holdings!"

"It's your funeral," he returns. "Potentate will sure make trouble for you."

"Sign over a deed," I says. "Here's a check for eleven thousand."

We couldn't sign a deed on account of him not owning the land. But we made out a form of contract and signed her up.

So there we were, and I was right joyful over it. Instead of spending at least fifty thousand for land alone, as I had figured on, I had all but eighty acres of High Valley for a total of sixteen thousand.

And not shook down yet, neither!

## CHAPTER IV

### TRAPPED

"SO YOU really are Jenkins—Tom Jenkins!" William looked up from his copy of our agreement and gave me a cheerful grin. "I don't suppose—Hullo! By jingo, ain't that bird a beauty?"

We looked up. About fifty feet away from us, and walking with a dignified strut right across the road, was one of them birds I had seen up to Simcoe's place—Chiny birds, as the old snoozer had called 'em. This one sure had wonderful colorings and long tail feathers.

I jerks out my Colt.

"Dog-gone it, I'm a heap tempted!" I says. "Simcoe says them birds are great eatin'—and if she eats like she looks, they must be! But I don't hanker to bust any more game laws; this here State has got different kinds of laws for every section—"

Williams busts into a laugh.

"Yes," he says, "you'd look fine shootin' that bird with your young cannon! I'll bet you five even that you can't hit him above that ring on his neck! If you can I'll pay the fine if the warden's deputy catches us. By gosh I'll bet you a hundred even!"

"You're on," I says and throws down on the bird. The top of his head comes off clean as a whistle.

"You owe me a hundred," I says.

"And everybody hands up!" says a voice from behind.

We twisted around to see the game deputy standing among the bushes with a gun trained on us, but chiefly on me. By the look in his eye I judged he meant it. So, not without a chuckle, I obeyed. Williams had agreed to pay the fine, anyhow!

"This here," said the deputy after we elevated, "is a fine bit o' work! I see plain how them quail were killed this morning. You Jasper-Jenkins, did you kill 'em?"

"Sure," I says. "If you'd asked me before, 'stead of crawfishin' around the subject, I'd have told you straight out. My name's Jenkins, but this is my car. My middle name is Jasper, and I use it sometimes."

"I see," says the deputy. He had a mean eye, a tuft of whiskers on his chin, and his finger was too stiff on the trigger to suit me. "Drop that gun!"

I drops her, pronto.

"Listen to reason, will you?" I says. "You got me wrong; I admits it. I ain't famous as a breaker o' game laws, and them quail simply caught me at a foolish moment. I'm willin' to pay for it. Name what the fine will be, and I'll fork over."

Williams spoke up.

"That's right. Give Jenkins a chance! He's acting square enough. Told me this morning that he'd settle up and take his medicine."

"What in time d'you gents think I am?" says the deputy. "A fool?"

"I'd hate to disagree with you on that verdict," I returns right smooth. "But what's the cause o' this here outburst? Ain't my proposition reasonable? Them quail—"

"Them quail," says the deputy real solemn, "ain't got nothin' to do with it—nothin' a-tall—except mebbe as an additional charge."

"Good gosh!" I says. "Additional to what?"

He jerks his free hand toward the Chiny bird.

"You know what that bird is, don't you?"

"No," I tells him. "I never seen one in my life before to-day, and I've seen all kinds. What's this bird?"

"It's a Chiny pheasant," says the deputy. "A Chiny pheasant, with which the gov'ment has propagated these here mountains! That's what it is."

"Conceded," I says. "I'll accept your diagnosis." I turns to Williams. "Pardner, it looks to me like this here is your funeral! You agrees to take over the fine—"

"That's right," assents Williams. "I owe you a hundred and what the fine comes to."

"There ain't goin' to be no fine," says the deputy.

"How come?" I asks.

"This ain't a State affair," he tells me. "It's a Fed'ral offense, and the only penalty they is is a penitentiary sentence. So rise up an' travel to town with me."

"Good gosh!" I says. "Do you mean that?"

"Don't ask me—ask the jedge!" says the deputy real sour. "Williams, I want you for a witness. Don't you guys get fresh, now, or this gun goes off!"

Poor Williams looks at me. His face was a yard long.

"I'm out of it," he says. "I said I'd stand the fine, but San Quentin wasn't mentioned. I'm durned sorry, Jenkins! They sure hit strangers hard in this county—hit 'em hard. I never knowed about this penitentiary thing, though."

Well, I done some quick and fancy thinking. It looked like I was up against it this time and no mistake—and all from bein' a blamed fool.

"Joel X.," I says, "go take a little walk. Me and the deputy have private business."

The deputy scowled, but Williams walked over to the two cars and stayed. I turns to the deputy.

"Pardner," I says, "I figger on starting a ranch in these parts. I got a heap of coin to bring into the county banks. If you lay me away it'll hurt this county a heap."

"So much the better for my reputation," he says. "Glad to hear that news!"

I took a fresh breath.

"Now listen!" I says. "This here is strictly between the three of us. I got some certified checks in my pocket for different amounts. I ain't so set on myself but what I can own up to my own mistakes and admit I been a blamed silly fool. Likewise I can keep my mouth shet. So can Williams, if I'm any judge. Now, feller, it's your ante."

The deputy frowned.

"Are you offerin' to bribe me?"

"Yes," I says. "I am. With big money."

He studied me a spell. Finally he shook his head.

"It won't do, I reckon," he says. "You ain't got money enough to square it. I'd have to leave these here parts for good; I couldn't take no chances. Besides the felony o' tryin' to bribe me, you're offerin' to cheat poor folks out o' their dinner."

"How do you figure that?" I says.

"Seized game goes to the poor-farm kitchen," and he grins.

Well, I could see good and proper that he was hooked. It was only a question of coming to a proper settlement. We talks for a while.

"You got to look at it this way," he concludes. "It's the pen for you, certain; like Williams says, strangers gets the limit in this county. Local folks don't matter; we believe in preservin' our game for home consumption."

"Well," I says, "I belong to the local union, seein's I own the land right above here, what used to belong to Simcoe."

"Oh!" he says, fingering his whisker tuft. "That's different. But I'd sure have to leave these parts! I'd have to have a big enough check to start me up in business somewheres else. And it couldn't be in my name, neither."

"That's easy," I says. "I'll endorse a certified check, and you can cash her under any name you please. How much will buy your business?"

"Ten thousand ought to do it, I reckon."

I sat in cold sober thought while he eyed me.

Ten thousand! It was a durned high price to pay for a bird with pretty feathers. On the other hand, I was not hankering to get a free suit of clothes with stripes running the wrong way. Seemed to me that I did remember something about pheasants being Federal property; but down in the part of the State where I come from peacocks and pheasants were not running around loose.

However, the next move was now up to me. And she was a forgone conclusion; I had to put up or take my medicine. So I reaches into my pocket and unpinned the roll of certified checks that was hooked to my suspenders by a safety-pin. Fortunately I had come provided with checks in various and sundry denominations. Without letting that deputy see more than I could help, I found a check for ten thousand, and hauled her out.

"Got a fountain pen?" I says.

The deputy called Williams, who furnished pen and ink. I signed the check and handed her over. The deputy put up his gun and looked at Williams.

"You'd better run me into town," he says. "I'll take the early morning stage out."

"All right." Williams turns to me. "You're lucky, that's all! I'm sorry this come up. Stop in for dinner to-night, will you? I live right behind the office—next house. We can clean up them papers and talk over gettin' that eighty acres away from Potentate."

"All right," I says. "And I'll collect that hundred."

Williams found a spare tire on Potentate's car and stole it. Them two gents faded away through the brush and left me to ruminate on my folly.

I ruminated for quite a spell. The more I done so, the more I begun to scent a polecat around the premises.

Maybe the encounter with that game deputy had sobered me a mite. Anyhow, I begun to see the light of reason on what I had done. As it stood I owned all this here valley except a strip of eighty acres across the middle, and Potentate owned that strip. He could sure make trouble if he had a mind to.

"And he'll sure have a mind to!" I thinks. "He can raise all kinds of legal ructions with me, and can make me buy him out at his own figure. Now could it be possible that I have miscued? Could Williams and John Q. be collaborators on this here deal?"

That notion hit me like a cold rain.

Yes, sir! The more I thought about it the more certain I was that I had stepped plumb into a bear-trap—and there was no getting out!

CHAPTER V

TO GET EIGHTY ACRES

I SAT THERE and looked at those two cars, with the dead pheasant off to one side, and thinks to myself that I had got shook down after all.

What was to prevent Williams and Potentate from pretending to be enemies? Not a thing. That would simply be good business for them. They had this High Valley property all framed up for the first sucker that came along—and I was it. Potentate would hold out that eighty-acre strip and either ruin the whole works or get an outrageous price.

Looking at it this way I could see easy enough that I'd been a considerable fool all morning. Renfrew had warned me off this Williams, and so had old John Parker, but I had been too stuck up to pay proper heed. No wonder Williams had asked me to stop in for supper! Then was when the harpoon was to be stuck into me good and plenty.

"Pinky," I says to myself real sorrowful, "when old John and Steve Moran get a hold of this here deal you're goin' to be in the soup! And there ain't no come-back, neither. Not a chance in the world. They got you hog-tied an' squaw-hitched proper!"

There was nothing to be done about it except to take my medicine. I was signed up in an agreement with Williams, which same amounted to a contract. If I busted it I was liable for the whole works.

With a sigh I decides to verify my suspicions before taking any action. To do that I had to get back to civilization. To do that, again, I had to move John Q. Potentate's flivver. So I set about the job of easing his car out of my way.

I must admit that I was none too gentle about doing it. When I had started his old rattler into life I pointed her at the brush to one side of the road and made her climb. She done noble for as much as a minute—riz up and tackled that scrub like she was determined to do or die. She done both. When most of her had grabbed the brush with all four legs she grunted and give up the ghost.

Just as I was climbing out of the saddle I hears a yell and looks around. There come John Q. himself, wavin' a shotgun, and behind him was poor old Simcoe.

"Leave my car alone, you thief!" yells Potentate. Then—

"Bang! Bang!" He lets go with both barrels of the gun.

My first notion was to perforate him quick and sudden, and I started to do it. He had not hurt me, however, and just as I was throwing down on him I got an idea. Yes, sir, a real, live idea! Or, as the Boston feller said, an idear.

So I waits. Potentate comes busting up, then halts right sudden when he sees my gun. He makes a grab to lift his shotgun.

"Go easy, feller!" I says. "She's clear unloaded now, and safe. You and me are goin' to hold a palaver."

He stood there panting and glaring at me. Old Simcoe nosed along with his whiskers flying until he seen the gun likewise and halted.

"Hold on, Jenkins!" he orates, and waves a bit of paper at me. "Here's that there check you give me. Give back my land!"

"What's this?" I says.

"Give it back!" The poor old snoozer caught his breath, for the gun had winded him. "You got to give it back, see?"

"Nope. I'm blind in that eye," I says. "What's the notion, anyhow?"

Simcoe pointed at Potentate. From the look in his eye I judged he was real frightened about something.

"He wants it!" he says. "You got to give it back so he can have it."

"Why, ain't you satisfied with the deal?"

"Sure, sure!" The old boy looked powerful hungrily at that check. "Sure! But John, he wants the land."

I tells him short where John can go to homestead all the land he wants.

"John ain't running me," I goes on. "Nor you neither, is he? Then what's all your holler about?"

Simcoe combs out his whiskers.

"Why," he says, "it's like this. John, here, he knows about that there still of mine. He says if I don't git the land back an' sell to him he'll give me away to the off'cers. Pardner, you wouldn't let an ol' man like me git stuck in jail, would ye?"

"Nope," I tells him. "And Potentate ain't goin' to do it."

"Is that so?" retorts Potentate. "Well, you'll find out that I am! What's more, I'll have you took up for carryin' concealed weapons! We don't want no gun-toters in this here county!"

I begun to get the little scheme all straightened out.

Potentate wanted to keep that land of Simcoe's tied up. Sure! Him and Williams had not figured on me buying it at all just yet. In fact, they had not figured on me buying anything at all.

So long as I had that contract with Williams I had to keep it or get released. When I found that Potentate owned the strip across the middle of the valley, and likewise controlled Simcoe's land, I would holler for help. Either they would sell out to me, or, what was more probable, I would pay through the nose to get out of the Williams contract. So, at least, they figured.

"Simcoe," I says, "come here a minute."

He come. The poor old boy was uncertain whether I meant to shoot him or take back my money. Either way, he was mighty unhappy.

When he was close enough so's I could whisper without bein' overheard by John Q. Potentate I elucidates matters. Simcoe stared at me, blinked his old eyes, clawed his whiskers, and finally emits a joyful oath when he understood. Then he reached to his hip and brought out a bottle.

"Pardner, will you drink on it?" he says solemn.

I refuses. He tips the bottle of homemade hooch and takes enough to paralyze a steer. Then he gives me the bottle to hold, turns, and walks in on Potentate. The latter looks a bit startled.

"Put me in jail, will ye?" says Simcoe. "Durn your measly hide! I hear tell that you've done some fist fightin' in your time. That right?"

Before Potentate could answer old Simcoe hauls off and whales him in the bull-moose nose. Then the old boy begins to dance.

"I'll learn ye!" he sings out. "Think I'm too old to fight, do ye? Put me in jail? Come on, ye skunk! I'll—"

Potentate lets out a beller and starts to clean up the old boy.

Well I don't know when I've enjoyed anything like that there ruckus! My sympathies was all one-sided at first, for it looked like John Q. could stiffen Simcoe with one hand. In about three minutes, however, I begun to feel real sorry for the village bad man.

Beyond a doubt that hooch had hit Simcoe like a pipe of marihuana hits a greaser. And I'm here to say the old snoozer was some agile on his feet! He run Potentate ragged—hit him, kicked him, whanged away at him from all sides. In no time at all he had the big gent bruised up and bleeding.

Potentate naturally done his best, but I'd have hated myself to stand up against that human-whiskered cyclone. In about a minute John Q. was on the defensive, and in another minute he was off it. Simcoe hit him under the ear, knocked him against my car, kicked him across the road, and then jumped on him.

"I'll learn ye!" he cackles, and he sure did learn him.

Finally I had to step in and pull Simcoe off his prey. I gives him the bottle and shoves him into my car to wait. Then I goes back to Potentate.

John Q. looks up at me feeble, moans, and slowly comes to his feet. He began to feel of his face and frame, but I takes his arm and indicates an object to him.

"You see that?" I says.

He blinks and grunts an assent.

"Now see what you done, shootin' guns regardless!" I says. "I'm going to take you in right now and lay a charge against you. What's more, Simcoe will be witness. You know what the penalty is, don't ye? It's the pen! And you'll sure go."

"My land!" groans Potentate, staring at that dead pheasant. "I didn't go—"

"Shut up!" I tells him. "You climb into that car. Here, Simcoe! Take this here gun and shoot this gent if he tries any tricks, sabe? I'll drive you both into town, and we'll land him behind the bars before sundown! No talk, you! Climb in!"

He was sure flabbergasted. I kicks him into the car, gives Simcoe my gun to hold on him, and then throws in the dead pheasant for evidence. What between the lickin' he had got, and the realization of what he thought he had done, that gent was real tame. Yes, sir! He was so tame that he begun to beg.

I told him to shut up and begun to drive home.

Old Simcoe sure enjoyed that run back to town. Every five minutes he would poke John Q. in the ribs with the gun, which same Potentate did not enjoy a whole lot. Besides Simcoe had finished the rest of that hooch. Every time we jounced on a stone Potentate thought he was goin' to get shot.

It was along toward supper time when the town hove into sight. John Q. had lost all his fight and was about as spunky as a cat that's been swimming in the bathtub all day. Just outside town he gives me a prayerful plea.

"This—this here will plumb ruin me!" he wails. "They're awful hard on any one that's caught shootin' them birds!"

"Sure!" I says nice and cheerful. "That's why you're goin' to catch it."

"Leave me go!" he begs. "I'm a deacon in the church, and it'll make a scandal! I got a family to pervide for. You wouldn't go to hurt innercent children?"

"Well," I says, "that's quite an argument, and no mistake! Maybe, if you was to sell me them eighty acres real cheap—"

"Oh, my gosh! Drive right over to my office, next the barber shop!" he says.

I done it.

## CHAPTER VI

### THE SHAKEDOWN

IN THE pleasant glow of sunset I stood outside Potentate's office and done some mighty pleasant glowing my own self.

Just think what that one dead pheasant had done! It had influenced old Simcoe to turn like a worm and do some fancy hitting; then it had influenced John Q. to sell me those eighty acres at a nominal, reasonable rate. He had sure been influenced, too! Just now he was limping home and calling for the arnica.

Simcoe had departed for the hotel, him having confessed to a hankering after the fleshpots of high life, now that he had some money to spend. As for me, I was plumb satisfied with the way things had shaped out. All of High Valley was mine, and there was going to be no holdup nor shakedown, neither.

"It sure is great to have brains, Tom Jenkins!" I says to myself. "You made a blamed fool of yourself this morning, but you sure evened things up before night. And now it's your turn to call Joel X. Williams' busted flush—she's certain busted!"

As I turned and headed for Williams' house I had to chuckle. Potentate had denied to the last that there was any collusion betwixt him and Williams; just the same I was sure of my deductions, as the feller said in the detective story. And wouldn't Steve Moran grin when he collected that bet off old John Parker! Nobody had shook me down, after all.

It was a pleasurable moment I felt exactly as a feller does when he has stayed on two pair and faith, and then draws her full. I was feeling so good that I clear forgot somebody else might have drawed cards likewise.

Well, I turns the corner and approaches Williams' house. He was out in front helping his wife corner a pig that had broke from its corral. Naturally I helped in the job, and when we got it done there was introductions, and so forth, everybody flushed and happy. His wife was a right smart little woman. She left us a moment later, havin' the dinner to attend to.

I went up on the stoop with Williams. We sat down and rolled one. I had meant to say nothing and let him flounder, but I judged it might be best to settle matters right off, so as to avoid making him feel bad in front of his wife. So, the time being good, I lights my cigarette and orates.

"I just come from Potentates's office," I says. "Him and me concluded a deal."

"Huh?" Williams looks hard at me. "Thought you'd been warned off o' that scoundrel! How bad did he sting you?"

"I ain't stung," I says and chuckles. "You might as well quit callin' him names, pardner. That was a fine little trick you had all laid out, but I've seen cold decks rung in before you was in long pants!"

"I don't get you," he says, staring hard at me.

"That's all right. I'm satisfied," I tells him. "I can see through a brick wall most generally, when it's got windows. I seen right off that you and Potentate were pullin' that fake rivalry stuff—"

"Listen!" he breaks in, beginning to roll his eyes. "Listen! For the love o' Mike, *listen!* Fake rivalry stuff? You don't think him and me are on speakin' terms, do you? Good gosh, man! Why he's quit goin' to lodge ever since they made me the grand flappin' turtle; and last week my wife and hisn come together and we like to never pried 'em apart."

There was somethin' convincin' earnest about this gent.

"Dog-goned if you don't talk like you meant it," I says. "Look here, didn't you and him frame up that High Valley deal on me?"

"Frame up nothing! I wouldn't no more trust him to go in on any deal than I would that pig out yonder. I'd a durned sight prefer the pig! What deal you talkin' about!"

I begun to believe that my deductions had maybe gone too far. I can tell when a man really means his words.

"I doped it out," I tells him, "that you two gents had me framed, him to keep that there eighty-acre strip and club me with it."

Williams chuckled. "Listen, brother! What I said is the truth! Besides I never knew that you had any interest in High Valley until I met you there to-day."

"That's so. Anyhow, I done bought the eighty—"

And I tells him about what had happened, and how that dead pheasant had come to be utilized.

"So you're all settled—got all the land you want?" he says.

"Yep."

He lights the cigarette and breaks the match.

"You sure are a fast worker," he says. "Old John Parker warned me—but I didn't see how it could be done so fast. Yes, sir, I'll hand it to you for—"

"What's this?" I says. "John warned you? Warned you what? How come?"

He grinned at me.

"John wrote me you were comin' under the name of Jasper," he says. "He warned you against me because he figured you were pig-headed and contrary enough to look me up on that very account. You see, John wrote that he wanted me to sting you somehow—"

"My gosh!" I says, staring at him. "My gosh! But go on."

He begun to chuckle and pointed at the corner. Two figures were coming in sight, and I recognized one of them for Tom Renfrew.

"I'll admit you were too fast for us," says Williams. "Tom and me were going after your scalp, proper. Renfrew, you see, was layin' the groundwork by pretendin' to hate me. But you were too durned fast, that's all! We figured you'd poke around for a week, anyhow."

"So John Parker was pullin' another of his jokes, was he?" I drew a deep breath and leaned back in my chair. Then I grinned at Williams. "Well, it's all right, anyhow! You ain't trimmed me, after all."

"Is that so?" says Williams. "Is that so? Listen, brother! You been trimmed for ten thousand—and the check's on the way to old John Parker this minute for any disposition he sees fit to make! You set back and look at your cards again. You done slipped up."

"What?" I says, gulping hard. "You— Good gosh! You don't mean to say—"

"I do." Williams got up and took my arm. He led me to the steps where Renfrew and the other gent were approaching. "Mr. T. Jasper Jenkins, meet my friend Tom Renfrew! And, on the other side, meet my brother-in-law."

I reaches out to shake hands, when I realized that the brother-in-law was that there game warden's deputy what I had bribed with ten thousand dollars. I like to fainted when I begun to see the shakedown, and everybody was hollering with laughter but me.

"Are you a deputy?" I says to the feller with the whiskers.

He was not. There was no hope whatever. I had been shook down, that was all! Just as I realized this Williams leaned over.

"Listen!" he says, tryin' to look mysterious between laughs. "Listen! All of us is havin' a dinner party to celebrate the shakedown, sabe? And, Pinky Jenkins, we're havin' a real dinner in your honor. Six roast—"

But what's the use going on? That's the whole story—except that I never got the ten thousand back. Nope. Old John Parker says I deserved to lose that for breakin' the game laws like I done, so he sent it to China to feed babies with.

Which same was all right with me.

So long!

A NEW DEAL IN DOUBLE ACE

*PROLOGUE.—Deponent, T.J. Jenkins, whose residence is Running F Ranch, County of Coyote, State of Nevoming, being duly sworn, deposes: That to the best of his knowledge and belief the facts related and set forth by him hereinafter are true and exact statements, inspired by no malice and containing nothing but the truth. Witness his hand and seal, given in my presence this first day of July, 1923.*

*(Signed) T.J. JENKINS.*

*Witness: ED BOUNCE, Sheriff.*

*[SEAL]*

*Attest: J.F. HASKINS, Notary Public, City of Double Ace, County of Coyote, State of Nevoming.*

### CHAPTER I

O LD JOHN PARKER and me sure run into something fine and fancy when we hit Coyote County, but it was maybe all our own fault for leaving California like we done. This was the way of it. You remember Old John, maybe. He was chief scout in all the late Injun wars, and put down the rising at Walla Walla in '79. Well, I rode over to his place to tell him about the offer I'd had that day, and found him miserable as all get-out.

"If I was young and spry like you, Tom Jenkins," says he, pulling a long face, "I'd go back to the cow country. Dang it, I'm homesick!"

I rung the bell for the Chink to bring us a drink, which he done. Then I looked up at the wall and sort of agreed with Old John. He had all his militia and army commissions framed up there, along with a big picture of me that was took at Broken Bow in '89.

"If I was just turned fifty like you," he went on, "I'd sure say good-by to this here danged sunshine state and go back to the cow country. You and me are sufferin' from too much money, Tom. I sold some land this week down to Calistoga and done put another danged eighty thousand in the bank. What good's it to me, anyhow?"

"Listen here, John," I tells him. "I'll own that there's too durned many settlers and such-like around here. A real-estater come to me to-day and offered a hundred and sixty thousand cold cash for the H Bar L. I've a notion to hold out the brand, which same has been registered in my name for the past thirty year, sell him the ranch, and start life all over again back in Idaho or Wyoming or maybe Utah. The short-grass country is too far east and all settled up anyhow. I'll go if you will."

"Gosh, Tom," he said, wistfully, "I'd sure like to! But I been rollin' around on the cushions of that danged Rolls-Royce so much I couldn't sit a hoss no more, I reckon. 'Sides, I'm old and sure get the rheumatiz hard—"

"Don't get no rheumatiz on the other side the Rockies," I tells him, and he brightens.

"That's so! Look here, Tom! Remember that time you and me was express guards on the Del Oro shipments, in '94, and done chased them hold-ups clear over into Coyote County and collected the rewards besides gettin' back the dust?"

"I'd ought to remember it," said I. "That was what give me my start, not to mention a chunk of lead that still bothers me in wet weather. What about it?"

He dug out a copy of the *Stockmen's Journal* and turned to an advertisement.

"Here's the very thing to suit you, Tom! Fine ranch twenty miles from county seat, no railroads, no sheep, no nothin' but landscape. No danged tourists or real-estaters neither. Good buildin's, five thousand head mostly Herefords, six thousand acres good land and some that don't count, good goin' concern with registered brand, water to burn—says 'all the water owner can use'—reasons for selling strictly personal. Don't come hunting bargains, it says; fair price asked, fair value given. Write Mrs. Sarah Colfax, Double Ace, Coyote County. S'pose you write her you're coming, Pinky."

That name made me homesick some more. Nobody but Old John had called me Pinky for a long while; around here it was Mr. Jenkins, or Tom, and it got wearisome. I looked at John and he sized up solid. He was a trifle old, maybe, but nobody was ever quicker on the draw, and he was six wildcats in a scrap. He had only one trouble—he was too blamed fond of a joke at somebody else's expense.

"I don't hanker to deal with no lady," I says. "Remember that time in Reno when you spotted a cold deck, and there was a lady lookout and nobody dast to shoot her and hell was raised all around in consequence? I don't deny that the ranch place looks good—"

"But see here!" sang out John, shoving his finger at another advertisement. "This here would just suit me—bank for sale in Double Ace! That's the county seat, Pinky. One hundred per cent of the stock for sale. Owner's got Bright's disease. I allus did hanker to sit in a bank winder and twiddle my thumbs, and I've got a notion to buy this here bank."

"Looks like all of Double Ace is for sale," says I. "Howcome nobody there wants to buy the bank? But let's you and me go look over things. You got a chauffeur who ain't earning his keep by running that big car of yours. Send him acrost the mountains with the car and we'll go by train—"

John grabbed my arm, and his face brightened up in a grin.

"For gosh sake! Listen, Pinky. None of that fooling, savvy? You and me goes, and we goes as pilgrims, and we starts life all over! Won't hurt us to go look, anyhow. I bet they still got hosses in Coyote County that's worth buyin' saddles for—I'm sick o' these danged automobiles! We'll send that danged chauffeur with the car, all right, but he can take his time comin' by trail, and we'll put a load of our good licker in the car. If he gets caught and the car confiscated, I don't give a durn, and if he don't, we'll sure irrigate Coyote County. Remember the sheriff who helped us collect them rewards? Bounce, his name was."

"Reckon he's dead long ago," I says. "John, you're a durned fool to—"

"Sure, and that's all the fun there is in life, bein' a durned fool," said he, with a grin. "If you and me goes over there large as life, Pinky, they'll hold ghost dances and git our scalps. I'll write 'em we're coming, and then we'll sneak in and sort of size up things for our own selves. If they know we got a wad in our jeans, they'll dance our scalps certain, but if two old jaspers amble in, two old white-haired pilgrims that ain't got enough git-up betwixt 'em to lick a mule—"

"You speak for yourself," I says. "I ain't white-haired by a long shot, and I got enough git-up-and-git to lick anybody that don't like my looks. You're the one to go get you a new outfit of goat-glands."

"Is that so? Dang you, I'll set into any game you pick and back you off the boards, you mahogany-faced Piute!"

Whenever Old John calls anybody a mahogany-faced Piute, he means business, so I smoothes him down. We agrees to sell out and leave the sunshine, which is mostly rain and fog, and start life over again back east in Coyote County. That's howcome we done so. I sold out, kept the brand in my own name, arranged with my bank in San Francisco to wire me money if I needed it, and it never once occurred to me about Old John's love for joking. It was wet and cold in San Francisco, and he was groaning about his rheumatiz, and I thought for once he was starting life with a serious mind. But I should have known better.

So John and me crossed the Rockies, or most of 'em, and connected with the stage that run to Double Ace. We had on our old clothes, and John had let his white whiskers grow for a couple of days, and some women in the Pullman remarked that ticket-agents had ought to be careful who they sold seats to these days and wasn't it a shame the way the workin' classes were running the country, so we judged that we looked all right. John always favored his feet some, and he had a shiny pair of new shoes that squeaked, but I wore some old high boots that I got in Medicine Hat in '99 and never could wear out; only they smelled a little of sheep dip on account of somebody stealing them once and me not getting them again until he was dead. The ladies was glad to see us leave the train, I guess.

The stage was waiting—a flivver fixed up with a long body and a boot behind for baggage. Nobody else got off the train but us, and the driver looked mighty disappointed. He was a hard-jawed young citizen, that driver was.

"Lookin' for anybody?" I asks him.

"Not this trip, I guess," says he. "You two fellers together?"

Old John snorted. "Do I look like I was with this here excuse for a human?" he says, pointing at me. "If that ain't sheep dip I

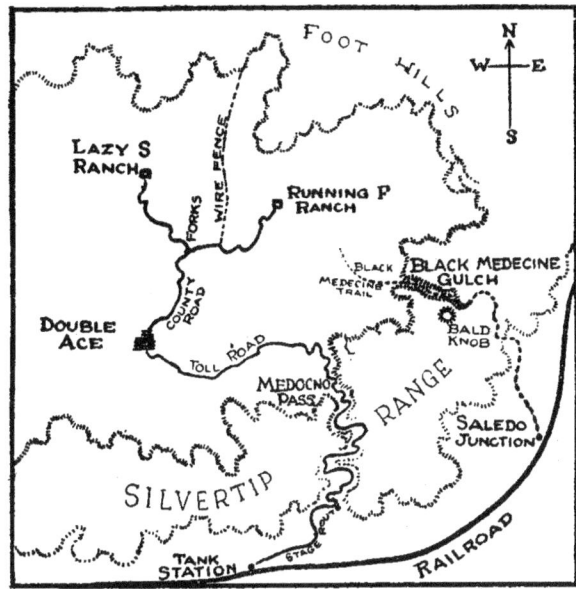

smell on his boots, I'm a liar! I ain't never mixed with a sheep-man yet, and I don't aim to. Where's your stage?"

"Other side the platform," and the driver jerked his thumb. "Throw in your grip. You got any baggage?" he says to me. I showed him the saddle I had hauled off the train, and it was a real old-timer.

"Kind of thought I'd meet a couple o' rich pilgrims this trip," says he, as we went over to the stage. John was crawling into the back seat. "Double Ace is excited as hell. One feller coming to buy the bank, and another feller with him to buy the Running F Ranch. Looks like Double Ace is picking up after all. Thought sure they'd be on the train."

"What's peculiar about all that?" I asked. "Don't property ever change hands in Double Ace?"

"Not this partic'lar property," says he, with a nasty grin. "Who might you be?"

"Moses or Pharaoh, only I'm not. Tom Jasper is me. I was up in this here country a few years back, and come along this time to get me a cow job."

"Skelly is my name," says he, and looks at Old John. "You huntin' a job, too?"

"Not by a dummed sight," says John, pointing to his grip. "I'm sellin' Hassayamp Oil, what was invented by old Hassayamp Simpson down to Phoenix, guaranteed to remove any ache, pain, bunion or spavin in five applications and the Lord have mercy on your soul!"

Skelly grunted and climbed in the car, and I got in beside him, and in another minute we were puffing away from the junction and heading for Medocno Pass, which same gives entrance to Coyote County.

"You was askin' me about property changin' hands," said Skelly after a bit, "and about a job. You let me steer you right, and we'll see about the job. Property's different. My dad, Reno Frank Skelly, owns this here stage line and other things, and has his own notions about who had ought to buy into Coyote County. We don't aim to have no outsiders come in."

"Oh!" says I. "That's human, ain't it?"

He took that for a compliment, which it wasn't.

"Yep. It's different with fellers like you, of course. We'll speak to my dad to-night about that job. You ain't busted?"

"Not quite," I tells him. "I aim to hit the hotel until I get me the job."

"My dad owns the hotel," he says.

I was sort of taking to the notion that I'd like to kick both him and his dad where it would do them the most good, but by good luck I kept my sentiments under cover. Come to find out, this young Skelly had intended to talk the prospective buyers into taking the next train back to San Francisco, and he had a line of talk that was convincing. He was dead stuck on himself and on his dad, which same I gathered was the greatest man ever lived, and the wealthiest in Coyote County. Still, there was something blamed mysterious back of the whole business which I didn't savvy at all.

"You work in with my dad," says he, "and you'll be well taken care of. Know anybody in the county?"

"Not a soul." I figured Sheriff Bounce was dead and gone years ago.

"What sort of a job do you want?"

"Foreman's, if she suits me."

"Best ranch in the whole county is the Running F. If you was to get the foreman's job there, but was really workin' for my dad all the while, I s'pose it'd be all right with you?"

"Certain, certain!" I tells him, beginning to smell a mouse right there. "I ain't no killer, y'understand; outside o' that, I ain't got no principles a-tall."

The kid grinned his nasty little grin. "Fine! The feller that was comin' to see that ranch, though, is a killer—got that repytation. An old-timer, they say, name o' Jenkins. My dad looked him up. Seems like he was run out o' the Panhandle in the old days, had a ten-year Montana sentence suspended on him for his share in the sheep war, and got in bad in the silver country around Reno 'count of a couple of killin's. They say he made his pile by robbin' somebody and is a rich man now—"

"Who says so?" I asked him. Just then Old John Parker lets out a snort.

"I says so, by gosh!" he sings out. "I've heard o' that feller Jenkins! He was durned near lynched in the Bitter-Root country for hoss-stealin' and is wanted for murder in two Nevada counties this minute!"

"That's him," said Skelly, with a nod. "I'm to warn him against comin' into the county, o' course; chances are he won't come, but again, he may. The feller with him is pretty near as bad, they say—"

"Who says so?" spits out John real sudden.

"My dad. Done looked him up—feller name of Parker. Old John Parker—"

"By gosh, I heard o' him down to Phoenix!" sings out John. "Used to be a pony express rider in the 'Pache days, chief scout for Gen'ral Howard—"

"I've heard of him, too," says I, turning around for a look at John. "They say he's the biggest liar unhung, that he was drummed out of the army for cowardice, that he'd steal the pennies off a dead man's eyes, that he was run out of Walla Walla for robbin' a blind woman and hasn't got no more heart than a crow. That's him!"

"That's him, all right," said Skelly, while Old John Parker made noises in his throat. "You two fellers have knocked around, ain't you? Well, you see how it is. We don't want them birds in the county a-tall. Especially, my dad don't want 'em."

"Why not?" I asked him.

"Different reasons. My dad has run some no-account folks out o' the county, see? There was a dispute between his riders— he owns the Lazy S—and the Running F boys, and some shootin' was done. Colfax, that owned the Running F, done got killed somehow. They're a bad bunch up to that end the valley. But my dad's got the town 'bout cleaned up now, I bet you!"

After this, young Skelly sort of got a brake on his tongue and wouldn't say much more of interest, but he had said enough to make T. Jasper Jenkins, which was me, plumb thoughtful as he steered the flivver through the pass. Yes, sir, plumb thoughtful! I began to be real glad that I had the old forty-five in my pants, even if she wasn't loaded.

CHAPTER II

I'LL NEVER to my dying day forget how we come into Double Ace along about six that night, and what I heard about myself when we lit.

Double Ace was a right smart little town, with some good stores and converted saloons. What used to be the old dance hall was now the hotel, with additions. Everybody in town was out on the street staring at the stage, and young Skelly leaned out to the right and kept yelling that "they didn't come." There was a heap of interest aroused, but most of it was in front of the hotel, where there was a small crowd headed by a lady about thirty-odd, right good-looking, with a long quirt in her hand and fire in her eye.

"They didn't come!" yells young Skelly as he draws up. The lady steps forward.

"Who are these men? Either of you men named Pinky Jenkins?"

Somehow, I began to feel right glad that I hadn't mentioned to Skelly that I was usually called Pinky.

"No, ma'am," said Old John. "This here excuse for a cowman is named Jasper. I'm Doc Jones, and to-morrow night I'll be mighty glad to see you around when I start in to sellin' Hassayamp Oil, the only genuwine and real remover of all pain and spavins from man and beast, the undiluted product of the glorious state of Arizona, which same I hails from—"

The lady walked off, mounted a bronc hitched just beyond us, and rode away.

"She's sure layin' to get that feller Jenkins!" said somebody in the crowd, amid a general laugh. "Seems like he wrote her he was comin' to look over the Runnin' F and her likewise, and if she was in the market might take her with the ranch. Said he had two wives in Salt Lake City now but would be glad to connect up with her as number three, and gosh, ain't she mad! Too bad he didn't come. I'd like to see that there quirt of her'n in action on him."

I gives John a look. "For two cents    "

"Don't forgit that there saddle of yours, Jasper!' he cuts in, then grabs his grip and goes into the hotel. I followed him, and all around me heard nothing but the name of Pinky Jenkins and his matrimonial proposals, and how he was a killer. But I was thinking of Mrs. Colfax, who was right good looking, and when I run into Old John at the hotel desk I gives him a cussing out that he'll remember. Some feller nearby started to inform me that this was no way to speak to an old man, so I knocked him up against the wall and he lost interest in the proceedings. Then I looked around at the crowd.

"I don't aim to horn into trouble, gents, and I'm right anxious to have Double Ace know me as a gentle harness-broke citizen, but I don't aim to let nobody give me orders without they're payin' for that there privilege. If you gents—"

Young Skelly had been whispering to a man, who now came forward. It was Reno Frank, as I could see with half an eye—a tall, broad-shouldered man with a bad eye, a wide grin, the general air of a bartender, and expensively dressed. He grabbed for my hand at once.

"Mr. Jasper, I'm proud to meet you and welcome you to our midst. As the president of the Double Ace Chamber of Commerce, I welcome a future valued citizen. Let this slight trouble be forgotten!"

"You win," I says. "She's forgotten. Show me where to hang this here saddle and get my head into the feed-box, will you? Reckon I'll have a room, but make it as far as possible from that ornery old medicine man. If he didn't have one foot in the grave—"

"By gosh, I'll lick you any day in the year!" roars Old John, shaking his fist at me. "You mahogany-faced Piute—"

Reno Frank led me away while the other gents got John calmed down. He was mad clean through, on account of what I had said to young Skelly about him getting drummed out of the army. Like every gent that likes a joke, John didn't like it when it was on him.

Neither did I like the joke he had played me. He had written Mrs. Colfax from San Francisco or else from the ranch, and had probably signed my name to the letter; and he had sure played hell with Pinky Jenkins. If the widow hadn't been so easy on the eyes, I might not have cared; but young Skelly had made me think there was some kind of skullduggery going on here in Coyote County, with the Running F bearing the brunt of it, and after seeing the lady herself I was right set to go to the bottom of it and take a hand.

I washed up, took another look at Main Street from my window, and liked the looks of it fine. There were mighty few autos in sight, and quite a few cow-ponies hitched to racks, and here and there a gent that looked like he might be a real cowhand and not a moving-picture hero. Thinks I, to-morrow I'll get me some overalls and a bronc and see what this here county looks like. Gosh, it was good to be starting life over again!

Old John said the same thing when I met him in the diningroom hall. Nobody was in sight, so when I runs into John I stops and gives him a word.

"John, I'm right sorry about that there army remark. Didn't mean to get under your hide—"

"And I'm right sorry about writin' the widder in your name," says he. "How'd I know it would be took so deadly? You and me can't afford to fight, old-timer. Slide into my room later on to-night and we'll licker up. I brought a quart along. You and me needs to bury the hatchet."

That was true enough, and I was mighty glad he had got over his mad, but we agreed to remain enemies in public. It looked to both of us like trouble in the air. So we drifted into the dining-room and took separate seats.

Me being late, I was pretty soon left all alone at my table, when along comes Reno Frank Skelly and sits down by me. After a few preliminary remarks, he asks about my past history, so I let him have what I judged would suit him best, saying nothing very definite and giving the general impression that I had left my last job for the sake of my health. He nodded and laughed.

"My boy was tellin' me about you, Jasper," he says. "Now, the Running F is needing a foreman right bad; the owner is that there lady what met the stage with a quirt to-day. How'd you like to land the job with her, do a little work in my interest, and

stay on as foreman after I take over her ranch? I figger on takin'
it over one of these days."

"What's there in it?" I asked him.

"A thousand cash when I take over the prop'ty."

"You're on," I says, with mental reservations. "Nothing barred
except federal offenses. I reckon you can manage to keep your
men out o' jail."

"I'd ought to," and he laughed again. "The Sheriff is a
cripple—an old has-been who don't count. His deputies are all
my men, and they do the work. Judge Haskins is depending on
me to send him to Congress next year, so the courts are likewise
safe."

"Who's the sheriff?" I asked him.

"Feller named Ed Bounce. He used to be a killer of bad men
in the old days and they keep him in office because of his repytation. He needs the money. Well, let me wise you up a bit on
this ranch business! Y'see, me and Mis' Colfax don't quite hitch.
I got a mortgage on her place that comes due in six months,
and the interest date is the first of next month. My land is next
to hers, and it's got water she needs, and she's got grass I need,
and the two outfits don't get along none too good. So don't let
on to her that you're a friend o' mine."

"I wouldn't let on that to anybody," says I. "I'll ride out to
her place to-morrow, most likely. I got to get me a cayuse and
a lariat—"

"A which?" says he.

"Lariat."

"Oh! You come from down south, eh? That word just ain't
known up in these quarters, Jasper. Up here, the boys talk about
a 'rope.' You come down to the livery stable in the mornin'—I'll
be there. I own it. I'll fit you out with a real hoss, feller, and
price won't be no object. So long."

He rose and left me. I'm here to orate that Reno Frank Skelly
was a self-made man; the only trouble was that he had not made
himself better than he did. By all accounts he was a top-notch

cowman and he had a good head; he was a husky, vigorous gent who liked to dress well but could wear overalls without hurting his dignity none, and he had a name for using a gun. Just the same, he was bad. Mean. A regular high-class hoss with a mean eye.

So old Ed Bounce was still in the land of the living! That was news, and when supper was over I accumulated my hat and set forth to do some detective work. I couldn't run any risks by marching up to some gent and asking where the sheriff lived, because everybody in town would hear of it, but after a while I nosed out the trail and walked down the back streets to a little shack. It had a big front window, a lamp was burning on the table, and Ed Bounce was sitting reading. It was close on to thirty year since I'd seen him, but I knew him again right off— spite of his white hair and wrinkles and specs. He had a face like a square chunk of wood, sawed-off sharp, and mostly chin. I came up close to the door and then ducked into the shadow.

"Douse that there light, Ed," I says. "This is Pinky Jenkins, and I don't crave no publicity around here."

"Fer gosh sake!" said he, and the light went out. I came inside and we shook hands in the dark. Seems like he had sort of expected me to hunt him up, though he had been afraid that I'd never strike Double Ace. He had heard that I was coming to look over the Running F, of course, but had kept his mouth shut about me.

We had a heart-to-heart talk, and both of us learned some things. Ed Bounce was crippled and clear out of any action whatsoever, but his old brain was clear and sharp as a whip. When we had renewed old times and brought our general affairs down to date, I told him about me and John Parker, and what we had run into here in Coyote County.

"These ain't the old days, Pinky," says he, after a silence. "If they was, I'd say go to it; you and John Parker were the best roughneck fighters and gunmen I ever knew. But you and him had better pull your freight and shove for home."

"I ain't asked for advice yet, but for facts."

"Facts are hell, Pinky. You know I done met up with the worst bad men this side of the divide, but none of 'em was so bad or dangerous as Reno Frank Skelly. Why? Because he's got brains and can use 'em plenty. First, he's a rich man. Next, he's got plenty men workin' for him, and political influence, and court influence and gosh knows what all. Next, he's got guts, no end of 'em, and treats his own men right; they like him, 'cause he won't ask 'em to do what he won't do."

"Boot Hill has seen plenty like him."

"Sure; but he ain't on Boot Hill, is he? Nobody's going to carve his headstone in a hurry. That kid of his is about as bad, only meaner. Now for facts, Pinky. He's had a feud with the Colfax outfit. His men killed Colfax and are sure ridin' the Running F hard. He's got a mortgage on the ranch. She's tryin' to sell out, and he don't want her to, being as he wants the place himself; but she wouldn't sell to him if he was the last man on earth. So he's tryin' to crook her all he can, and he's sure done a plenty."

"If them facts are what you call hell," I says, "I'm willing to go there."

"That ain't all. You may get by with this assumed alias of yours, but once you come into the open, you'll be done for. Pinky, them riders of his ain't honest men or honest fighters; they're killers! They done shot Colfax in the back. They're dirty little cowards—"

"Like the feller that shot Mr. Howard and laid poor Jesse in his grave," I puts in, and he chuckled.

"Yep, that's the brand exactly. Don't think that the situation calls for somebody to buck Reno Frank; it don't. Plenty have bucked him. The last feller that tried was Jack Williams, who opened up a bank here. Jack's a good fellow and nervy to boot, but they sure got his goat. One thing after another come up, and finally they tarred and feathered him one night—"

"Who did?" I says. "Where was the sheriff?"

"Where he always is, crippled up. Gang of masked men did it, and the sheriff's deputies were in the gang, you bet! Williams has agreed to get out in thirty days, sell or no sell. Skelly won't buy the bank off him and won't let nobody else do it; swears it's goin' bust. Skelly has a bank of his own up the street, sabe? He'd drop me, only it'd cause a lot of commotion and I threatened to shoot him up proper if he done it—I would, too! So he lets me be, and I let things drift and don't interfere."

"You ain't what you used to be," I says.

"I know it," and his voice was bitter. "But what can I do, Pinky? Not a durned thing. He's run or bought out the best men in the county, and the leavings ain't worth a whoop in Halifax. The best men here now are his men. He laid out to run Coyote County, and he's doing it. No redress in the courts. The town has run down consid'able in the past year, Skelly and his men steal the road funds, so folks are slow to buy autos, and the railroad spur line was never built because nobody would subscribe to help out, Skelly bein' set against it. Long as he can keep the county shut off from the world, she's his to run, and he knows it."

"So you advise to let him be, eh?"

"I do, Pinky," he says, kind o' mournful. "Even if this was the old days, and you was in your prime—"

"Now listen here," I put in. "I ain't got one foot in the grave by no means, Ed Bounce, and I don't admire to be told that I'm a dodderin' old fool. As for John Parker, he ain't exactly spry when the rheumatiz gets him, but any other time he's liable to loosen up with a surprise for any galoot that happens in his way."

"Never mind," he says. "That ain't the point. The point is that Skelly has an organization that works like greased lightning. Why, I don't dast write a letter that don't praise Reno Frank! The postmaster has everybody spotted and opens all mail—"

"Can you prove that?"

"Hell, no! If I could it wouldn't do any good."

"Well," I says, thinking it over, "when me and Old John started out in life, we sure riz by climbing over other gents. Now we've started life all over again, Ed, we don't look for no soft pickin's. Still, Parker ain't what he used to be. He'll likely drop in to see you to-morrow, so you discourage him a heap. Make him give up this here Hassayamp Oil stunt and go back to 'Frisco. Me, I'll sashay over to the Running F to-morrow or Monday and most likely take a job there, and sort of feel the cards as they go out and maybe pick where they're marked. If things look too bad, I'll go away. S'pose you tell me the name of one feller who I can trust to do an errand for me in the big outside world."

"You can trust Jack Williams, only his nerve's gone. He's got a week left to leave town in."

"Albright," I says. "You slip him word to ride out towards the Running F next Thursday morning—this is Sat'day, ain't it? Yep. I'll meet him on the road. Don't spill who I am, of course. Looks to me like Tom Jasper had better watch his identity real careful."

"You're a danged fool," said Ed Bounce.

"I always was, so we'll agree right there. So long! See you later."

After a while I eased into the hotel and finding nobody in the upstairs hall, slipped into John Parker's room. Doc Jones, as he now was, had shaved off his white whiskers, but left a stub of mustache under his nose. I told him what he looked like, and he told me to go there, and he got out his quart of liquor and we oiled up.

He listened to all I repeated, and then chortled over it.

"Pinky—"

"Shut up! I'm Tom Jasper, you ornery coyote!"

"All right. This is rich, Tom! You and me are goin' to have ructions. I got both my old guns here, and I'll sure get 'em greased up to-morrow. I'm goin' to buy that feller's bank, savvy?"

"If you do," I says, "don't count too much on me. I aim to spend a while up the valley and I can't come runnin' into town to keep young Skelly from shovin' your white hairs into the grave."

"That so? Durn you, who's askin' you to come? Don't forget them two wives in Salt Lake City—"

I heaved a boot at him and left him cussing. But that night I did some tall thinkin' before I went to sleep. It looked like trouble ahead and plenty of it. I needed all my nerve and more than that—my brains!

CHAPTER III

I RODE UP the valley Monday morning feeling like twenty years had been lifted from my shoulders. Reno Frank had kept his word and provided me with a fine cow-trained bronc at a fair price, Coyote County looked remarkably good to me, and a box of cartridges in one pocket balanced the forty-five in the other. By the looks of the valley, time had sure turned backward in his flight, too.

It was a relief to be jogging along an old-fashioned road that wasn't meant for autos, with regular cow-country all around and no wire fences running every which way. By the time Double Ace dropped out of sight, I was real happy. Most of the valley was taken up by three or four fair-sized ranches; Skelly had consolidated several into the Lazy S, which was making money, and the Running F had been making money until Colfax died, a year previous. The others didn't count, being shiftless outfits that dragged along somehow and stood in with Skelly.

I met nobody at all on the road until about eleven in the morning, when I was looking for the fork that led off to the Running F. It was early summer, the country was rolling and green, the lonesome buttes looked mighty good to me, and the cattle in sight looked better; so all in all I was feeling like old times. I loaded up the old gun and took one or two shots at objects in passing, and was as glad as any kid to find that my right hand had not lost its cunning.

Just as I was rolling a cigaret and wishing Old John had come along, a patch of cottonwoods beside a creek ahead suddenly gave birth to two riders, who jogged into the road and came toward me. A worse pair of leather-pullers I never did see. One had a bad squint and red whiskers, the other had a zigzag scar down the side of his face; neither face would have disgraced San Quentin prison, and anyone could see that neither gent knew much about horses, although they were rigged up in leather chaps. They drew up a little ways ahead of me, filling the whole road.

"Howdy, boys," I said, real mild and pleasant, me feeling that way. "How far ahead is that turnout to the Running F?"

Squint-eye, who was swinging a quirt from his left wrist, gaped at me.

"Huh? See here, you ain't that feller Jenkins?"

I lighted my cigaret. "You say I ain't, so that settles it. My name, pilgrim, happens to be Jasper. Who might you two gents be?"

Scarface leans over and catches his pal's arm.

"Lay off," he says in a low voice. "He's all right—he's ridin' one o' Reno's stable."

Squint-eye shook him off, but not before I noted the word he'd used.

"I ain't ridin' no stable," I says. "Good gosh! You talk like an Easterner I met up with once over in the Tetons. From down east he was, somewheres near St. Louis, and every time he was talkin' about hosses, he'd say stable—"

"Never mind how we talk, partner," said Squint-eye. "What you goin' to the Running F for anyhow?"

"If I was to tell you, I reckon you'd know."

"None o' that!" says Squint-eye, hitching his pony forward. "Come across and come quick! You talk."

"Well," I says, "I'm talking right now, and I don't admire to be questioned by no cross-eyed son of Jehosaphat in movin'-picture cowboy costume. What you need is a bath in the crick and someone to wipe off them red whiskers and see what jail you got out of—"

It was right unfortunate for that cuss, me happening to forget myself from force of habit. Of course I was a mite hampered by having no gun-belt on, but when his hand slid in under his shirt I unlimbered and done it quick. His gun jumped off into the brush and he give a howl as his hand dripped blood and his pony began to plunge. Then Scarface let fly unexpected. He would have got me sure only his bronc jumped likewise and spoiled his aim, and before he could shoot his little flat pistol again I had him by the neck and dropped him into the road.

There was considerable excitement for half a minute. Squint-eye, he fell off his horse and yammered over his busted hand, which was consid'able busted. I dismounted and grabbed the quirt off his wrist and give him a lick over the face that sent him running down the road. Then I turned on Scarface, who was fumbling in the dirt for his little gun, and hauled him up by the collar.

"What you need, pilgrim, is this here quirt in the right place—"

So I give it to him until the blood spurted. He began by cussing me like a coiled diamond-back and ended up by yelling for help like he meant it.

"Now," I says, with a last cut, "go on back wherever you come from, and if there's any more like you want to run in a cold deck on Tom Jasper, come right ahead! It's a durned good thing for you I didn't lose my temper and start to shooting. Your partner won't handle no more guns for a while, and if you get in my way again you won't never handle any. Git!"

I told a lie there, of course, for I had lost my temper good and plenty. Scarface went running down the road after his friend, and I gathered their horses and took 'em along a ways with me. Both broncs carried the Lazy S brand, so with one thing and another it was plain that two of Reno Frank's men had met up with me. Not that I cared. When I had picked up their pistols, I mounted again and herded their horses as far as the patch of cottonwoods, then turned 'em in to graze, bridles off.

Surprises never come single, however. No sooner had I started again and turned the bend by them cottonwoods, when I come face to face with a rider—and it was Mrs. Colfax. We both pulled up short and stared. She was dressed in khaki, was right smart looking, and now I saw that she had big blue eyes which looked frightened. I felt right sorry for her, her being what you might call a terrible pretty woman, and able to handle herself, too.

"Who was that I heard shooting?" she cried out. "Is anybody hurt?"

"Yes'm," I says. "No, ma'am—that is to say—"

"Stop twisting that hat in your hands and talk sense!" she shot at me, and I saw that she had me placed now. "You're the man Jasper who came in the stage yesterday! Who was shoot-ing around the bend there?"

"Nobody, ma'am. That scar-faced horn-toad aimed to shoot around the bend, I reckon, only the bullet went wide and wouldn't curve on him like he'd figgered—"

"What's the matter with you? Will you talk sense?"

"Yes'm," I says, and laughed. After a second she laughed a little, too. "Two gents fell off their hosses, ma'am. One of 'em done got helped off, so to speak. Then they calculated they wanted to walk to town anyhow, so they started walkin'. If I was you, I wouldn't waste no partic'lar sympathy on them galoots. They need it, I reckon, but they hadn't ought to get it."

"Huh!" says she, and looks me over, "What's that in your hand?"

I held up my fist, and there was the quirt that I'd forgotten. It was all blood.

"Now," says she, "you hand me the truth, and hand it out quick!"

So I did, and her blue eyes scorched right into me. When I got done, she said:

"Know who those men were?"

"No, ma'am."

"They were two of Skelly's men placed here to watch the road and see who came to my ranch. Did you say you were going there?"

"Yes'm."

She wheeled her bronc. "Then come along. I aim to beat the dinner-bell."

Neither of us talked as we rode, for she set me a good pace. I could see that she wanted to ask questions, but being a uncommon sort of woman she held off; so did I. She was sizing me up as we went along, and I was sizing her up, and thinks I: "Reno Frank sure picked somebody to scrap with when he picked her! Yes, sir. She's got a temper, but she's got it squaw-hitched, and she's got a right pretty dimple in her cheek, and blamed if I ever see a woman could sit a hoss better—"

Before I knew it we were drawing up to the ranch-house, which same was a right smart of a house set on a loma above the creek, corral and barns and so forth setting a mite farther down the creek. Nobody was in sight.

"I told 'em not to wait dinner for me," said Mrs. Colfax, as we climbed down and I got the corral gate open. "Pretty place, ain't it?"

"Right pretty, ma'am," I says. "Set on a this loma this-a-way—"

"Loma!" She gives me a quick look. "I ain't heard that word since I was over in California as a girl. You come from there?"

"Used to work with the Miller & Lux, and up the San Joaquin farther, ma'am."

She said no more, nor did I, and pretty soon we goes up to the house and she shows me where to wash up.

"Come in when you're ready, Mr. Jasper. Since my husband's death we all eat together in the dining-room; my boys are friends, not hired hands."

"I judged so already, ma'am," I says.

"How come?" she snapped, but I pretended not to hear, so she went on.

Right there I hauled T. Jasper Jenkins up short. The old fool was fifty and should have more sense. I told him so as we communed with nature and hunted a clean spot on the towel. He should know better than to go saying silly things to a woman at his age.

"Fool yourself," says he, sort of irritated. "She ain't no common kind of woman, with her seat in the saddle! Besides which, she's durned pretty—"

"And when did you begin to look at a pretty woman?" I says. "You ornery old cow-hand, when did you begin to get gay with the ladies? If Old John Parker could see you now!"

"Well, he ain't here to see," he shoots back. "Besides which, no snub-nosed old rickety puncher is giving me orders, so shut up."

I shut up, and went into the house. Mrs. Colfax met me and we came to the dining-room where eight riders were going for grub like they'd never seen it, and a Mex cook was grinning all over her brown face. The boys rose up as we come in, and I judged there was considerable discipline at mess time.

"Boys," says Mrs. Colfax, "this here is Mr. Tom Jasper. I don't know where he's from or what he wants, but he met up with Logan and Woods by that patch of cottonwoods in the road, and they tried to corner him, so he blew off one or two of Logan's fingers and gave Woods a quirting. Somebody make room."

"Good for him!" sings out somebody, and they crowded over to make room. I judged Logan was Squint-eye and Woods was Scarface, and so it was.

Everybody was plumb excited over the story, and I gathered from one thing and another that those two gents were imported bad men who had caused the Running F a heap of trouble. However, after a while things calmed down, dinner being more important to me than talking. I used my eyes if not my tongue, and took note that it was a right promising bunch of boys, mostly young fellers, though two was grizzled old-timers. Them two was wearing guns openly.

Pretty soon everybody drifted out, leaving me and Mrs. Colfax to finish eating in peace. She tells me to roll a smoke, which I done, then says she'd have given ten dollars to have seen the fracas in the road, I grinned at that.

"I'd give another ten to see Reno Frank's face when them bad men tell him about it!"

"You know Skelly?" she asked.

"Yes'm. He's my best friend in Double Ace."

She sort of sat up at that and shot me a quick look. "Oh! What you doing here, then?"

"Why, ma'am, I heard tell you needed a foreman, and I'd sort of like to apply—"

"Who told you that?"

"Reno Frank."

"The impudence—" When she met my eyes, she drew in on the bridle and checked herself. "You dare say to me that he's your best friend, that he told you I needed—"

"Yes'm, and then some," I told her. "He arranged with me to get the job, and then do a little work for him on the side. Seems like he figures to be owning this here ranch before long. As to him being my best friend in Double Ace, that ain't saying much—it's merely quoting him. I think maybe he's a mite ignorant on the subject, my own self, seeing as I've got a pretty blamed good friend in Ed Bounce, only nobody knows that—"

"Stop that tongue rattling!" she said, with a look from her blue eyes that bored into me. Then she began to laugh, as she understood things better. "You know Ed Bounce, do you?"

"Yes'm."

She got up and went to a telephone on the wall, and called a number.

"Hello, Ed!" she said. "There's a man here named Tom Jasper applying for position as foreman. Says he knows, you. What can you tell me about him?"

She listened for a minute, then looked at me, and I saw a smile brimming up in her blue eyes. She rang off and turned to me, laughing, and shoved out her hand across the table.

"Ed says you're the worst liar and cattle-thief and general no-account rascal unhung, but I'd better hire you—so I will. Glad to meet you, Tom!"

We shook on it, then began to talk wages and such. I was hired.

## CHAPTER IV

SPRING ROUNDUP was over a long time ago, and so far as I could see by loafing about during the afternoon and sizing things up, there was nothing about the Running F to justify keeping eight riders and a foreman on the books all summer. Fences appeared to be all in shape and she looked like a lazy man's job until, later in the afternoon, I had a bit of straight talk with Mrs. Colfax in her office.

"You might's well start in by understanding things," she said, after pumping me a while and finding my local knowledge sort of hazy. "I haven't got an awful lot of money in the bank, Tom, and the first of the month is interest date—and the interest on the mortgage is payable to Reno Frank's bank. I've got a scheme all framed up to meet that interest, but not a soul knows about it—and won't until I know you just a mite better. Tell you about it to-morrow night, maybe."

"You seem to reckon on knowing me a heap better to-morrow night," I says. Her blue eyes sort of sized me up.

"I aim to. You're going to town to-morrow morning for me, and if you come back alive after what you did to Logan and Woods this morning—you and I will sure make a pair to draw to!"

"Thanks," I said, "but don't forget Reno Frank's a good friend o' mine."

"His men ain't, and they'll have a say if they're in town. Don't worry! You're sure going to have work ahead of you to-morrow. I've had some hopes of selling the ranch, or of getting a pardner to help me run it, rather; I hate like sin to lay down and quit before that man Skelly! Still, nobody seems anxious to buy."

Her eyes snapped at mention of Skelly. I told her about the stage driver, young Skelly, and how he had likely discouraged any possible buyers. She just nodded.

"Of course. That road over Medocno Pass is a private road, and the company is owned by Reno Frank, and it has a mail contract. Last time I tried to ship out any cattle, half of 'em were scared out off the road and went down into the cañon. You can't tell me anything I don't know about that skunk Reno Frank and his boy! Now, pay attention. If you see Reno Frank in town, pretend to be working with him, sabe? If we can find out just what he aims to do, we can block him. I'm going to make a fight for water this summer, and he's going to grab my grass if he can—"

"I seen your advertisement," I said thoughtfully. "Seems to me it specified plenty o' water here, ma'am."

"It said: 'all the water owner can use,'" and she laughed a little. "It's the truth. We could use a sight more if we could get it! If you've got a gun, take it with you to-morrow—oh, of course you've got one! Perhaps a couple of the boys had better go with you—"

"Thank you, ma'am, but I guess not," I broke in. "A gang always makes trouble, while one man can slide from under. I'm law-abiding and peaceful, and while sometimes I'm liable to forget myself, still and all I figure to go a long ways around trouble."

"Yes, you look it," says she, in a dry tone. "You look like an old friend of mine, when I was a girl down below Fresno—Ike Moran, an old-timer from the Pecos country."

"Good gosh—Ike Moran!" I broke out. "Why, ma'am, me and Ike were buddies for ten year and more, and his boy Steve and I—"

I choked the rest back and like to bit off my tongue, for her blue eyes were glued on me mighty sharp.

"Yes?" she exclaimed. "Funny I never heard Ike mention anyone by the name of Jasper! I'd heard that his boy Steve was partners with an old-timer by the name of Pinky Jenkins—"

"Yes'm," I said hurriedly. "But that was after my time, I guess. Well, if you get your list ready, I'll get off early in the morning. Want me to take a team?"

"No—all we want is the mail, and I'll have some letters for you to post. Holy Pete goes in every Saturday for the general load."

I escaped, wiping my fevered brow, as the story-books say—I sure had come a close one that trip! A minute more and she'd have nailed me for Pinky Jenkins. However, a miss is as good as a mile, and after this, thinks I, Tom Jasper will guard that slippery fool tongue of his mighty sharp!

We had a right smart game of stud in the bunk-house that evening, and a good time was had by all except me, which same dropped about thirty dollars. Those two old-timers were partners from over in Utah, and along in the shank of the evening one of them, whose name was Holy Pete, looked across the table at me as I was dealing, and spoke up.

"I've seen you somewheres before this," says he.

"If you have," I tells him, "keep it to yourself. I been in one or two jails, sure."

Holy Pete screwed up his eyes, while everybody else laughed.

"It wasn't no jail," he orates. "I dunno where it was, but it was a long while ago. Seems to me like it was over to Saint's Rest, one time."

Right there I stopped the deal. I had unpleasant memories of Saint's Rest, though they were not recent by any means and belonged to my unregenerate youth. It was not likely that Holy Pete had happened to be there twenty years previous and had seen Pinky Jenkins clean out a crooked faro game and leave Utah two jumps ahead of the sheriff and the saints—but it was possible.

"Look here, Pete," I says. "You ain't no chicken. You're old enough to know better than to go shooting off your mouth. If you want to pry into my past, you step right outside and you can try all you durned please. If you don't, shut up!"

The old-timer hadn't meant to get me riled up, and apologized, but I could see he was still trying to place me, inside his head. That's the hell of having a past. A man just can't get away from it. However, Holy Pete shut up and all passed off happily.

Come daybreak, I got an early bite from the cook, got the letters from Mrs. Colfax, slung on the mail sack, and started to town. It made me feel bright and cheerful—like the good old times, before every ranch had a flivver and punchers took to wearing pliers instead of chaps. I jogged along right smart, meeting nobody on the road and seeing nothing of Reno Frank's men, and along in the warmth of the morning I came to Double Ace. As I wanted to look up Old John Parker, and might be in town all day, I turned in the bronc at the livery stable. First person I ran into was Reno Frank.

"Great hemlock!" He grabbed my arm and pulled me into the livery office. "Jasper, what you mean by shootin' up my men? Why didn't you tell me you could use a gun? If I'd known that, I'd have sent you up to my own ranch—"

"Your men!" I said, looking a heap surprised. "Them two galoots yesterday? How was I to know they were your men? Anyhow, I ain't responsible when anybody throws down on me."

"No," said he, and laughed. "I reckon you ain't, for a fact! But the rest of my boys are sure lookin' for your scalp, and how'm I to hold 'em back? I dassn't tell 'em that you're working for me, because nobody must know that—"

"Leave her ride, leave her ride, feller!" I said. "The more your riders pick on me, the more sure everybody will be that you and I ain't exactly friends. Ain't it so?"

He shook his head, looking worried. "Yes, but I don't want you killed—"

"You and me sure agree on that point, Reno. If I was you, I wouldn't worry over Tom Jasper. You worry over them Lazy S boys of yours. If them two I met up with are samples of the rest, my sleep ain't exactly uneasy."

"Well," said he, "if you want it that way, all right. Anyhow, we understand each other. You got the job?"

"Yep. Got any orders for me?"

"Not yet. Thursday night after sundown you slide down the crick aways to that patch of willows half a mile below your ranch-house. My foreman will meet you there and he can slip you the good word. Savvy? I'll have to let him into the secret, but I can sure trust him."

"All right," I said, and went on about my business. I judged that Reno Frank was more than a little anxious about my health, but I had no intentions of letting him hang any crape on his hat for T.J. Jenkins.

When I had mailed the letters and got my sack for the ranch, I left it at the livery office and went on down street to the hotel, in order to be first at the trough when the feed was passed out, and to see Old John. I passed an empty platform plastered over with big signs about Doc Jones and Hassayamp Oil, and I judged John had got busy.

When I got to the hotel, the office was empty, so I slid right up the stairs and went to his room. I swung the door open, and Old John swung on me with a pistol and blamed near took his thumb off the hammer.

"What you mean, scarin' a feller that way?" said he. "Howdy, Tom. Come in."

I looked things over. He had about a thousand little glass bottles and corks, and was drawing machine oil out of a couple of five-gallon cans setting on a chair. He locked the door after me, and then chuckled.

"Tom, my medicine is mighty strong!" said he. "Durned if I didn't sell a hundred bottles of oil last night at a dollar a throw! There's a dance to-night, and everybody will be in town, and I'm goin' to make a cleanup. Better stay and see the fun."

"Not me," I said. "Where's that quart of liquor? Gimme a drink, John."

All he gave me was a look. "Why, Pinky—I mean, Tom—you know danged well there wasn't no quart left in that bottle! How long d'you expect—"

"Why, you white-whiskered old hog!" I said. "You mean to say you drunk it all?"

"No. I made Hassayamp Oil with it yesterday, and everybody said it was grand. They'll get real oil to-night."

"You're a fool, then! If they don't get you for bootleggin', they'll sure get you for not keeping on bein' a bootlegger. You can't—"

"Cool off," he says. "Never mind me; I'll hoe my own pun'kins, and if anybody tries to dance my scalp, let 'em watch out! I've seen Ed Bounce. He tells me you've landed the Running F job. That so? I heard there was a shootin' on the road yesterday too."

"Well," I said, relaxing after making sure no drink was in prospect, "well, John, it seems like things were sure moving in this here county." I went on to relate what had happened and what was likely to happen, while he sucked his pipe and grinned at me. When I got through, he eased his feet off the table and chortled some more.

"Say, I've seen Jack Williams, feller that wants to sell the bank. Him and me and Ed Bounce had a talk together last night. Williams is leavin' town Friday. He'll be out to see you

Thursday morning, like you wanted him to. I've bought the bank off'n him, but we're keeping it quiet. I don't figger on opening her up until next Monday morning."

"You'll open up a slice of hell, then," I said.

"Sho! I got you down for forty per cent of the stock. It'll cost you eight thousand, and if we bust this here county open, Tom, we'll make a cleanup! And I got a chance to bust her wide open inside of two weeks."

"What is it?" I said.

"None of your danged business. Want to come in on the bank deal?"

I got my money belt out from next to my hide, and fished for pay dirt. I had come with a small bale of certified checks in various denominations, to be prepared against whatever might happen, so I found one for five thousand and another for three thousand and passed them over.

"You know anybody within a hundred miles of here—old-timers?" he asked.

I thought that over for a minute. "Guess not, John—not very many. There's Swede Simmons over to Silver Cañon—he owns them ruby silver outcrops and runs the mine himself; he's still alive. Then there's Bill Hoffman. Maybe you've heard of him—Diamond Bill of Tucson, he used to be. He was a gambler but has reformed. He's a preacher now and last I heard of him he was settled down in Pahrump Valley. Why?"

"You set down and write 'em to get here a week from next Monday, and bring their guns. We sure need a preacher—I had most forgot about that. You know there ain't a church in this here entire community? No, sir. Reno Frank run out the only preacher there was. I heard of Diamond Bill down to Phoenix; he's just the man."

I stared at him. "Good gosh, John! What'll I tell 'em to come here for?"

"To help bust Coyote County open and ask no questions, you danged old fool! Here's some paper. Set down and write 'em."

Old John was on the warpath and no mistake, and I've never known him to get led off on a false trail, neither. Fact is, I've a heap more confidence in his judgment than in my own, which explains why I wrote the letters like he wanted—sight unseen. He wouldn't loosen up a bit as regarded his plans. When this was done, he stowed away the letters and lighted his pipe.

"Now, Tom," says he, looking a mite worried, "we got a problem to face. You know, I told that danged chauffeur of mine to bring the Rolls-Royce and a load of hard liquor? Well, what's going to happen when he comes with that there palashul car into this here community? Hell's goin' to pop, that's what! I been lookin' up the roads, and I figger he'd ought to be here about Sunday."

"For gosh sake stop him," I said.

"I don't dast. There's no telegraph service to the outside; telegrams go over the long distance 'phone to the railroad. Ed Bounce told me that Reno Frank's daughter is the chief operator, and his wife's sister's husband is the postmaster. He's done got us squaw-hitched for sure. Besides which, while I'd like to stop the car, I'd hate like dangnation to stop the liquor. I'm an old man, Tom—"

"I'm glad to hear you say it," I broke in. "Have Williams send a telegram from outside, savvy? Wire that cussed chauffeur of yours at every hotel between here and California, and be sure you catch him. Tell him to slap a coat of black paint over that there car and make her look as near like a wreck as he can. Tell him to drive over Medocno Pass after dark, slide right through town here without stopping to hitch, and to come right on to the Running F Ranch. My gosh! Tell him to take the name of Pinky Jenkins. That's an idea, Tom. He'll be Pinky Jenkins."

John like to split his sides laughing over that, but just then the dinner bell banged out, and I lit a shuck for the feed trough.

## CHAPTER V

SOMEHOW IT has always been my cussed luck to run into trouble just when I was aiming to be peaceful with all the world. Right there at the dinner table, for example. Opposite to me there sits a smart alec drummer what had come in the day before, and he was consid'able breezy with his mouth. I didn't pay no attention, until all of a sudden, while everybody else was laughing at his cracks, he looks at me and speaks up.

"Say, if you wouldn't mind liftin' your head out of the trough long enough to hand me the sugar—"

I'm ashamed to say that I gives him the sugar, crock and all, square between the eyes. There was a little excitement, what with one thing and another, until he come to his senses and staggered up.

"Now, pilgrim," I says to him, "I don't aim to be spoke to by any funny man like I was a hog. You ain't much to blame because you don't know better—"

"I'll sue you! I'll sue you!" he hollers. Just then Reno Frank slips out of the crowd and beckons me aside. As I had about finished my dinner, I went out with him.

"Jasper," says he, real sorrowful, "you see how it is. You'll have to stay out of this here hotel, that's all. I got to run you out for the looks of it, after you shot up my boys yesterday. This here commotion will make folks talk—"

"Run, then," I says. "But mind, Reno—run gentle! By gosh, I mean it!"

He saw that I meant it, so all he did was to walk out to the door with me and let everybody think I had decamped without an argument. Then, as I stepped out into the street, if I didn't come face to face with that scarred-up Woods!

Scarface gave me one look, and then began to back up.

"Quit it!" I told him. "You reach for a gun and I'll perforate you! I don't want no trouble, so quit it."

He let his hand fall. "All right," he said, with a nasty look. "But one of these days I'll pay you out for that quirting, Jasper! You wait."

"Waiting is my best bet," said I, and went on. Before I had gone ten feet, a gent tapped me on the shoulder and threw back his coat to show a deputy sheriff's star.

"Your name's Jasper?" said he, and a mean skunk he was in looks. "I got orders from the sheriff's office to warn you that we folks in Double Ace are civilized. We don't want no gun-toting around here, and no bad men neither."

"Why, good gosh!" I said, staring at him. "I want peace as much as anybody else does! I'm the peacefullest critter ever set a saddle—it ain't my fault if everybody picks on me—"

"None of your back talk," he snapped. It was all a staged affair, of course, just for the looks of things—so everybody would think that Reno Frank and his men were out to get the new foreman of the Running F. Only, I forgot about this part of it. "You get out o' town and stay out—"

"You go plump to Halifax," I says, beginning to get riled up. He reached for his hip, and I hit him under the ear. Before he had picked himself up, two other deputies were holding guns on me, and one of them located the gun in my pants.

"Come along," they said. "You're under arrest for toting a gun, resisting an officer and raising hell generally. We'll let the justice settle your hash, feller."

"Who's the justice—Reno Frank?" I asked, real sarcastic.

"No. Ed Bounce. He's sheriff and justice likewise."

Well, consid'able of a crowd trailed along to the sheriff's office. When we got there, Ed Bounce put on his specs and looked me over as the deputies told their story. He took my old gun and looked her over likewise.

"Gun's confiscated," says he. "Pris'ner, got anything to say?"

"You gimme back that gun or I'll show you what I got to say!" I said.

"Contempt o' court—ten dollars. Toting a gun, ten dollars. Resisting an officer, ten dollars. Raising hell generally around town, ten dollars. Another ten to make her an even fifty. Fifty bucks or fifty days in jail. Which is it?"

I didn't have fifty in cash on me, and had more sense than to show what was in my moneybelt. Ed Bounce asked if I had a job, and I said what job I had.

"All right," said he. "You got three hours to raise the money. Where's your hoss?"

I told him, and he sent the deputies off to take charge of my bronc as security for the fine. Then he shut the door, which left the two of us alone, and grinned at me.

"Pinky, you're a durned fool!" he said. "Here's your gun. Fer gosh sake, can't you act like a white man instead of a danged Piute? Quit raising ructions or I'll have to take Reno Frank's orders and jail you—"

I explained my relations with Reno Frank, and he grinned. "You aiming to stick it out here, are you?"

"For a while," I said. "Where can I raise that fifty?"

"I'll lend it to you and collect off John Parker." He got excited for a minute "See here! I ain't a mite of good any more in a scrap, but if you and Old John start in to bust Coyote County open—you figger Ed Bounce right in!"

"As I expected," and I shook hands with him. "Ed, do something for me?"

"What?" he said, peeping over his specs.

"Gimme a deputy's star and a job as special deputy. I'll keep it blamed quiet, you can be sure! Only, it might come in powerful handy, Ed. I don't aim to give it no publicity, but in a bad pinch—"

"I'll do it, and Reno Frank be damned!" said he, and he done it.

So I went out and paid my fine and saddled up the bronc and, thinks I, now we'll ride home again and keep out of this blamed town! Before I had the bronc out of the stall, along comes Reno Frank. He had heard about me getting arrested, and was wearing a broad grin. It faded as he came up to me, however, for he had bad news.

"I just got a 'phone call from the ranch, Jasper," he said. "The foreman ain't there. The cook called me up to say that four o' the boys were coming to town and were aiming to get you. Now, Jasper, them riders of mine ain't just what you'd call house-broke gents. I know you ain't anybody's fool, but I sure don't want to see you ride into them four boys."

"My gosh, no more do I!" said I. "Seems like everybody in this danged county is anxious to pick a fight with me. Why?"

"Darned if I know," said Reno. "Here's that fifty you had to pay the justice—I aim to treat you square, savvy? Now, them boys of mine have got the ranch flivver, so you can't get away from 'em. You wait here for thirty minutes. They'll be in town by that time—"

"Listen!" I said, real earnest. "Reno, I don't want no scrap, but I don't figger on hidin' my head in a livery stable—"

"Did anybody ever say you was too proud to fight?" said he. "Then call him a liar for me. You consarned fool, learn some sense! Never mind squinting at me, now; you can't start any roughhouse around here! Cool off."

"All right," I said, and led out the bronc. "But I'm heading up the valley, not into a manure pile. I ain't going to hurt your danged men, and if they hurt me it's my own fault. So long! I'll be down the crick Thursday night."

As I rode out of town, it looked to me like my program was dated for some consid'able time ahead. Thursday morning was the time for me to meet up with Jack Williams on the road, and give him any letters or telegrams for the outside world. It was clear enough that Old John had told Williams who I was, and I hoped he'd keep quiet. Then, on Thursday night, I was to meet the Lazy S foreman down by the creek and get instructions from Reno Frank as to what kind of deviltry I was to pull off. Come Monday, Old John Parker meant to spring the news that he'd bought the bank off Williams, and open her up, which same spelled heap big trouble. Sunday or Monday at the latest, the chauffeur was due to arrive with the Rolls-Royce. By a week from next Monday, looked like a bunch of old-timers would drop into Double Ace—what for, I couldn't exactly see. Old John could hardly expect them to pull guns and form a vigilante committee; but that was his funeral, not mine. And in the meanwhile, Mrs. Colfax had some sort of a scheme up her sleeve to raise enough money to meet the mortgage interest on the first of the month, which was only eight days away; to be exact, the first came a week from Tuesday, the day after Old John was to open up his bank.

"Double Ace is going to see some high jinks first o' next week, sure enough!" I thinks. "Right now, the main object in view is for me to keep shy of them four men from the Lazy S, but I got a clear view of the road and there's time enough to think about that when they show up. Looks like Ed Bounce is perking up. Dog-gone him, that there star on my bosom sure makes me feel good!"

It did, for a fact. I had felt sorrowful over the way Ed Bounce had been laying down in front of Reno Frank Skelly, but now things looked different. He took a big chance making me a deputy, because if I sprung the information on the public, Reno Frank would sure raise Cain with him. If there was any killing pulled off, however, and things come to a real showdown, that there star would do T.J. Jenkins a heap of good. Ed Bounce might be done for in body, but give him half a chance and he would back up our play to the holy limit.

Me and Old John were sure starting life over, and having a sight of fun doing it, but I set to figuring on those four men from the Lazy S. It was pretty sure that they knew me from description but not from sight; same time, they'd sure have a full description of my hoss, and they might come into view any minute now. Never having been exactly famous for sticking to the truth when she looked painful, I rode on until I came to a little coulée leading off the road, and led the pony up the coulée a ways until he was clear hid. Then I came back to the road, set on the bridge, rolled me a smoke, and kept my eye peeled.

Just in time, too, for about half a smoke afterward there come a streak of dust from up the valley, and a flivver hove in sight comin' like a meteor. It was the one, all right, and in her was four gents of the same general brand as Woods and Logan. Where Reno Frank had raised all them prison birds I didn't know—later I found he got 'em from Omaha.

Well, the flivver slowed down like a bucking steer and halted alongside me.

"Howdy, boys," I says, before any of the four got a chance to speak. "How far is it to Lazy S?"

"Who in hell are you?" spoke up one of 'em. "Ain't you that feller Jasper?"

"Who's Jasper?" I asked. "Me, I'm Mose Peggmills from Mormon Wells, down in the Mojave—consid'ably down, too. Say, you got some queer gents in this county."

"How so?" says one of the four.

"Why, comin' in from the railroad, the stage driver and me got real friendly. I'd heard over to Rawhide that I might get me a good job in Double Ace, so on I comes. The stage driver took me to his dad, a feller named Skelly, and Skelly give me a job on his ranch. Said it was only a little ways out o' town and I could get me a hoss there. So I set out to walk, and good gosh! I been walking since breakfast. Where is that danged ranch anyhow, gents?"

The four looked at me, then at each other, and began to laugh. It looked to them like Reno Frank had played a good joke on a pilgrim, so they kept the joke boiling.

"Only about half a mile further," says one of 'em. "You turn off to the left right ahead here—you'll see the track. So long!"

They started up the engine and went whoopin' off toward town, leaving me chuckling to myself. I got out the bronc and we rode on home, and nothing more happened.

Dropping off the mail sack on the porch, nobody being in sight, I went on and took care of the horse, and when I came back from the corral Mrs. Colfax was opening her mail. She told me to come up and set, which I done, and then she opened up on me.

"Well, what happened?"

"Nothing, ma'am."

"Don't you lie to me, Tom! A friend of mine in town called me up and said you'd been arrested on Main Street. Who did it?"

"Deputy sheriffs."

"What for?"

"Pure cussedness, ma'am. I wasn't doin' a thing."

"Hm! How 'bout assaulting an officer?"

"That was an accident, ma'am. Ed Bounce done fined me, and that was the end of it."

"Hm! Did you get thrown out of the hotel?"

I gave her a look, and seen somebody had spilled everything to her, so I up and told her what had happened. She began to laugh, and we had a right good time until she remembered business, and waved a letter at me.

"This here is a notice about the interest money coming due the first. I have a man ready to hand me a check for a hundred head o' cattle the minute I can deliver them to him at the railroad. Now, Tom, if you were in my shoes how'd you deliver those cattle? I can't use the toll road—Skelly has me shut off completely."

I squinted out at the creek and remembered how me and Old John got our start by trailing the gang of express robbers.

"Well, ma'am, looks like there's two things to consider. First off, the road. Used to be a trail leadin' out through them hills," and I pointed to the Silvertip Range closing in the east side of the valley, twenty miles away. "It used to run by Black Medicine Gulch and then come out above Hidden Springs."

"You seem to know a lot about this country, for a stranger," says she.

"Yes'm. I was here quite a spell back—thirty year more or less."

"Well," says she, laughing at me, "your idea about the Black Medicine trail is the very thing I had in mind. Four of the boys have gone there to-day, to go over the trail and see if it's in shape for cattle to cross. It hasn't been used for a good many years, you know; in fact, it never was used to amount to anything, the Silvertip road being shorter and better. Trouble is, Reno Frank has men watching that road. If we take any, we have to take the Black Medicine trail. But there are difficulties in the way."

"Like which?" I asked.

"It's twenty mile from here to the hills. The minute we start any cattle that way, some of the Lazy S men will interfere. Again, after we go over the trail, we must go a long way around to reach the railroad; thirty miles at least, and no good water."

I figured over that for a minute or two.

"Reckon you know as well as I do, ma'am, the difference between drivin' cattle by day and by night. S'pose, now, the trail's all right. Well, between now and Thursday we'll cut out the steers you want to ship, and work 'em gradual up the crick toward the hills."

"Toward a water-hole, you mean," she broke in. "The crick comes from a spring five mile back. Go on."

"Thursday night after dark, four of the boys and me will take them cattle over the ground between and along into the trail. We can cover it easy by night, ease 'em over the pass and out the next day, rest 'em up, take 'em on Friday night and get to railroad on Saturday morning. Jack Williams is leavin' town Friday. He'll take a message for you; wire your buyer to be on hand with a certified check. She'll go off like clock-work."

Mrs. Colfax stared at me, her blue eyes shining.

"I believe it will!" she said slowly. "But why wait for Thursday night? And why won't the Lazy S men cut in ahead of us?"

I tells her about my instructions from Reno Frank.

"I'll give that Lazy S foreman a medicine talk about them steers, ma'am, and he won't suspect nothing. Besides, they won't be watching for a night drive—why, what's the matter?"

Her face had changed suddenly. "That foreman—Lon Beaumont! He's the man who shot my husband. We never could prove it—but we know it—"

"Oh!" I said, and began to roll me a cigaret. "I'm right glad you told me that, ma'am. Yes'm, right glad!"

"Why?" she asked quickly. But I didn't tell her why.


CHAPTER VI

WHEN I set into the job of range bossing and general overseeing, I found there was a heap more to do on the Running F than I had thought for, and less men to do it with, four of the best being gone.

Between then and Thursday I sure humped myself—mostly on getting the shipping cattle cut out. The ranch was a right straggling piece of ground that ran back up to the foothills— half of it good ground and the rest of it mostly mountain and rock. Mrs. Colfax had run a fence between her ground and that of the Lazy S, adjoining to the west, but otherwise it was all open range, and she covered most of it with me. Her aim was to pick out the primest stock she had, because quite a bit of fat would be run off before we got 'em to railroad, the way we were going. Then this stock had to be edged over to the eastward so's to be all ready to light out with 'em for the Black Medicine trail. That some of the Lazy S men would sort of get a line on our idea was a foregone conclusion, but they wouldn't dream that we were going to go by Black Medicines. That trail had been unused so long that it was supposed to be impassable and was clear left out of the reckoning.

Wednesday morning something turned up that just fit into my hand like an ace of hearts into a four-card flush. I was riding down the west line fence with Mrs. Colfax, when we made out a man riding toward the fence across our land. Mrs. Colfax went white as a sheet—not with scare, but with mad. She reached for her quirt.

"Hold on, ma'am!" I says. "Who is it?"

"Beaumont."

"Gosh—wait a minute! Let me go speak to him. You'll spoil the whole works if you don't. No sense in passing the bet when you got an ace in the hole, is there? You set here and leave me have a word with him."

Her blue eyes went right through me. "What do you mean?"

"I mean it's our chance to make a big play! Wait here."

I wheeled my bronc and started for Beaumont. He seen me coming, and slowed down. He was a big, strapping feller and looked to me like a right good man in an argument; none of your city-raised gents, neither, but a range man clean through. He drew rein and kept his eyes on me as I came up.

"I'm Tom Jasper," I told him. "Has Reno put you wise about me?"

He nodded and stood pat.

"Then," I went on, "listen to what I got to say, and don't waste time. I got orders to shoo you off our land, sabe? The missus was going for you herself, but I steps in. Look here—tell Reno that we're collecting a couple hundred head o' cattle and drawing 'em down the valley to ship. We aim to start with 'em Thursday night, midnight, and run 'em out over Medocno Pass—we figure on gettin' through the pass with 'em by Friday noon. Surprise party."

"Good for you," he says, with another nod. "That's important news, Jasper. We knew you boys were up to something, but couldn't quite make out what. Now, about them orders from Reno—"

"Let that ride until to-morrow night," I says, jerking a thumb back towards Mrs. Colfax. "No time now. I'm here to put you off the Running F and do it quick."

He grinned at that and gathered up his reins.

"All right, I'm goin'. See you to-morrow night."

"I sure hope you do," thinks I, riding back to the lady. "And you'll see more'n you figure on seeing, too!"

When I had joined Mrs. Colfax, she gives me an inquiring look, and I reports what has been said.

"It was a whale of a chance," I concluded, "to get the coast cleared. Reno's boys will most likely be away over the other side of the valley in Medocno Pass, waiting to stampede your herd—and we'll have a clear road by the Black Medicine trail. Sabe?"

"*Si,*" and she laughs a little, but with a sparkle still in her eye. "Tom Jasper, you're a quick thinker."

"No'm," I says, "I'm a right quick liar though, in a pinch."

She gave me a quick look. "I wish everybody was your kind of a liar, Tom! Are you married?"

"No, ma'am. Somehow I ain't never met anybody that took my notion before."

"Before what?" says she.

"Why," I said, thinking quick and feeling myself getting red over that durned thoughtless remark, "why, before—before prohibition, of course. There's that bunch we been looking for, ain't it? Over there beyond that cañoncito—or I reckon I'd better say coulée and act like I belonged in this here country."

So it went off all right, but to think of how careless my tongue was getting made me feel scared and no mistake. Somehow when I was riding alone with Mrs. Colfax I clear forgot all about being T.J. Jenkins—I was just with her, that was all, and words popped out of me before I thought. There was something about her that kept a man from feeling bashful and backward—maybe it was because she was just as good as any man on the range.

Wednesday night old Holy Pete turned up, looking consid'ably frazzled. He had been one of the four gone to inspect the trail, and he brought in a right good report on road conditions. The other three had stayed to work. It seems like the old trail was in pretty good shape except for one place where the rains had clear washed out ten foot or so, and another place where a bridge was clean gone. Mrs. Colfax had sent them with tools, so they had set right to work and fixed up the washout. Holy Pete reported it was no boulevard by a durned sight, but two cattle could go abreast. There being plenty of timber close to hand, the other three had stopped to fix up the bridge over the twenty-foot break. They figured on having it all in shape by next day.

That night Mrs. Colfax gave out the orders, and I picked Holy Pete and his partner, with a young rider named Curly, to go with me. Mrs. Colfax wanted to go likewise, but as I pointed out to her, the value of good drivers lies chiefly in their cussing ability, and her being along with us might hinder us a whole lot. Holy Pete had once drove up the old desert trail to Salt Lake City, so he knew his business proper.

There was no poker game that night, all of us being due to sleep early and late on account of the work ahead. But before the bunkhouse lamp went out, I calls Holy Pete and the other four boys to order, and sets out to them just how I was pretending to be working with Reno Frank, and what had happened that morning with Beaumont. Likewise I tells them about my date with Beaumont for next evening, and we holds a pow-wow and does a ghost dance, as Old John would have said.

"I don't aim to lay down my hand to Reno just yet," I tells them, "so we got to make this here play real careful. If we make delivery of these cattle and get the check, then I'll call Reno and have a showdown; but first we want to go easy and see what Beaumont has to say. You gents obey orders, and if anybody slips up I'll sure tan his hide proper."

Next morning I came mighty near forgetting my date with Jack Williams, for things were humping around the place.

However, I slid out and saddled and rode down to the county road, and started towards town. Before I had went a mile, I sighted a flivver and it proved to have Williams at the wheel. He was a good-looking young sprig, but weak around the eyes and draggled out; it was plain to see that he had once had nerve, but it had been taken out of him. He hauls up, and when he found I was Jasper and I found he was Williams, everything was right. He was mournful about me and Old John, saying that we'd be lucky if we got out of Coyote County alive, and it seemed like Old John had been in a big row Monday night.

John had sold consid'able Hassayamp Oil and would have sold more only he sneaked over to the dance and got tangled up with a deputy sheriff. Williams claimed that Old John had shot a big surprise into Double Ace, for he had climbed all over that deputy and laid him out cold; then one of Reno's henchmen started to pull a gun on Old John, and the dance was ruined. John started out to lick everyone in sight, and notched up four before they got him down.

"Durned lucky for all concerned he didn't have no gun with him," I said. "Is he in jail?"

"No," said Williams. "Out on bail. He gets tried Tuesday. He wasn't drunk, but that's the charge—it's a jail offense in this state, you know. They'll jail him certain."

"I'll bet you a hundred dollars against a plug of tobacco they don't," I said. "Old John don't really begin to use his brains until he gets back up into a corner! Wait and see."

"I ain't waiting," he said, and grimaced. "I'm going our to-morrow morning. What's this about me sending messages for you?"

I gave him some letters and telegrams that I had fixed up.

"You send 'em by to-morrow night sure," I said, and he promised he would. So, there being no more to say, we parted, and I was a free man until my evening engagement.

The boys were looking forward to something better than a cattle drive that night, and at supper there was quite an exchange of winks and knowing looks. Mrs. Colfax was by no means blind, and she knew about me meeting Beaumont that night—we had put off starting the drive on account of it. So after supper she took me into the office.

"Tom, what's up? Are you boys framing up something for Beaumont?"

Her blue eyes told me there was no particle of use in lying.

"Yes'm," I said. "We aims to grease that skunk up, feather him, tie him on a hoss and send him into Double Ace."

"I thought as much. Well, I refuse to allow it."

"How come?" I asked her.

"Are you running this ranch, Tom Jasper, or am I? That's how come. What's the plan?"

I told her just what it was, and she listened right sharp. When I had finished, she nodded her head and gave me a smile that didn't show the dimple at all. I'd hate to have her smile that way, with me in mind.

"I'll take charge of this business myself," said she. "You trot along and keep your appointment. This is my affair, not yours."

It was, too, for the boys were all dead certain that Beaumont had shot Colfax down, only they could never get any proof except hoofprints. So, after a smoke, I slid out of the house and started down the creek towards a bunch of willows half a mile from the buildings, or maybe a bit more.

The night was hazy with cloud, and promised to be dead right for our purposes, if rain didn't come on to spoil the Black Medicine trail. When I got to the willows, nobody was there, so I hung around a spot I had selected—an opening with trees and brush close about. After a bit I heard a horse and lighted a cigaret. Lon Beaumont got off his bronc and came forward on foot, give me a hail, and joined me.

"Douse that cigaret," he says. "I ain't running into suicide. What time you going to start your herd to moving?"

"Midnight."

"Then we got lots o' time." He came closer to me and dropped his voice. "Good thing you give me the news yesterday. I'll pay you back right now. You keep in front o' that herd when she hits Medocno Pass, savvy? The farther front you get, the better for your health."

"Is that a warning?" I says, drawing him out so anybody who was close by could catch the whole thing.

"You bet you it's a warning, feller!" Beaumont laughed. "We aim to send them cattle into Medocno cañon and the herd drivers with 'em. There won't be nobody to tell tales but you, the evidence bein' that the herd took the riders over with 'em. Our whole durned outfit is on the way there now."

That was good news.

"Well," I says, "you'll sure see me leadin' the string! Now, what's the general orders? What does Reno want me to do, anyhow?"

"To be ready for anything. Mrs. Colfax is tryin' to get this herd out to railroad so's she can pay the interest on her mortgage nex' Tuesday. If it don't go through she's plumb liable to find the money anyhow; you take a woman with her back agin' the wall, and she can scratch a waterhole in hell. Reno don't figger on takin' no chances. You get her off'n the place Monday night certain. We aim to burn out the Running F and do it good. Then we got to chase into town on another job—mebbe you'd like to go along?"

"You fellers seem right busy," I said. "If Reno is so dog-goned set agin' Mrs. Colfax, why don't he up an' shoot her, like he done her husband?"

Beaumont swore softly. "They's limits, that's why! Reno ain't any angel, but he draws the line at shootin' a woman—'specially if it ain't necessary."

"Oh!" I said. "Well, what's this other job?"

At that, Beaumont began to laugh. "Say, Reno got one pulled over him this afternoon sure! You know that old snoozer Doc Jones—the med'cine man? Well, they say he's a sassy old galoot, and Reno had the boys pinch him Monday night for bein' drunk, that same bein' a jail offense. He was out on bail with the trial to come next Tuesday, but this afternoon he passes the word around that he'd like to have the trial right off quick. He allowed he would claim he got the liquor from Reno, and could prove it. Since he wa'n't drunk at all, that sure put Reno in a hole—one man's lie is as good as another man's in court. So Reno had to call it off. Case was dismissed this afternoon. But we're goin' to run the old snoozer out o' town Monday night, after we get through here. Give him a coat o' tar and feathers, savvy? We might arrange for you to get in on the party—"

Right there an electric torch broke over us, and about three feet away was Mrs. Colfax and Holy Pete, holding guns on us.

"Not a move!" she says. "Elevate, both of you! This is a fine mess, ain't it! So you're sellin' me out, are you, Jasper? I s'pose you been telling this Texas killer about our drive, eh? Well, here's what I think of you—"

And she laid out to tell me in plain words what she thought of a traitor who'd sell her out. Even though it was all for Beaumont's benefit, her language sure made me fidget. Then she snaps out an order.

"Tie up Beaumont. You, Curly, jerk this Jasper gent down to the crick and put a bullet through him and leave him there. I've quit fooling."

So a couple of the boys jerks me off into the night, and after a minute or two Curly fires his gun in the air.

"You're dead," says Curly, real soft. "Sneak back and watch what's going to happen. The missus is out for blood, feller."

So I sneaked up on the party, real cautious.

## CHAPTER VII

WITH ALL his faults, Lon Beaumont was a real range man—he sure had guts. He could swear that I'd been shot down, and could look for nothing better himself, but he stood quiet and said not a word as Mrs. Colfax questioned him. Then she sprang a little surprise that shook him for a minute.

"I think we'll escort you out of this county, Beaumont," she says. "Boys, get ready to start the drive right off—we'll not wait for midnight. Tie Beaumont on his boss and rope him good, and blindfold him. We'll take him along with us."

She said this, of course, having overheard that scheme to run the herd and drivers into Medocno cañon. Beaumont's heavy face showed for a moment just how bad he was shook up by her words. He had not suspected that she was going with the herd, and didn't want to see her go; nor himself either. But if he made any argument he would give away the scheme and betray his boss, which is clear against the first principles of the range. I judged Mrs. Colfax was no more than testing him out and giving him a taste of purgatory, for she laughed at him as he stood there licking his lips. He had sand, though; he never uttered one word.

Two of the boys dragged him away, the electric torch went out, and I walked up to the corral with Mrs. Colfax. She was so furious for a while that she could hardly speak.

"Burn me out! Run my herd and drivers into the cañon—oh, the murderers! Tom, we can have the law on him for his—"

"You can't law nobody for his intentions," I reminded her. "Now, the thing for you to do is to turn this gent loose."

"Why so?" she snapped.

"He'll pass the word that I'm dead, and a dead man can be a durned useful object at times. Also, he don't know that you overheard any of that talk, especially about burning you out. It would suit me just fine, ma'am, to be setting on the dark side of the corral with a Winchester when them Lazy S men start to burn you out! Yes'm, it would. I can't imagine nothing more suitable to my disposition. Two or three neighbors on hand to view the party and identify the remains would be pretty good, too; and there'd be no comeback from the law."

She stopped short and stared at me. "Tom Jasper," she said slowly, "thank heaven that you're sitting into this game with me!"

"Yes'm," I told her. "Them's my sentiments exactly, only put more elegant. If you and me"—dog-gone that slippery tongue! "Excuse me, ma'am—I got to get my outfit."

I went away in a hurry, leaving her staring after me, and cussing myself for not keeping my tongue in better care.

In another ten minutes we were off. Mrs. Colfax and the rest of the outfit were riding with us as far as the opening of Black Medicine trail, for we aimed to keep the herd humping and needed swing men; once into the trail, I could handle them with the three men I'd picked. So, taking my three men, I rode on ahead to get the herd rounded up and on the start. Mrs. Colfax followed with the other two men and Beaumont, so's he would get no idea that I was still alive and kicking.

Thinks I, next Monday is all set to be a lively day, what with Old John opening up the bank and one thing and another. The only question is whether I can get back in time to buy chips in the various and sundry games that will be starting.

With Holy Pete, Curly and the other old-timer, we got to the gathered herd and fell to work getting the durned critters started. I never did see such ornery cows when it come to getting them formed up and the point started, but after consid'able cussing Holy Pete started into the Chisholm Trail song, and then I knew all was well. By the time Mrs. Colfax came up, we had 'em swinging forward into the night in good shape, and there was nothing much left to do except steer them right and keep them humping.

"You're a first-class cowman, Tom," said Mrs. Colfax, coming up the right flank and joining me.

"Thanks," I said. "You still got Beaumont along?"

"Yes."

We had good open country all the way, but none the less I set out ahead of the trail herd to make sure we met nobody, also to keep out of Beaumont's hearing. I knew we'd have no great work once we got the herd into the cañon, for that trail was nothing but a hand-hold all the way to Hidden Springs, halfway across. After that, it followed the bed of a dry cañon and was good going. Once we got the herd started, they'd keep going and have no chance to mill until they got to Hidden Springs, and then it wouldn't matter much. I figured to rest them there anyhow.

Having no stars and no nothing to guide us, we had to work by compass, and did a right good job if I do say it. As things turned out, it was lucky that I was out ahead, for along after midnight I connected up with the three riders who had been building trail for us. They reported the job done, and all clear to go ahead. I warned them about spilling any information where Beaumont could hear, and sent 'em on back to the herd.

By two in the morning we were in the cañon opening, and that was pretty smart work, having come about twenty miles. Of course, in the old days a thirty-mile drive was nothing for rangy old longhorn steers to cover by night, but these cattle were civilized critters and the trail came hard to them. There were a hundred and twenty head in the bunch, and after sending Holy Pete on ahead to keep things clear that way, I joined Mrs. Colfax and watched the drive go past. Then I made out two of the riders lighting a fire over to one side in a little draw.

"What's that for?" I said.

"For me," said Mrs. Colfax. "Send Curly to keep prodding those cows along, and stick around to see what happens."

Since all we could do was to keep the cattle humping two abreast as far as Hidden Springs, I sent Curly on the job and followed over to the fire. There I kept out of sight, for when the flames licked up they fetched in Beaumont and took off his blindfold and ropes likewise. He stood there rubbing his wrists, wondering where he was and what was going to happen to him. He found out right quick.

Mrs. Colfax came into the firelight. She had taken off her khaki coat and looked mighty slim and pretty in her khaki blouse and riding pants. She had her quirt on her wrist.

"Beaumont," she says, "you're the man who shot my husband last year. I have no proof of it, but I know you're the man. Now, my riders have orders not to interfere, no matter what happens. I'm going to give you punishment that you'll remember. Stand up and fight, any way you want—"

Beaumont took a step back. "My gosh!" he said, "I can't fight no woman—"

"But you can shoot a man in the back," says she, and brought the quirt across his face.

What followed was no ways pretty to see, and it was durned hard not to step in and take a hand; but Mrs. Colfax had issued orders that she meant to be obeyed, and they was sure obeyed plenty. Not a one of us moved. It was her affair, as she had said, and we all calculated that she was competent to handle it.

In spite of everything, it came hard to her to lash a man who wouldn't fight. For a minute or two Beaumont stood there, a great bulking brute of a man, glaring at her and trying to hold himself in. Then he started to dodging the quirt but didn't have any great luck with it, for Mrs. Colfax drove him around the fire and got in two slashes that fair maddened him.

He whirled around, fending off the quirt with one arm.

"Quit it!" he yelled hoarsely. "Or I'll have to go for you—"

"You come right ahead, you coyote," she snapped at him, and curled the quirt around his bare forearm.

Beaumont went right up into the air. "You damned she-wolf!" he cried out, and then started for her.

It looked mighty uneven, in spite of her having the loaded quirt, for he could have broken her over his knee to all appearance. But as he started forward, she laughed, and right then I knew that Lou Beaumont was going to get his needin's. I'll back off any day from a scrap with a gent that cries like a baby, for that means trouble; but the gent that laughs when he fights is sure going to raise hell before he goes down. And it was that kind of a laugh that she gave.

Beaumont went for her hell-bent, and she stepped right into it and quirted him over the cheek and the blood spurted. He grabbed her arm, held her off, and tried to twist the quirt from her—then she was into him teeth and toenails, smashed her other fist into his jaw, and twisted clear. The quirt bit him again, and Beaumont went clear out of his head with fury.

He jumped for her, and no blame to him either, like he would to any man—and one blow from his fist would have done the trick. He couldn't land the blow, however. She shifted back and forth, danced around him, and kept the quirt flying. He was all a mass of blood by this time, cursing and sobbing, and suddenly she brought the quirt square across his eyes.

Beaumont gave a scream and put his hands to his face—then lunged for her and got her. His big paws closed on her neck and drew her up close to him.

"Now, by gosh, I'll send you after him," he panted out. "You hell-cat!"

I heard more than one click of hammers being cocked, but right then Mrs. Colfax showed her stuff. He was sinking his fingers into her white throat, and she let him do it, while she got the quirt off her wrist.

Then—smack! The loaded butt of that quirt smashed him over the head. She hit him a second time, and he let go of her and staggered back. She stepped in on him and give him a third clip that took him under the ear. That was all Lon Beaumont knew about the evening's entertainment—or I should say morning's—for he curled right up and went to sleep.

The rest of us let out a howl and surrounded Mrs. Colfax, but she waved us off.

"Leave me alone," she panted, rolling down her sleeves, and then with a shudder flung the quirt away, dropped down in a huddle, and began to shake with great sobs.

We looks one at another, and drifts off into the darkness, after kicking out the fire.

"Reckon he's blinded?" asked one of the boys, as we rolled cigarets.

"Nope," I said. "But he will be next time I meet up with him. You boys heard what he said. It wa'n't no legal confession, I guess, but it's all I need."

"Yes," said somebody, "only you're dead."

"I'm comin' alive Monday," I says. "And Monday the lid is goin' to blow off in Double Ace. You boys set close to home. Good gosh!"

"What's the matter?" asked somebody. The matter was that I had clean forgot about that cussed car and chauffeur of Old John Parker's, which was due to arrive Sunday morning or Monday morning, if they came over Medocno Pass at night.

"Nothing," I says. "Only there's more hell to pay than I had figured on."

I told Holy Pete's pardner, who was going with me, to get mounted, and then walked in on the embers of the fire. Mrs. Colfax had got rid of her tears and was standing up, and I held out my hand to her.

"Well, ma'am, I guess we'll mosey along on the trail. I aim to hit Saledo Junction with them cows early Sat'day morning, collect off your buyer, and get started home."

She gripped hard on to my hand for a minute, and I felt she was trembling.

"I'm right sorry about all this," and she jerked her hand toward where Beaumont lay, dead to the world. "It's something I shouldn't have done. Somehow I just saw red—"

"By gosh, you done yourself proud!" I says. "Yes'm, you sure did! You blindfold that feller and rope him on his hoss and turn him loose. The hoss will take him home, and he won't know where this place was, and Reno Frank never will understand how we sneaked them cattle out of the county under his nose. You ain't hurt Beaumont none to speak of."

"I'm sorry you're going," said she. "When will you be back?"

I let go her hand, realizing that I was an ornery old fool.

"Depends on circumstances, ma'am—but we'll be back Monday night, and you can bank on that! You be sure and arrange that there little party we spoke about. The only thing that can keep me from being there is jail, and from what I seen of the jail in Double Ace I wouldn't place no bets on that being able to hold me. Of course, we may be home quicker'n we figure on. Is there a bank in Saledo Junction where I can cash that there check I get?"

"Yes, but they don't know you."

"They will," I says. "You take good care of yourself and keep the boys to home, and stay there your own self. So long, and good luck!"

"Same to you, Tom. So long!"

I walked to where my bronc was waiting, slung up to the saddle, waved the boys good-by, and hit out for the Black Medicine trail.

CHAPTER VIII

TO CUT a long story short, as the Injun' said when he scalped the preacher, we got them cattle into Saledo Junction before sun-up Saturday, having lost not more than a dozen head going over the trail. I got over to the Pilgrim's Rest House, woke up the buyer, and sat down to a right hearty breakfast with his check in my pocket.

Next I interviewed the agent at the railroad station. All this while I had been worrying over Old John's car, but now I found a way out. The agent tells me there's a train at nine-twenty going west. So, having to stop into the bank when she opened up, I said to hold that train, since she was sure to be on time.

"Can't do it, partner—"

"Listen!" I said. "I got to visit the bank. You hold that there train until nine-thirty and there's fifty dollars in it for you. Now can you do it?"

"Don't ask fool questions," says he, grinning.

So I moseyed back towards the bank and picked up the boys. Now, Saledo was real excited over that drive herd from Coyote County and consid'able of a crowd collected, and while I was waiting on the bank steps with the three riders, out of the crowd bust a little old man with white hair flying, and he came for me on the jump.

"By the great horn spoon—if it ain't Pinky Jenkins!" he bellowed. "Pinky! Remember me? Remember Pecos Hardy, and the summer we was up to Medicine Hat—"

"Jenkins!" said Holy Pete, staring at me. "By gosh, I thought I knowed you!"

Well, there was the fat in the fire and no mistake. I cussed Pecos and shook hands with him in the same breath; come to find out, he was working a small ranch over in the Skeleton Range. I remembered what Old John had said, and took him off to one side.

"Listen, Pecos! Remember Old John Parker—do, eh? Well, John's over to Double Ace, and if he ain't in jail he's in trouble. Going by the name of Doc Jones. You get over there next Monday, savvy? He's got a game on. So've I. My name's Tom Jasper right now."

I went back to the three boys and gave 'em a lecture. How they did grin! They promised to keep shut up to Mrs. Colfax, and then the bank opened, and in I went.

There was consid'able argument. The cashier called the president, and the president looked me over, and Pecos Hardy swore to me, and there was red tape a-plenty. However, at last I cashed Mrs. Colfax's check, and one of my own for ten thousand. Then I took Holy Pete by the neck and shook him into paying attention, giving him most of the money.

"Give this here money to the missus, sabe? Tell her I met a feller who wants to buy a half interest in the Running F and this is advance money. I ain't going back with you. I'm going up the railroad a piece and maybe will come back through Double Ace. You boys drift home, and drift rapid! If you ain't there by to-morrow night I'll give you hell. And if you spill one word to Mrs. Colfax about me being Pinky Jenkins, I'll give you double hell. So long! Hey, Pecos! Shall I tell Old John you're coming?"

"You bet you!" says he. "With both guns on, Pinky—"

That was enough, and I streaked it for the railroad station, where the train was whistling to beat creation. Old John would be glad to see Pecos Hardy again, especially if there was trouble. Pecos used to be sheriff down to Socorro, time the Big Bend going started up into the Pecos country, and if anybody could unwrap a gun quicker than Pecos I had yet to see the gent.

The agent got his fifty and I got my train, and we started over the grade.

When I bought my ticket from the conductor, for the desolate water-tank siding where passengers for Double Ace dropped off, the man ahead of me in the smoker turned around and gave me a look; then, a minute later, spoke to me.

"Heard you mention Double Ace," says he. "I'm going there. Know if I can get a stage over this afternoon?"

"I know you can't," I said. "This train don't bring folks for Double Ace, mostly. The stage don't wait to meet it."

"Then I have to spend the night in a hotel?"

"No," I said. "You don't. There ain't none. All there is is a platform and a water-tank and a road. If you're going out, you buy your ticket from the stage line in Double Ace. If you're coming in, you pray for luck. Never been there before?"

"No," said he, kind of short, and turned around again. He was a hard-faced hombre, with a good straight eye, but if he wasn't inclined to talk, then neither was I.

Not having had any sleep to mention lately, I slept about all the way to our destination, which we reached slightly before three in the afternoon. The train had a diner, so I got a snack and had them put me up some lunch besides. When I got off the train, there was nothing in sight but the station platform. The other man got out, too, and when the train was gone he came over to where I was resting my feet and rolling a smoke.

"Anybody coming to meet you?" he says.

"I hope not," and I lighted my cigaret. "Anybody coming to meet me would be a sure sign o' bad luck. Thinking of getting a ride, eh?"

He laughed, then eyed the road toward the pass and looked sort of anxious.

"You're not going to stay here all night, are you?"

"I aim to," I told him. "Unless you'd sooner have the platform, in which case I'll set under the water tank. You might get a ride, though; there's the highway over to the left, and I expect a car heading for Double Ace might branch off now and then."

He stood humming a little tune for a minute, then he sat down.

"Got the makin's to spare? Handshaw is my name. Not Handsaw, but Handshaw."

I supplied his needs and looked him over.

"Used to be a feller o' that name over to Virginia City in the old days—Sassafras Handshaw was him, on account of him always trying to get sassafras tea—"

"My dad!" says Handshaw, his eyes widening on me. "You knew him?"

"Real well," I returned. "Him and me drifted to Boise one time and darned near got lynched by mistake—"

"Then you're Jenkins—Pinky Jenkins of the H Bar L!" With that, he grabbed for my fist, beaming all over. "I've heard my dad tell of you a dozen times, and how you and him sneaked out of the jail in Boise, and how you got drunk and claimed to be sheriff of Broken Bow—"

"Wait," I struck in hastily. "Wait! That's enough. I'm an old man and respectable and got money in my clothes. Never mind them recollections. Your dad dead?"

"Five years ago. You ain't living in Double Ace?"

"No," I said with some truth. "No. You going there on business?"

He nodded. "Yep. I'm U.S. Marshal by deputy. We got a call from Double Ace to come in and collect a feller there name of Doc Jones. Claims to be selling patent medicine, but it seems that he's running hooch."

"Hm! Who called you in—Skelly?"

Handshaw nodded and gave me a curious look. "Know him?"

Well, it was easy enough to see that Sassafras Handshaw's boy was his dad all over, so the two of us had a right good talk. All at once I thought of something and fell to laughing.

"This is Saturday, ain't it?" I said. "Then you needn't figure on no stage in a hurry. Stage don't run Sundays."

"Durn the stage!" says he, and laughed. "I'll roost here as long as you will, Pinky! What was that you said about Skelly planning to burn out Mrs. Colfax?"

We talked some more. Along about the time darkness fell we understood each other pretty thoroughly. Handshaw was working on behalf of the state prohibition authorities, but after hearing what I had to say he decided to leave Doc Jones alone and go along to look Double Ace over on general principles.

"I'll lay low for a while, Jenkins," said he. "Of course I'm not going to be used by Skelly or anyone else as a cat's-paw; before I do any arresting I'll be dead sure that it's not a frame-up. So this Doc Jones ain't what he seems, eh? Well, I'll enjoy seeing the fun."

One thing impressed me real strong—Handshaw was honest as daylight, feared nobody, and was set on doing his durndest prohibition duty. Them being his principles, with which same I hadn't any right to quarrel, made things look a mite queer. I was gambling that the Rolls-Royce would come along between now and the time I got starved out; and the car was loaded with Old John's hard liquor; and here was a deputy U.S. Marshal set to enforce prohibition—and square about it! I tells him about the car, that evening, and how we come to send it—but I said nothing about the liquor, you bet.

I can't say that I enjoyed the evening, for it was cold as blazes, up there in the hills. Seeing a freight train stop for water was no excitement. However, we built us up a fire, made a meal off the grub I had fetched, and stuck her out. When the night passed and daylight came along, I was thankful. Time was when it would have meant less than nothing, but with short rations and no blankets I felt the cold in my bones. To make things worse, daylight brought a thin, fine drizzle of rain.

The big water tank was a blessing, for Handshaw got a chill, there was no timber at hand, and the best we could do was to get under the tank for shelter. And how that boy could cuss! He laid over anyone I have heard for quite a spell. I wasn't exactly happy my own self. And never a sign of anybody on the road, although several cars went by on the highway across the tracks.

It got wetter and wetter. Along about ten o'clock a freight stopped for water, and the crew piled off to have some fun with the two hoboes they sighted. We did not guess their intentions until a chunk of coal took Handshaw under the ear and laid him cold. About two minutes later the train crew was roosting here and there about the premises, dodging hot lead, and when I judged matters were evened up I showed the conductor my deputy's star and told him to lead me to the caboose, which same he done. The freight went on its way, and I went back to Handshaw with two dinner buckets. When he came around we had a right good meal and felt consid'ably better.

This put in the time until early afternoon, when the passenger train pulled through without a stop. Handshaw was cussing me by this time, and I had pretty near given up hope. We rustled up some wood and built us a fire, sitting out in the wet to enjoy it, one side wet and t'other steamy. His chills kept getting worse and worse.

Then, just when things looked blackest, along came the Rolls-Royce.

I didn't recognize her at first, but saw a car pitch out of the highway and head for the Medocno Pass road, so I jumped out and waved her. The chauffeur, for a wonder, knew me right off and slowed down.

"Howdy, Mr. Jenkinsh!" said he. "Fine shpring wezzer, ain't it? Have a drink?"

To put it blunt, he was far gone. I knew that Handshaw, friends or no friends, would gather in Old John if he got wise to the load aboard that car, so I jumped on the running-board and hit the chauffeur under the ear. Then I tumbled him into the back seat atop the case goods, took a bottle out of his pocket, and went over to Handshaw with a drink. He put it down and damned his principles, for he was shaking right smart. So was I.

"Climb in," I says. "We go, and go quick!"

That was a lie. We went, right enough, but the road through Medocno Pass was no road to take fast in rainy weather—she was slippery as the conscience of a sheep-man. As we went along, I looked the car over and saw that the chauffeur had sure performed the job allotted him. She was daubed with black paint and mud and looked like a wreck instead of the thirteen thousand she had cost Old John.

She looked worse before I got through the pass. There were no skid chains aboard, and gosh how she slid! Twice we went clear off the road, and once the rear end hung over the cañon, but Handshaw's powerful cussing saved us. Going down the other side of the mountain was worse, for all I could do was crawl and pray, and the praying was better than the crawling. Night came on before we near got down, and that made it worse.

However, all things have an end, and finally we got down to level ground and I threw in the gas. Handshaw was right sick—

had a fever, too—so I went straight ahead for Double Ace. It was pretty late when we got there, and I avoided the main street and pulled up in front of Ed Bounce's shack. Ed was up and about, and when he had put out his lamp I went inside.

"My gosh, I heard you was dead!" he says.

"I am," I told him. "Listen, Ed! Can you ride in a car?"

"Sure."

"Then get into your slicker."

I helped Handshaw out of the car and dumped him in the shack, then pulled out the snoring chauffeur and dumped him in a rain-puddle. Pretty soon he was sober and listening to me real hard.

"Don't ask any questions," I said. "You got to make up for bein' drunk, sabe?"

"Yes, sir," said he.

"Your name is T.J. Jenkins, and you've come here to buy a half interest in the Running F Ranch, on which you've already paid down about nine thousand advance. This gent," and I showed him Ed Bounce, "is the sheriff of Coyote County. He'll show you where to drive and what to say—and if you don't talk turkey you'll get pinched! Get in the car and get ready."

I turned to the sheriff. "Ed, go along out to the ranch with him. To-morrow night the Lazy S men are coming to burn Mrs. Colfax out. I aim to be there, and to have you on hand. Don't tell Mrs. Colfax anything about me being here. This feller with me, that I've got to nurse, is the U.S. marshal's deputy. Hide that car somewhere around the ranch. Send her back here about sundown to-morrow to get me and Old John. All right—go! Get out o' town before somebody spots the car!"

So off they went, and in I went to get Handshaw to bed.

## CHAPTER IX

BY THE time I got Handshaw into bed, I could see he was in bad shape, so I went to the telephone, called the hotel, and got Doc Jones on the line. No better doc ever worked, unofficial, than Old John Parker. He let out a yelp when he heard my voice.

"Get some chills and fever medicine and come over to the sheriff's shack," I says. "Don't mention no names. And come a-humping."

He done it, too, for by the time I had some water boiling he was there with a bottle of moonshine under one arm and some powders in his pocket. He mixed Handshaw a stiff hot one, fed him some quinine and a cannonball, and said he'd likely be out of bed in two or three days. Then we settled down to tell each other the story of our lives.

He had not much to tell. It seemed that the news was spread that I'd been shot by one of the Running F men, but as no body had been found there was nothing to be done about it yet. Folks had heard about Beaumont getting a drubbing from Mrs. Colfax, but there was nothing to be done about that, either. No man is going to prosecute a woman for licking him. John was going to open up the bank in the morning, but no one else in town knew it except the former cashier and bookkeeper, who would keep quiet to save their jobs.

Then I told John my say, or most of it. He was hopping mad because I had not taken a case out of the car, but I soon switched him off that, and finished by telling him about the tar-and-feather party that was scheduled for the next night, with him the chief mourner.

"The mahogany-faced Piutes!" says he, jumping up and down and cracking his heels in the air. "The ding-danged sons of blanks! Feather me, will they? I'll show 'em! I'll dance their measly scalps, by gosh. I'll show 'em what med'cine talk looks like—"

"You give me some medicine talk right now, and do it pronto," I says. "John, what's in your mind, anyhow? What are all them old-timers going to do when they get here? You can't set out to reform a town with a gun. Whatever your notion is, let's have it."

"All right," he says. "So far, these folks think that I'm a simple old fool of a patent med'cine man, savvy? I been blowing around consid'able about one thing and another. They think I'm in my second childhood—"

"That's natural," I says. "But go on, John, go on."

"So," he went on, after giving me a look that could bite, "Reno Frank and his friends have been kidding me in public, having a lot o' fun and so forth. Two-three days ago Reno was prodding me in the hotel lobby, so I offers to buy the stage line. You should have heard 'em holler! Reno gives me an option on his stock in the company and takes a dollar; he got his lawyer over and drew up a contract and everything. Well, Tom, you never seen so much fun as them fellers had with me! It was as good as a show for them. Reno says mebbe I'd like to buy the telephone company, too, so I says I'd take an option on that, and by this time there was a crowd in the hotel, laughing fit to kill."

John grinned at me and tested out what was left of the moonshine, and smacked his lips.

"Reno sure enjoyed himself, Tom. You never seen a man enjoy himself so much as Reno done, showing off before his friends that-a-way! He gives me an option on the livery stable and the hotel and his ranch, and somebody got a blackboard and begun to figger up, and every time the lawyer drew up a new option you could hear the yells from here to Californy. Everybody in town was there to kid the old fool along. Come to end up, I had options on all Reno's prop'ty, total amount somewheres around a hundred and ninety thousand. Then one and another bought chips, Reno bein' froze out. The drug store man, he slaps an option on me at ten thousand, and the newspaper man speaks up. They got a new blackboard and begun figgering up all over again. I got an option on the gen'ral store, the hardware, the restaurant—my gosh, I can't count 'em all! There was fifty-nine different options which same cost me one dollar a throw. No cold decks, neither; I know some law, and that lawyer done his job noble. The total amount was close to three hundred thousand—somebody shoved in another ranch on me towards the last."

If I had guessed that scene was coming off, I'd have broke a leg to be there and see Old John make himself the laughing-stock of Double Ace. When I got done with my own grin, I asked how he hoped to take them options up.

"That's the p'int! I ain't exactly poor, nor you neither. We got half a dozen old-timers coming, ain't we? We holds a ghost dance and splits up the jackpot, savvy? Then we gives Double Ace a new deal, Pinky! Yes, sir. That there all comes off next Monday at five in the afternoon, as specified in them there options. And Reno figgers I'll be tarred and feathered before then, does he? Durn his hide! No wonder him and his friends had so much fun!"

"Hold on!" I said. "You can't make 'em stick to them options, John! First, they're all made out in the name of Doc Jones—"

"D'ye take me for a ding-danged fool?" he snapped at me. "Any name you sign to a paper before witnesses—so long as it ain't a check—is good in court; that's common law, you ornery cowhand!"

"So is a pistol—too durned common in this here county," I says. "You ain't going to be alive next Monday, John."

"With you and me and Pecos Hardy and half a dozen more old-timers on the job? You guess again!" he snorted, but I knew better. John had sure put one over, but at the same time it looked to me like he had miscalculated on his dates. He was too stubborn to see it, though; the more a body argues with him, the more set he becomes, so I quit trying.

We made a few plans together, and then he went back to the hotel.

Next morning Handshaw was powerful weak. It wasn't the chills and fever, neither; John had been so enthusiastic with his quinine and powders and cannonballs and things, that the poor boy was laid out. That was just as well, for it kept him out of mischief and out of sight likewise.

No signs of strife happened along from the outside world to tell me that Old John was getting shot up in his bank, or elsewhere. Noon came, and still all was peaceful, and I began to get nervous, for I had one two little jobs on hand that were bound to get done that day. John had promised to call up—

It was two sharp when the telephone rang.

"Get busy," he says. "I see him coming from the hotel now. Wait—he's stopping to speak with somebody. No hurry. So long."

I went into the bedroom and buckled on one of Ed Bounce's gun-belts. Handshaw looked up from the bed, and asked a question.

"You lay quiet and don't show your nose," I told him. "The sheriff will be back sometime to-night. If anybody comes looking for him, say that you're his sister's son from Abilene and you're sick and tell 'em to go to hell. So long."

With which I left him, pulled my hat down over my face, buttoned an old slicker around me, and started out into the thin rain that was falling. I was fairly well disguised, and nobody paid me any attention as I walked down the back streets and came to what had been Jack Williams' bank; from the rear it was not much to look at. I ducked down the the nearest alley and came along in back of the bank, and Old John was at the back door to meet me. He made the peace sign and ducked inside. I followed.

"The employees are taking a vacation to-day," he sang out from somewhere, for my benefit. "Make yourself to home—he's coming now—'nother feller with him—"

Then there was silence. I shut the back door after me and reconnoitered.

I was in the back room of the bank, separated by a high partition from the front room. In the middle of the partition was a door ajar, to which I went, looking through into the front room as I got rid of my slicker.

Across the big front window was painted a sign, which I could read backwards: "This Bank Open To-day. Col. Jno. Parker." A grill ran down the sides and across the end in front of me, so I sneaks in and subsides behind a peep-hole. In the front window-space was set a desk, and at the desk was Old John. He had a fresh shave, his hair was greased down, and he was wearing a boiled shirt. There was nothing on the desk in front of him except his old forty-five, '86 model. He had a cigar in his teeth, and looked the living picture of health, prosperity and general comfort.

Just then Reno steps in, and I settles down at sight of the gent with him. It was Beaumont—his face still red and scarred. Reno walks over to the desk.

"Morning, Reno," said Old John, real cheerful. "Want to make a deposit?"

Reno was cold and out for business. "No. I want to understand things. I hear that you ain't Doc Jones at all. Is your real name Parker?"

"Some of it." Old John removes the cigar and chuckles hearty. "It's right on the window, Reno. I done bought me this bank, and here I set."

Reno glanced around, supposed naturally that the place was empty, and spoke his mind.

"You won't set long," he said. "You ain't wanted in Double Ace, Parker. We know your record and all about you."

"Who's the 'we,' Reno?" asked Old John.

"Chamber of Commerce, Retail Merchants' Association, and me," said Reno. "This is a fine trick you played on us! You got three days to get out of the county."

"It ain't enough," said Old John. "I got my money tied up here—"

"Three days," said Reno, real cold. Out across the street was gathering quite some crowd to see the interview. Several of the Lazy S punchers were in the crowd.

"And then what?" asked Old John.

"And then I ain't responsible, Parker. Best I can guarantee in the meantime is that your neck ain't in no danger. After the three days, I don't guarantee it."

"Oh!" says John. "Why don't you have your fellers start to shooting? This here glass window would make a durned pretty smash, not to mention me."

John was beginning to get his mad up, as I could see. Reno laughed.

"Nothing like that, Parker! We don't—"

John grabbed his gun. "Nothing like that, hey? You mahogany-faced Piute, trailin' in here with your hired killer to give me orders—I'll show you where to git off! I don't give a durn for you nor nobody else. You and your gang try to start something, and I'll dance your scalps proper! Run me out o' town, will you? By jings, I'm goin' to run you out!"

Reno gave him a curl of the lip. "You're an old fool, Parker. There'll be no gunplay whatever; been too much of that lately. You'll go like Williams did—"

"Not by a durned sight!" said John. "I s'pose you figger ridin' me on a rail with a gang of masked vigilantes, hey? You just try it, feller—try it! That's all."

Just then I opened the little door in the grill and steps out.

Beaumont looked at me, batted his eyes, and give a yelp as he backed up against the window. Reno turned and his face went dirty pale.

"My lord!" he said, like a gasp. "You—you're dead—"

"Nope," I said. "Not yet. John, go call in a couple o' gents off the street to be witnesses. Move lively."

John scuttled to the doorway and bawled at the crowd that Reno wanted 'em, and they begun to drift over. Reno and Beaumont stared at me, goggle-eyed.

"You ain't dead?" said Reno. "Then—then—"

"Reno," I says, "you're a plain, ornery skunk. I ain't dead, and I ain't what you think neither. I'm Tom Jasper Jenkins, and if you got any doubts on the subject you start trouble and you'll find it coming. Right now, I ain't got any business to settle with you, so keep out. You, Beaumont! You're the gent I aim to deal with."

They stared at me. John stood in the doorway juggling his gun. Behind him were some plain citizens and some not so plain, among them being Scarface Woods. I jerked my thumb, and Reno, who looked wild in the eyes, got the idea and stepped to one side. Then I looked at Beaumont, and he looked at me. He had been pretty badly rattled for a minute, but he saw I was no ghost and it cheered him up.

"What's all this, anyhow?" he says. "You been double-crossing us?"

"That's it," I says. "If Reno wants a showdown he can have it, but you and I have an argument to settle first."

"That's news to me," and he gave a short laugh. "What about?"

"About Colfax, that you shot in the back," I told him. "You said a plenty the other night when Mrs. Colfax was quirting you, and you're the gent that done it. Bad man, ain't you? Real bad. Go sneaking up on a rancher and throw down on him when he ain't looking—"

"He went for his gun!" says Beaumont.

"That's a lie. He was shot in the back. Now, feller, go for your gun—go for it!"

Reno wanted to interfere but didn't dast, and John kept one eye on me and the other on the crowd, which had begun to thin rapidly. Beaumont licked his lips, saw that I had a gun but was not reaching for it—and went for his own.

I came blamed near waiting too long, because I wanted everyone to be plumb certain he reached first. Not having any time to draw, I tips up the holster and lets him have it, and his bullet skimmed through my hair. Beaumont drops his gun and goes down, and the bullet smashes the plate glass window behind him.

"You folks seen it!" yelled Old John. "Beaumont drawed first—"

"This is murder!" said Reno. I let the holster drop and gave him a look.

"Murder, is it? Since when? You got a gun in your pocket, Reno. Go on and reach for it."

Not him. Reno had brains. He only shook his head, walked across to the door, and Old John let him go out into the crowd. Next minute John locked the door, then he unlocked it again, dragged Beaumont across the floor, shoves the body outside, and once more locks the door.

"You blamed near give me heart failure, Pinky," said he, "waitin' that way! Three o'clock. Now what? How long before they'll bring a mob to string you up?"

I set down on a corner of the desk and rolled me a smoke. "Not before to-night, John. Sheriff ain't to home, and Reno Frank is still mixed up in his mind. By the time him and his men get through milling, they'll think twice before tryin' to arrest me. I'm goin' to walk straight down to the livery and get me a hoss—and you'll see there won't a soul look crossways at me! You go back to the sheriff's house after a while and see if Handshaw needs anything. The car will be along to get you about sundown, and chances are that nobody will see you leave. Bring one of Ed's Winchesters with you."

"But, Pinky!" says he. "I don't want to go off and miss that there feathering party! I wouldn't miss it for a million—"

"There won't be none," I tells him, going after my slicker. "Those birds are going out to burn the Running F to-night first. What's left of 'em won't have no further ambitions when they get home. The lid's off, John. Unlock that door and let me out."

John unlocked the door, then he happened to see busted window.

"You durned careless reprobate!" he yelled. "Now look what you done—look at this here window! You ain't to be trusted with a gun—one foot in the grave—mahogany-faced old Piute—"

I left him raving and started down the street. And as I had expected, nobody looked twice at me. Probably Reno was just as glad to have me hire a horse and start for the Running F, with the evening's plan in mind.

If I had had enough sense to telephone out there first, I wouldn't have been half so joyful, however. I was feeling cocksure and stuck on myself, prob'ly, and was due for a big tumble off my high horse.

CHAPTER X

IT WAS a good animal I got from the livery, and sure had to be good, because I went, and went fast. I wanted to get clear away from town before Reno or his men tried to nab me for the shooting and other things; and I done it.

Along toward sundown I left the highway by the fork leading over to the Running F, maybe three miles away, having met nobody on the road. Then I heard a gun go off ahead, real rapid, like it was being fanned—only nobody knows how to fan a gun any more, these days. Then the car came into sight, booming merrily along the dusty road.

I can tell you, I drew that bronc out of the road in a hurry! The car's top was down, and that fool chauffeur sat at the wheel with a glassy-eyed stare like he was petrified. He was, too; worse petrified than the stone trees up to Frank Bouquet's place by Calistoga. In the back, Ed Bounce was standing up, waving a bottle of rye in one hand and getting out a fresh gun with the other. As I looked, he let out a yell and began to fan her. He done so, by gosh! Ed Bounce, Sheriff of Coyote County, was as petrified as the chauffeur.

"Whoop-eyow!" yelled Ed, as the car came down at sixty mile an hour, and let off his roll of cartridges. "Whoop-eyow! Cl'ar the road—"

That was all I heard. Neither of them saw me or heard me yell. As the car went away, she give a leap and Ed went down on his ear. Crippled! I'll tell the world he was crippled. He knew just one thing in life, probably, and that was to go and get me and Old John like I had impressed on his mind.

I put for the ranch-house. It was mighty queer that Ed Bounce would go and get himself drunk at such a time; but as I came close to the buildings thinks looked still queerer. Not a soul was in sight, the corral gate was open and the riding-stock gone, and the place had a cold and empty look. Nobody answered my hail. I rode up to the house, and saw two cases of whiskey setting on the porch, looking like the only tenants.

You could have knocked me down with a feather. I had figured on finding some of the neighbors on hand and Mrs. Colfax ready with everybody on the place to meet the burning-squad that night, this being due to come off in no great time. Instead of which, nothing!

I let the poor brute drag himself toward the water-trough and I went up on the porch and looked around. Nothing but the whiskey was in sight. There had been three cases in Old John's car. Where was the third? A minute later the answer came, as a voice reached from the inside the house giving first a gurgle and then a groan, and after that a wild yell.

I went in. Nothing showed up until I came to the dining room, and then a plenty displayed itself. The third case of whiskey, or parts of it, was setting on the table, and in Mrs. Colfax's chair was Holy Pete. He was a sight to behold. His left arm was in a sling, he had a bloody bandage around his head, he had nothing on him except a pair of boots and a gun-belt draped over his shoulders, and he was hitting the table in front of him with his one good fist. He looked up at me and never saw me.

"That's one," he mumbled. "There goes the biggest Gila monster—gosh! Got him! Durn my hide, pilgrim, I got him! Look at that thar sidewinder makin' faces at me—git out'n my way, sidewinder! I eats 'em alive. Sixteen rattles and a button—no, and I ain't goin' into the Aztec Fryin' Pan this trip. I got to go over to Death Valley and look up that thar lode. Ain't no desert rats goin' to scare me out. Hey! Look at that scorpion—got him!"

"And if something ain't got you, I'm a liar," I says. "Wake up! Where's everyone?"

Holy Pete looked at me and blinked.

"Now lissen!" he says, real calm. "I done told you once, Ed Bounce, that I don't stand for no man's interfering—stop wavin' back and forth, and lissen! I ain't goin' back to bed. I ain't goin' to do nothin' I don't want to. I—put 'em up, durn you! Now I got you—"

And blamed if he didn't have his gun on me before I knew what he was up to.

"You won't take a drink, huh?" he says. "Ed Bounce, you set thar and drink half a bottle—and do it quick! Whar's that durned chauffeur gone to? Set down, durn you, or I'll sure as hell perforate you—"

I sat down. T.J. Jenkins knows when a gent means business. And I began to see why Ed Bounce was paralyzed, not to mention the chauffeur. Holy Pete shoves his gun in my face and grins. I didn't grin, for he had the hammer back under his thumb.

"Drink, durn you!" he says. "Talk prohibition to me, will you? Sheriff, are you? By gosh, I'll show ye how we uset to drink down to Mojave! Pick your bottle and drink!"

I groped for a bottle. It was plain enough' now about Ed Bounce, but I had something else to do than please this lunatic.

So when I got my fingers on the bottle, I knocked Holy Pete over the ear and the poor old rascal went down, his gun missing me by an inch. Then I worked fast and hard. Something had happened, something mighty bad. I sung out for Tia Maria, the cook, but she was gone. I got a couple pails of water and doused Holy Pete proper, then left him to recover while I took a look around, In the office I found a big sheet of paper pinned to the desk—Mrs. Colfax had left a note for me.

"Dear Tom: Pete just got here, badly shot up. I'll have to let everything else go, take all the boys, and ride over to Bald Knob at once. Ed Bounce says he'll bring you out from town in the car. Do the best you can, but don't take any chances. We'll get back as soon as we can make it. I've sent Tia Maria off for the night. Luck to you,

Sarah Colfax."

The note was dated at three that afternoon. Why in time she had to take everbody and ride to Bald Knob, wherever that was, had me clear beat. Why had Holy Pete just got here at three this afternoon—and had he brought the money with him? That thought sent a jump through me.

I knew already what had happened after she had gone with the boys. Most likely she had bandaged Pete up and put him to bed. How he had got to the whiskey didn't matter much; the point was, he had got to it. Then he had put his gun on Ed Bounce and made Ed hit the firewater; while the chauffeur, of course, needed no urging. All this looked clear; but I wanted to know why Holy Pete had got shot up and how and what had taken Mrs. Colfax away.

Trying out the telephone, I found no response. The line was cut. How I cussed myself for not having called up the ranch from town that morning or afternoon! No use cussing, however, so I quit. A visit to Holy Pete showed that he was tossing around and exhibiting symptoms of sanity. Darkness was coming on, so I lighted a lamp, got two Winchesters and a box of cartridges from the office and set them on the porch, then went

into the kitchen and got some cold grub. With this, I came
back to the dining-room and waited for Holy Pete to come to
life. And a shot or two of liquor helped put down the grub.

Pete waked up presently. I hauled him into a chair, gave him
a drink, got a blanket wrapped around him, and he talked. He
didn't know me at all, was plumb wandering in his liquor, but
he was calm enough, and I talk was all about Curly and Bald
Knob and what had happened there. That way, I was able to
piece together the whole thing scrap by scrap, and the more I
pieced, the colder I got.

Seems like Holy Pete and his partner and Curly had rested
up at Saledo Junction until late Saturday night, then had set
out for home, meaning to get over Black Medicine trail Sunday
and reach home sometime Sunday night. The program was all
right, but the notes were mixed, as the feller said of the Jap
bartender in Nevada City.

Bald Knob, it appeared, was a rocky knob near this side the
trail entrance, about where Mrs. Colfax had quirted Lon Beaumont that night. The three boys got there the middle of Sunday
afternoon, not looking for trouble, when a volley came out of
the rocks and laid out their horses, and another volley done its
best to lay them out likewise. Holy Pete's partner was killed,
Curly had his leg broke, but somehow him and Pete got up to
Bald Knob with their guns and water bags, and stood siege
until dark. The money was all in Pete's saddlebags, and it was
clear gone.

I could figure out what had happened. Reno's men, Beaumont
among 'em, had probably trailed that drive herd after finding
nobody showed up around Medocno Pass, and had seen the
three riders coming home. They laid for 'em, got their horses,
got one of 'em, and treed the other two on Bald Knob.

Holy Pete rambled on. Curly's leg being broke, he couldn't
run. So Pete started off Sunday night, with an occasional shot
showing that they were being herded careful. He got through
the lines, and got a horse from the Lazy S bunch—and then

somebody jumped him. One bullet broke his arm, another busted his head, another drilled his shoulder—but he got away. Then the horse died on him, it having caught a bullet likewise, and the Lazy S crowd run him down. Pete crawled into a dry wash and got away. They thought he was dead. Come daylight started for home afoot, and didn't get there until three in the afternoon. Then Mrs. Colfax got the boys together and set out to save Curly.

"Thar's a woman for ye!" mumbled Holy Pete. "Damn the buildin's, says she, we got to bring in that boy—whoopee! Thar's a tarant'ler!" And his fist banged down on the table. He was clear nuts again, but he had given me his story.

I took a long, stiff drink and enjoyed it. Mrs. Colfax would not be back until midnight anyhow, and there was nobody but me and Holy Pete to stave off the burning party, and if anybody needed a drink, I did. It was easy to figure out that Beaumont had left two or three men to keep Curly treed, and had ridden into Double Ace to consult with Reno Frank Skelly, also to turn over the big bunch of currency that had been grabbed. I cussed myself again for having given Holy Pete that money in cash—but it had looked good at the time.

Anyhow, thinks I, there was a good day's work done when I settled that feller Lon Beaumont! Maybe he has killed Curly likewise. So Mrs. Colfax went to rescue Curly and damned the burning squad, eh? That was her all over, and I took another drink on it. All this while, Holy Pete was smashing his fist on the table and fighting snakes. Most times, it's the other way. He was the first one I ever saw who done all the fighting. These desert rats are all plumb locoed anyhow, as everybody knows.

I shoved back my chair to get up—and first thing I knew, something busted on my head. That crazy critter had hit me with a bottle! It staggered me, and he grabbed another bottle and hit me again. It put me clear down and out. As I went down, I heard him yell:

"Whoopee! That's the biggest diamondback I ever—"

Then everything was quiet, so far as T.J. Jenkins was concerned.

When I came to myself, which must have been a consid'able time afterward, I was right weak and dizzy. Holy Pete had my gun; it give a sudden roar, and something jarred my heel as I lay there.

"Dance, ye scorpion!" says he, "No durned reptiles is goin' to scare me! You wait till I git me another snifter—I'll show ye what shootin' is!"

I did not wait, but drew my legs under the table and started toward the door. It was all I could do to crawl; that blamed fool had cut my head open with his first blow, and I felt mighty poorly. All I wanted was to get out of there.

When I disappeared, he done forgot all about me. I crawled under the table to the other end, then crawled out of the room, then got to my feet and staggered out to the porch. The gun didn't matter, for I had two Winchesters out there. By some streak of cussedness, Holy Pete didn't do any more shooting. Forgot to, most likely.

I rolled me a smoke and set down on a case of whiskey to think things over. My horse was dead beat, but I could still get away. Staying here was suicide. Where I had made my big mistake was in letting Reno Frank walk out of that bank this afternoon; I could see it now clear enough. If that chauffeur brought Old John and Ed Bounce back in time, we could still fix the burners, but alone I couldn't hope to do a thing. Holy Pete was out of it—

Then I heard a noise. It wasn't much of a noise, not much more than a suspicion of a noise; but it was enough to make me take my foot in my hand and go away. Somebody's bridle-rings had jingled in the darkness. Sound carries far at night, and that sound didn't carry a bit too far to suit me.

A Winchester under each arm, I faded. It was surprising how weak and no-account I was from them blows over the head, too. It was all I could do to stagger down as far as the creek, but well up from the other buildings, and then I just collapsed in some willow bushes and lay quiet.

When I woke up, there was noises here and there and all around; murmurs of low voices talking, noise of boots scuffling up the dirt, a jingle of spurs. Somebody showed up about six feet in front of me.

"Not a soul around," said a voice. "Jenkins ain't here. Where's Reno?"

"Gone up to the house. His boy ought to have looked over the bunk-house by now—"

"Look out! There comes a light!"

Reno, or I judged from the talk that it was him, went up and rapped sharp on the door. Right after that, the lamp moved out to the doorway. Holy Pete was holding it in his hand, and he had slung off the blanket; how he could hold the lamp was a wonder, but somehow he done it. I felt cold and hot by turns, for I knew what was coming.

"Leave me 'lone!" he sung out, standing there with the light streaming over him. "I tell ye, leave me 'lone! There ain't nobody home but me and the rattlers, and I bet ye I can finish that thar case o' hard licker—"

I couldn't see what happened, but the light fell and smashed, and there came a groan. Then Reno Frank's voice leaped out.

"All right, boys! Nobody home! Set her off."

They done it.


CHAPTER X

IT SURE comes hard to admit it, but T.J. Jenkins, with two rifles, sat quiet while the Running F was burned out. Yes, sir.

Reno had his men in hand good and proper. Not one of 'em set foot in the house. The only thing they touched was the two cases of whiskey, which they dragged off the porch and set in the grass near Holy Pete, who was not killed but near it. They kept off the liquor, too, for Reno was there to be obeyed. His boy was there likewise.

I sat in among them willows, itching for the trigger but not daring. It would have done no good—I could not keep 'em off the whole place. The barn and bunk-house were fired, then they set fire to the house itself. By the light of the flames I made out that there were ten or a dozen men; they had left their horses down the creek a ways, and most of them had been masked, but they took the masks off on finding nobody home. They all had guns and rifles.

"All right, boys!" sung out Reno, as soon as the blaze took hold. He kicked Holy Pete. "Drag this durned fool out o' the way so's he won't roast. If you boys want to break open a case, go to it quick—and then get out o'here."

Did they want to bust into one of those two whiskey cases? They gave one joyful yell and then gathered around. The flames from the barn were beginning to light things up a bit, and Reno wanted to get off, for the house was fired in two places.

I just couldn't withstand the temptation, however, when I saw them rascals clustered around our good liquor, half-way up the knoll. Not being able to see Reno in the crowd, I let loose at the bunch of figures which were betwixt me and the house, and kept firing as fast as I could work the bolt. Also, I shot low.

The bunch scattered, most of them, and went for their horses. I dropped another one, then reports from outlying precincts began to come in as others of Reno's men along the creek opened on me. Bushes were no protection, and I rolled back into the creek and lay still. Two minutes later the whole crowd were spurring away, taking a few wounded with them, and I crawled out.

By good luck, I knew where Mrs. Colfax kept most of her papers, so I got into the house and managed to save them before the smoke and flames got too much for me. I blamed near stayed too long, for the fire was quicker than I figured on and cut me off. Still, I got through; my clothes was more or less burned off, but the blanket with Mrs. Colfax's papers in it came out alive, which was the main thing.

By this time there was a riot of flame mounting up the sky—barn and bunk-house roaring, and the house like a furnace. I rolled down the hill to the creek, then went back and got Holy Pete. He had been hit over his cracked head, and when I picked him up to drag him out of the heat, his eyes opened glassily.

"Thassal right, feller," he mumbled. "I allus knowed hell couldn't be hot alongside Death Valley. I ain't real warmed up yet—"

He went to sleep again. I got him down by the creek, then went back for a bottle of liquor from the smashed case, and settled down to watch the bonfire burn itself out, which it soon done. There were no neighbors to be looked for, because the only neighbors were friends of Reno. I had hoped to get one or two on hand to witness the party, springing it as a surprise, but even if they saw the glare they would not come over now. What hurt most of all was Old John failing me.

When things had burned down a bit, I went back and investigated the remains lying around the whiskey cases. Two of Reno's men had stayed here, but both were unknown to me; a third was lying down by the creek, and when I visited him I saw it was Scarface Woods. At first I thought he was safe from further trouble like the other two, but when I found him alive, I tied his hands and feet and let him rest. Several of the raiders had carried hot lead in their systems when they departed, too.

I might have looked after Scarface a mite, only about then my knees went back on me. What with one thing and another I was consid'able mussed up in health, chiefly by the two cracks over the head that Holy Pete had given me; also, I was scorched and blackened and still spitting smoke. So I staggered back to Pete and the whiskey bottle, and settled down to cuss my luck—or rather, Old John's whiskey. The cards had sure broken wrong this night.

There was nothing left of the buildings except a few red ashes when, along towards midnight, Mrs. Colfax turned up. She came with one rider, the other four having stayed to bring Curly along in a slung blanket, after setting his smashed leg. The moon had been up quite some time, and she needed no information on the extent of the damage. When I hailed, she came over to where I was.

"That you, Tom? Thank heaven you're safe and well, anyhow!"

"I'm safe if I ain't well," I says, and threw what was left of my coat where it was most needed to hide Holy Pete. "You lost a lot by goin' to get Curly."

"But I saved Curly," says she, and then got a sight of me, and let out a yelp, and I thought she would keel over.

There was consid'able talking. She had found Curly besieged by two Lazy S punchers, and standing them off noble; what was better, she had caught the two punchers clear off guard, and they had gone to the same place where Beaumont was. She went up to examine the two that had stayed to keep me company, and identified them as Reno's men.

"This is awful!" she said, but with her voice cool and quiet. "It don't seem possible that such things could happen in these days."

"That's what the feller said when G. Washington crossed the Delaware," I reminds her. "You got to send to town and get the coroner in the morning, and get me news of John Parker. Likewise, you got to pay your interest. Didn't get that money back?"

"No," she says, as she sat beside me and twisted her hands. "No, Tom. And everything I had went up with the house—"

"Not your papers and vallybles," I says, pointing to the bundle in the darkness. "I snaked everything out of the safe and your desk. Then, that feller Jenkins that was here, he give me a certified check. I got it in my belt now—"

"Please, Pinky!" said she, in a low voice, letting her hand drop on my wrist.

"What's that?" I says, a little startled. "My name ain't Pinky—"

"No use!" said she, and smiled at me in the moonlight. "Before you'd been here two days I knew who you were. And to-day Holy Pete told us. Why, did you think for a minute that we'd believe your fool chauffeur to be Pinky Jenkins! Nonsense! And Ed Bounce told me all about how your friend Parker wrote that letter—"

Glory be! I had come out all right after all, so far as she was concerned. We sat up and just talked until the other boys came in with Curly.

Morning came at last. Mrs. Colfax, after consid'able argument, had agreed to sell me half the property; for by this time I was going to stick until me or Reno Frank went under. Everything on the place was clean wiped out. About daybreak she saddled up to go into town and buy everything needful, and pay the mortgage interest. I gave her one of my remaining checks. She refused to take any of the boys with her, for fear they'd get into trouble with Reno's men, but promised to have some grub and supplies on the place before noon, along with the coroner and news of Old John Parker. So she departed alone, after promising not to start any ructions in town—for, take it from me, she was riled up.

What with me and Curly and Holy Pete and Scarface Woods, who had a slug clean through his body, there had been consid'able bathing and bandaging going on during the still hours of the night. As soon as Mrs. Colfax was on her way, I called in the boys and told 'em to get to work. Some tools were lying around, and a couple of old barns up the creek had escaped the fire.

"You boys get a shack rigged up for Mrs. Colfax," I said. "Start a fire here beside me and carry Scarface Woods over here. I want to talk to him. Anybody got a pencil?"

"Didn't you have fire enough last night?" says Curly. "Here's a pencil."

"You boys obey orders," I said, and they done so. Holy Pete was snoring, and Curly lay watching proceedings. Scarface was conscious and cussing as they laid him down beside me and then scattered to work. I got a blank sheet of paper from the blanket of stuff I had saved, and then sat down by Scarface and fed wood on the fire.

"What you goin' to do?" he says.

"Nothin' much. You were with Beaumont over to Bald Knob, weren't you?"

"What's that to you?" snarled Scarface. "Beaumont will sure fix you!"

"He won't," I says. "I fixed him yesterday. Funeral's to-day, I reckon."

This was news, as I hadn't mentioned it to Mrs. Colfax. When the fire got going good, I took off Scarface's boots and laid his bound feet by the fire, and showed him my star.

"Didn't know I was a deputy sheriff, eh?" I says. "When you get ready to talk, holler."

He cussed, but I rolled me a smoke and talked local politics with Curly. After a while Scarface quit cussing, and began to sweat and whimper, then all of a sudden he let out a yell.

"Fer gosh sake quit roastin' me! I'll talk."

"Sure," I says, and pulled his feet away. "Talk slow, while I write it down."

He done so. He had been with Beaumont over to Bald Knob, and named the other boys in that party, but claimed to know nothing about the money Holy Pete had lost. He likewise named all who had been with Reno the previous night. His friend and compadre Logan, off whom I had shot two fingers, had been in the crowd, as had young Skelly. I called in the other boys, and they cut Scarface loose and witnessed his signature to the paper, which I put into my pocket.

"Now," I said, "is there any place you could put this pilgrim for safe-keeping, over a week or so? I don't want him jailed. He's too good to lose."

"They's a cabin three mile up the crick," said somebody. "But it ain't ornamental."

"Take him up there," I says. "He won't be doing any walking around this week or next, anyhow; bullet went clear through him. One of you boys go up there every day with some grub, sabe? No, don't take his boots. He's better without 'em. Don't tell anybody you seen him, and when that coroner shows up, don't mention his signed statement neither."

"The blasted coroner is Reno Frank's man," spoke up Curly.

"That's all right. Tell him you haven't seen me and you think I was carried off by the burning-party last night. But hide away that whiskey before anybody comes!"

"Where are you going?"

"To sleep," I says. "Send after me when Mrs. Colfax gets back."

I was mighty near dead for sleep, too, so much so that I had stopped worrying over Old John Parker. I went down the creek a ways to that big clump of trees where Beaumont had met me, and I burrowed in among the trees and brush, fixed me a den like a bear, and dropped off in the arms of Murphy, as the Greek feller said.

When I came to myself the afternoon sun was dribbling through the trees, and two of the boys were shaking me awake.

"Come an' git it!" sings out one of 'em, real joyous. "Grub's here and Tia Maria is back and we got a meal fit to eat. Mrs. Colfax is here likewise. Come with the flivver that brought the supplies."

"Coroner come?" I asked, sitting up and yawning. They grinned.

"Come and gone. Took the evidence and wouldn't give no decision. Looks bad."

I went up the creek with them to where the new shack was being finished; she was not much to look at, but would serve. A ton of tents and supplies of all kinds lay off to one side, and all hands were setting down to one of Al Fresco's meals that the papers talk about—served on the grass-roots. Tia Maria was working over a sod-oven, and Mrs. Colfax waved her hand at me cheerfully from the coffee-pot on the fire. I went to her. I meant to ask about Old John, but my tongue slipped.

"You look mighty pretty, ma'am, with the fire-color in your face and the curls hanging around your ears! Yes'm. Have any trouble cashing that there check of mine?"

She looked red, sure enough, and shoved back her hair.

"No, not a mite. I paid the interest and deposited the balance. Reno was not in the bank, and the cashier was too astonished to ask any questions. And—Tom! Or I should say, Pinky—I have bad news for you."

Her blue eyes looked square into mine, and I nodded.

"Spill it, ma'am."

"I was given to understand that you're wanted. A warrant is out for you for the murder of Lon Beaumont; willful murder, according to the coroner's verdict. Other warrants are to be issued for last night's shooting, which are also called murders. The story is that a number of deputies with a posse heard you were here, rode here to get you, that you resisted arrest and killed three besides wounding several, then set fire to the house. Reno Frank Skelly will offer a reward for your apprehension, I judge."

"Shucks!" I said. "What's the bad news? What about Old John Parker?"

"In jail."

"How come?"

"That automobile got to town last night and was wrecked in Main Street. The sheriff was knocked senseless and taken home; they think he'll recover. The chauffeur was jailed for drunkenness and driving while intoxicated. Your friend Parker was seen on the street and a crowd got him. He shot two men and was jailed. Is all this bad enough?"

"Might be worse," I said, rubbing my jaw. "Didn't think to bring me out a razor, I s'pose?"

Her eyes twinkled, anxious though they were. "My lands, no! Now, what do you want to do? I imagine a posse will be here to get you to-night, and if you say fight—"

"I say eat, ma'am," I says. "Come along and don't keep the boys waiting."

The boys were consid'able sobered by all this news, and so was I. Reno Frank sure had coppered all our bets. Outside of Scarface Woods' confession, which he didn't know about, there was nothing to prove that I was not the murderer he made out. If they got me, I was due for a free trip to the penitentiary, and no mistake. Worst of all was that I needed a razor, for my bristles were out half an inch. So, what with one thing and another, we made a hearty meal but didn't indulge in much loud talk. As for resisting arrest, that was out of the question. Mrs. Colfax had all she could do just to get her place to running once more.

"What about your friend Parker?" she asks me.

"Leave him in jail," I says. "He's safer there than he is loose. Can you lend me two of your boys for the rest of the week?"

"The place is yours, Tom," she says. "What's your plan?"

"I'd rather not say, ma'am," I told her. "It ain't a plan at all; it's mostly a hope. We'll want the three best hosses and quite a bit of grub." I looked around at the boys. "You fellers got that whiskey hid away? Then don't let Holy Pete know where it is, when he gets on his feet. Which two of you boys will light a shuck with me?"

They all five lets out a yell simultaneous. I picks two of the best riders, Weary Steve and Bitter Root Perkins, and tells 'em to saddle up. Then, while I'm getting my outfit together from what's left, Mrs. Colfax comes up to me.

"Tom, please tell me where you're going!"

"I'm going to get me a razor, ma'am," I says, and I meant it.

CHAPTER XII

"WHERE YOU headin' for, Tom?" asked Bitter
Root.

"The Lazy S," I says. "You fellers lead me there acrost country,
not by road."

They looked at each other and at me, and then grinned. Those
boys had guts. They also had guns, and I had a Winchester in
a boot at my stirrup, though I figured my old forty-five was all
I would need. Still, I had clear quit taking chances.

After that, there were no questions asked. Sunset was not
far away, and we jogged steady and easy until, about dark, we
came to the fence. Weary clipped it and we went through. I
figured that all Reno's men would be in town, except maybe
one or two, but I aimed to make sure of my play before I dis-
carded.

It was along about eight o'clock when we sighted the Lazy
S, and Bitter Root pointed out the lay of the land to me.

"The bunk-house is where that light is," he said, "and over
to the left is the house; she's all dark, so nobody's to home. That
other light behind her is the summer kitchen—prob'ly the
cook's washing up now."

"As I figgered," I told him. "I ain't interested in the cook.
Sneak up on the boys."

We dismounted and Weary went ahead to reconnoitre. When
we were a hundred feet from the bunk-house he came back
with word that just one rider was there—a feller they called
Sundown Foster. Foster, he says, sat with one foot in a chair,
reading a book.

"All right," and I pulled my gun. "Foster is the gent I was
hoping to find, or one of 'em. You boys wait outside the door.
When I start him out, grab him, blindfold him and rope his
arms. No noise, though."

I walked in on the bunk-house. Foster was sitting with his back to the door and didn't hear me step in. Every time he turned a page of his book, he give a groan and felt of his foot. Second time he done it, I coughed, and he looked around at my gun.

"Put 'em up," I said. "Now get up and walk to the door."

He turned green in the face. "Durn you, I can't!" he sang out. "I got a bullet clean through my foot—"

"I aimed to put one there, and don't need to bother," I says. "Get up and walk! I'll show you the age of miracles ain't past by a durned sight! I'm a deputy sheriff and you're arrested for the murder of one man at Bald Knob, the theft of ten thousand dollars belonging to Mrs. Colfax, the burning of the Running F buildings and a few other things. Get up and walk or I'll perforate your other foot, you durned reptile!"

I flashed my deputy's star, and he turned greener than ever. He hobbled to the door somehow, though it sure did draw groans out of him, and then the boys grabbed him.

"Carry him along," I says. "Weary, you look like a hoss-thief. Drop him at the hosses, then come back and sneak a bronc out of the corral without any noise."

They done it. In ten minutes we had Foster roped bareback and riding with us. First bunch of trees we came to, I stopped.

"Now build a little Injun fire," I says. "I'll attend to this gent."

I got Sundown Foster off his perch and laid him with his feet, bandaged one and all, right adjacent to the fire. He was scared stiff.

"Great hemlock—you ain't goin' to torture me!" he sings out.

"Mental torture first," I says. "Listen to this." I read over to him the confession that I'd got from Scarface. "Now, Sundown, we need your signature and testimony that this here is all true. Give it, and I'll save you from the pen. Don't give it, and I'll roast your feet proper till you do. What say?"

He said it in a hurry, took the pencil I give him, and signed up. Weary and I hoisted him aboard the bareback and roped him there, then I gave Bitter Root his orders.

"Take this gent to that cabin up above our place and leave him to condole with Scarface Woods. Don't leave him no boots, though. Tell one of the boys to drop in on him every day and double the rations. Don't tell Mrs. Colfax about him. Then mosey along and meet Weary or me early to-morrow morning two mile outside Double Ace on the Medocno Pass road. Sabe?"

"You bet," he says, and swung off with his prisoner.

Weary and I headed south for Double Ace, but did not go near the town. Four mile this side of town was a feller named Billson, on my list. He lived alone and had a small place where he raised chickens and produce. We got to Billson's about midnight, found everything dark, and hammered at the door. There was some powerful cussing before Billson lighted a lamp and opened up.

"Why can't you let a body sleep once in a while?" he says. "Who's there?"

"Pinky Jenkins," and I shoved my gun in his stomach. "Don't drop that lamp! Here's my badge—deputy sheriff. You were in the party that burned out the Running F last night. You're under arrest. Anything you say will be used against you—and you're going to say a hell of a lot. March inside."

We marched with him, and inside of two minutes had him lashed hand and foot to a big chair. I left him there, sat down to the table, and wrote a note to Handshaw, which I gave Weary. The note told Handshaw to lay mighty low until next Monday.

"Take this into town. There's a U.S. marshal or deputy stopping at the sheriff's house. Find out how Ed Bounce is getting on, give this note to the deputy marshal; go meet Bitter Root and fetch him here—and don't wake me up if I'm asleep. I got a lot of sleep to make up. If you can raise an extry hoss or so, do it."

I went out and unsaddled, put my horse in the barn, and came back to where Billson was resting uneasy.

"Pleasant dreams," I says. "I'll keep the bed warm for you. Got a razor around?"

"Listen!" he broke out. "Be reasonable, Jenkins! You ain't goin' to leave me here—"

"You'll change your mind about that towards morning," I says. "And if you let out a holler, so help me I'll give you a gag that you'll remember! Guess I'll let the shave go till morning anyhow."

Making sure that he was lashed good and tight, I went into the other room, pulled off my boots, and slept some more.

There was nothing much to Billson except whiskers and pop-eyes; his sand was mostly dirt. About sun-up his groans waked me up—and he was suffering plenty. I let him groan, while I got me a shave, found some of his clothes to fit me, and started breakfast. I told him Reno Frank was dead and most of the crowd under arrest, and he believed it. Then Weary and Bitter Root showed up, tired but happy.

"Did you find that U.S. Marshal?" I says to Weary, and winked.

"Yes," he said. "He'll do just as you say. Ed Bounce is bruised up some but not hurt to speak of."

Billson's eyes got bigger and bigger. I sent the boys to occupy the bed, after we had absorbed breakfast, and I looked at Billson real hard.

"I dunno what to do with you," I said. "The jail's clear full and all the printed warrants on hand have been used up. I'd sure hate to take you into town in that there piece of a nightshirt. If I don't bring you, the U.S. marshal will give me hell."

What with pain and hunger and cold and general misery, Billson began to spill tears on his dirty whiskers. No wonder his razor was a good one; he'd never used it.

"Of course," I said reflectively, "if you were to make a confession and then disappear for a week or so—"

"Good gosh! Is that enough?" he broke out. "Lemme go! I got a brother-in-law living over to Cutoff Gulch in Pahrump county. I'll fan it over there and won't come back until you say so, if somebody will look after my chickens."

"Damn your chickens and you, too!" I said. "Who looked after Mrs. Colfax's buildings last night?"

He began to whimper. So presently I cut him loose. When he was able to move, he sat down and wrote out a confession, including names. I gave him some breakfast, then let him telephone to a friend in town, who promised to come out next day and feed the chickens. Then I threw some more scare into him and let him go. He saddled up his horse and went away in the direction of the mountains, and you never saw a gladder man than him.

Well, to go along and tell all that we done between then and Sunday night would be a whole book. Two posses were out looking for me, and once or twice I had a closer shave than I got from Billson's razor, but all went well. Thursday night we got Squint-eye Logan, the same whom I had shot the two fingers off of; but he made so much trouble I had to drill him in the shoulder. I sent Weary home with him to the cabin on the ranch, and Weary joined us Friday night in a camp we made on Coyote River. We laid up until Saturday night, then we grabbed a small independent rancher named Eli Woodson, who was a close friend of Reno Frank's, as he was going home from town. I smashed his foot with one bullet and trimmed his hair with another, and after some persuasion he signed up with us. Bitter Root took him to our private jail, and I dismissed him from the service with a message telling Mrs. Colfax to be in town Monday afternoon with all the boys.

Sunday morning Weary and I were up the Medocno Pass road, had a brush with a posse, and hid out in the hills that afternoon and night. We saddled up Monday morning, and along towards noon found the spot we were looking for toward the top of the grade. It was a quick hairpin turn in the road, with high rocks all around, and the stage had to take this section in low as she went up. We had no more than got stationed when we sighted the stage climbing a bend away below us.

"If you shoot," I told Weary, "you shoot durned straight. We can't take any chances this trip—it's draw to fill or lose the whole blamed pot!"

As the stage got closer, we saw somebody sitting alongside of young Skelly, and Weary allows it's a deputy. He has a rifle in his lap, so probably he's there for guard. I laid low until the stage got to the hairpin turn right below us, then I rose up.

"Elevate!" I said.

Young Skelly jams his foot on the brake and elevates, looking scared. The deputy elevated his rifle instead of his hands, and Weary plugged him dead center. Young Skelly let out a screech as the deputy keeled over and turned white as a sheet. I made him lift out the body and lay it alongside the road to wait for the down trip. He was scared stiff.

"You're interfering with the mails!" he wailed.

"No I ain't," I says. "But you're under arrest, young feller. Here's my badge—"

"They'll get you!" he whimpered. "Grand Jury's in session to-day and—"

"Suits me fine," I says. "You ride us up to the railroad. Weary, set behind this gent, and if he makes one suspicious move, perforate his hide. Push her, Skelly! Don't waste any time. There'd ought to be somebody waiting for us at the railroad."

Young Skelly sure shoved the stage up the grade. I was laying my whole bet, of course, on finding a crowd of old-timers waiting for us, which same Old John Parker had written to get here this Monday without fail. When, after a while, we got out of the pass and sighted the railroad station, I felt right dizzy in my stomach, because that platform was bare as a bone!

Then I remembered that the train had not come yet.

That Monday afternoon there was consid'able excitement in Double Ace. The whole town was stirred up over the doings of that there desperado Pinky Jenkins, the Grand Jury was taking

evidence toward indicting him and others, and they got Old
John Parker up before 'em to stand a grilling.

On the way to town, I stopped the stage at a ranch that had
a telephone, and called up the sheriff's office. Handshaw answered the telephone, and said Ed Bounce was just out of bed
and getting dressed to go before the Grand Jury, so I told Handshaw what to do and then got back to the stage.

"Let her go," I said, "and don't spare the spurs, Skelly."

Young Skelly was green as a cucumber, and no wonder.
Besides me and Weary, there was Pecos Hardy, with his white
whiskers waving in the wind; Swede Simmons, with a sawed-
off shotgun; Diamond Bill of Tucson, with a Bible in one hand
and a gun in the other; Piute Haskins, a U.S. marshall from
over the Nevada line, with his star shining; Redeye Burton of
the Circledot X, the biggest ranch in southern Wyoming; and
Lazy Jim Drayton, who was now U.S. district judge of Pahrump
County. Besides these, the corpse of Reno's deputy was setting
beside young Skelly and jogging his elbow, and young Skelly
didn't appreciate it a whole lot neither. We were one happy
party, I'm here to say!

At last we got to Double Ace, and instead of heading down
Main Street, young Skelly threw in the gas and went for the
courthouse, with the stage bouncing our gizzards out. As everybody was waiting at the hotel for the stage, there was no
crowd around here; in front of the courthouse was Mrs. Colfax
with the Running F boys and Handshaw, and Ed Bounce hobbling along on a cane. When the stage stops, Weary takes charge
of young Skelly, and I got Ed Bounce into action. Most of our
crowd knew him and were yelling at him, but he stops them
quick.

"Hold up your hands!" he said to all of us. "Swear and so
forth—now, by gosh, you're all deputies! Pinky, give your orders.
They got Old John in the Grand Jury room now."

"Then we'll go right along," I says. "Swede, you and Redeye
give Ed a lift. Come on, Mrs. Colfax! No time to talk."

You never witnessed in your life such a danged surprise as that Grand Jury got when we walked in on them. Besides the jurors, two of Reno's lawyers and the prosecuting attorney and Judge Haskins were there, all of them pecking at Old John Parker like a parcel of crows around a dead horse; but Old John wasn't dead. He let out a yell as we come in, then waited developments.

"I got evidence to lay before this here jury," I said, walking in. "Who wants it?"

Everybody set still as could be. Maybe it was because I had a gun in my hand. Weary drags in young Skelly, and the rest of us forms up. Judge Haskins turned sort of pale around the gills, for the bailiffs and attorneys and so forth had all ducked behind desks and he and the jury were unable to do likewise.

"What's this mean?" he sings out. "You're interfering with the court—"

"Not a bit, your honor," said Ed Bounce, hobbling forward. "I done been summoned to give this here Grand Jury my evidence, and here it is," and he waved his cane toward me. "Mr. Jenkins is a legal deputy sheriff of this county and has been one for quite a spell back. These other gents are distinguished citizens—one of 'em's a U.S. marshal. This here is Mr. Handshaw, deputy marshal from the capital of this here state. Pinky, the bets are all covered; lay down your hand."

I shoved away the gun and produced some slips of paper.

"Your Honor, and gentlemen of the jury here are confessions involving Mr. Skelly, senior, and Mr. Skelly, junior, and seventeen other gents, some of which is dead, Lon Beaumont died resisting an officer in the act of drawing a deadly weapon on same. Those gents who burned out the Running F were fired on by an officer in pursuit of his duty, which was me. Further, by the evidence of these here confessions you'll see that Reno Frank Skelly robbed Mrs. Colfax of ten thousand dollars cash, which same is now in his bank uptown, and conspired to commit arson on her buildings—"

"And that ain't all by a durned sight!" piped Old John Parker. "Whoopee! I got a Federal Reserve charter for my bank, dod-gast ye! I wants Reno Frank took in custody by that there deputy U.S. marshal for conspiracy to hinder my bank from opening—"

Just then one of Mrs. Colfax's riders, who had been stationed outside, opened the doors and slid into the courtroom.

"Reno Frank's coming!" he sang out.

It was right unfortunate for Reno that he was by no means sure of what was happening in the court-room where the Grand Jury was setting. He opened the doors and walked in, with six of his men at his back. Before they knew what was up, the doors were shut again and they had their hands in the air.

Reno Frank stood dead quiet, saw he was caught, and elevated.

"One minute!" I said, for some of the jurymen were durned uneasy as they read them confessions. "I'd suggest that the Grand Jury, in taking these here confessions into consideration, strike out all names involved except them of Reno and young Skelly and these here six gunmen with Reno. If Mrs. Colfax, as chief complainant in them charges of arson, theft and so on, agrees—"

"I agree," speaks up Mrs. Colfax, and gosh, how them jurymen did breathe easier! Four of them were named in the confessions.

Judge Haskins swallowed real hard, but he hadn't no choice.

"The prisoners are remanded in custody of the sheriff and his deputies here present," he said "The Grand Jury will request all officers and others to withdraw. Mr. Parker—"

"Charges against John Parker are dismissed, Your Honor," said Ed Bounce, and the judge had to agree with him.

We all trooped out into the hall, and everybody was shaking hands with Old John, and he was a joyful man. Then he went up to Reno, who stood ironed beside Handshaw, and pulls a bundle of papers from his pocket.

"S'pose we take up them options here and now," he says. "Come on, you fellers, split this here jackpot and get out your checkbooks! Don't ask no questions. Hey, Pinky! Where's Pinky Jenkins? New deal in Double Ace—come and git your chips, Pinky! Where is he?"

T.J. Jenkins, however, was somewhere else. Him and Mrs. Sarah Colfax were going down the hall together towards the place where marriage licenses were issued.

### EPILOGUE

*Deponent, John Parker, whose residence is the Parker House, City of Double Ace, County of Coyote, State of Nevoming, being duly sworn, deposes: That to his certain knowledge and belief the statements of record entitled "A New Deal in Double Ace," said statements having been delivered under oath by T.J. Jenkins, are untrue and slanderous to the reputation of said deponent and in contravention of an act of the State of Nevoming, entitled "An Act to Protect Banks And Bankers," etc. Quae cum ita sint, deponent prays that the Grand Jury of the County of Coyote be directed to make full and unbiased investigation of the facts surrounding the marriage of Mrs. Sarah Colfax to said T.J. Jenkins and where the liquor came from that was drunk at said marriage. Witness his hand and seal, given in my presence this first day of July, 1923.*

*(Signed) Jno. Parker.*

*SEAL*

*Attest: J.F. Haskins, Notary Public, City of Double Ace, County of Coyote, State of Nevoming.*

*Witness: Ed Bounce, Sheriff.*

# ABOUT THE AUTHOR

H. BEDFORD-JONES is a Canadian by birth, but not by profession, having removed to the United States at the age of one year. For over twenty years he has been more or less profitably engaged in writing and traveling. As he has seldom resided in one place longer than a year or so and is a person of retiring habits, he is somewhat a man of mystery; more than once he has suffered from unscrupulous gentlemen who impersonated him—one of whom murdered a wife and was subsequently shot by the police, luckily after losing his alias.

The real Bedford-Jones is an elderly man, whose gray hair and precise attire give him rather the appearance of a retired foreign diplomat. His hobby is stamp collecting, and his collection of Japan is said to be one of the finest in existence. At present writing he is en route to Morocco, and when this appears in print he will probably be somewhere on the Mojave Desert in company with Erle Stanley Gardner.

Questioned as to the main facts in his life, he declared there was only one main fact, but it was not for publication; that his life had been uneventful except for numerous financial losses, and that his only adventures lay in evading adventurers. In his younger years he was something of an athlete, but the encroachments of age preclude any active pursuits except that of motoring. He is usually to be found poring over his stamps, working at his typewriter, or laboring in his California rose garden, which is one of the sights of Cathedral Cañon, near Palm Springs.